Very many years ago, as a school boy in Jamaica, Viv Wellington began to have ideas sweep into his head when he would lie on his back on the lawn late at night gazing at the stars. One night he even tried to count them. Having grown up with these thoughtful enquiries, he decided long ago that we're here on earth for a purpose. The big question is, are we endeavouring to fulfil that purpose?

The author arrived in Britain and completed his schooling, then joined the R.A.F. During these years, he was able to view much of the world and some of its various cultural behaviour.

He is an ardent admirer of English and French classics, romantic and religious poetry, all types of music and most sports.

WHAT AM I
LIVING FOR?

V G WELLINGTON

What Am I Living For?

Vanguard Press

A CIP catalogue record for this title is
available from the British Library

ISBN 1 84386 186 0

*Vanguard Press is an imprint of
Pegasus Elliot MacKenzie Publishers Ltd.*
www.pegasuspublishers.com

First Published in 2005

**Vanguard Press
Sheraton House Castle Park
Cambridge England**

Printed & Bound in Great Britain

Acknowledgements

I wish to express sincere thanks to all my relatives and friends. Together, their persistent encouragement did inspire me to spend much time in isolation in order to complete this book.

Chapter One

"I certainly don't think you should get rid of it. After all, it's all you have; you need it to get around respectably. And besides, selling it would be a tragedy."

"Oh, but I can do without it. I don't go out nowadays. My life is confined to Diane and Connie."

"But selling it is exactly what you mustn't do, my dear. You ought to recover your old image, now that you're single, or let's say you're single for the time being. After all, a husband in jail is not-effective, quite useless, if you ask me. If you sell it you'll become housebound, bed ridden. It's the worst state to get into. Before long you won't even recognize yourself. You'll put on years in a couple of months. And God forbid, for a girl to get old without a husband, she might as well take an overdose."

"Once Pascoe's out, things will improve, I am sure."

"Pascoe will have to leave the country to start a business again, darling, you know that. In this country he won't raise two pence in capital. Listen to me, Jackie, the sooner you do something to improve your life, the sooner you'll get back to yourself."

Jackie was weary. She handed Mary a Martini. Mary was determined to make her realize the true depth of the situation. But Jackie was reluctant. She went back to the cabinet and brought the bottle over, then she planted herself in the armchair opposite Mary.

"Well," she said, hopelessly, "if I am going to restore myself to any extent I'll need money to start. I have nothing in my account, I'm ashamed to ask for an overdraft. All the same, I am desperate. Selling the car means getting cash. And besides, I would reduce my expenditure a great deal."

"Oh, the few hundred you'll get for it won't last long. It won't give you much security. In two months you'll be broke again. Then what?"

"But at least I won't have the car as an extra burden. I tell you, Mary, every time I backed it out of the garage, it cost me money. In two months it will need new tax and insurance."

"Look," said Mary, with determined emphasis, "You're an attractive girl. You're in this mess because you've neglected yourself. You can do anything you want if you go about it the right way. I think you should forget about selling the car. Just use your brains a little."

11

Jackie shrugged. "I've been doing that for thirty-two years and this is where it's got me: no money and a husband in Brixton prison. Any moment now the postman will deliver a letter from the estate agent. I'm a month behind with the rent. Oh, I dread the thought of it. My bills are unpaid. I don't see how I can meet them all without getting rid of the car. And I'll need to get rid of it before the week is out. I need money to clear up a lot of things.

"Well, I think you ought to try something else before selling the car. Perhaps I could suggest something" Mary sipped the Martini and looked at Jackie. "Do you know Penman?"

Jackie searched her mind. "Penman? Yes, I think so."

"He was the one who suggested champagne at the party last weekend."

"I remember him."

"Well, I wouldn't be surprised if he's keeping a notebook on you."

"You mean he hasn't anything better to do?"

"It's lucky for you that he hasn't, it should be a tremendous compliment."

"Why? I don't understand."

"He's filthy rich. "

"I don't suppose it makes any difference. I can't honestly say I gave him a second thought; I don't care for him."

"No one's asking you to care for him. All you have to do is be a little less respectful to him. Show some warmth. Last Saturday night your attitude was too correct. There was certainly no need to flirt, but you deliberately avoided a conversation with him. You never once smiled when he chatted to you. And mind you, he did say some very complimentary things. I suppose you could repair the damage by being warmer. Be yourself. No question about it, he'll sympathise with you."

Jackie sighed. "I don't see myself being anything but formal towards Mr. Penman. I have no business proposition to put to him, and I can't ask him seriously if he wants a secretary. I can only type with two fingers; and anyway, I am not likely to be interested enough in what he's saying to take it down on paper."

The obstinacy was unjustified. Naturally, Jackie was going through a difficult patch and was sensitive about who she confided in; but she had an advantage and ought to make the best of it, thought Mary.

"What if he makes a proposition to you?"

"I don't see why he should. With his status he shouldn't be vulnerable to women who find themselves in his company."

"At his age they prefer to think they're still capable."

"Oh, there's no question of that. He looks masterly and energetic. But he ought to be settled with a wife. Perhaps I'm disappointed that he should be eying me up in this way."

Mary was beginning to understand. It was not that Jackie disliked Penman. She had started off by respecting him. Now she was annoyed to find he had that particular weakness. "Maybe he's lost his wife for some reason. Perhaps he's single. If that's the case, you can't hold it against him."

"I might fine him amusing yet. I will make a point of finding out next time we meet."

"Ah, that's more like you, my dear, sensible and understanding. He might well need your sympathy, and there's only one way to find out: chat to him, learn something about him. Forget Pascoe, he's no good to you where he is. It's unfortunate, of course, but the fact is, he's absolutely ineffective. And he won't be much of a husband when he comes out."

Jackie recoiled a little. She was sensitive about her husband's imprisonment. "We're married, Mary, I don't want to forget that," she proclaimed solemnly.

"Marriage is only an ideal status, my dear, you know that. Goodness me. We have to live. We need to get that much out of life; no one will honestly deny that. You haven't had much since you married him. You could have had the girls without being married to him."

Mary had never liked Pascoe. He was too free and easy. His attitude had always been suspicious. When Jackie had told her she was about to marry him, she had felt quite sick. He was too fast and too callous. He was hardly capable of treating her right. Mary had been unable to do anything about it. She had merely obliged by being at the register office.

She was not surprised when Pascoe was in front of the judge for embezzlement. She had anticipated the seriousness of it and estimated that he would probably get two years, with a heavy fine. Then she was quite surprised and shocked at hearing about his sentence of five years and a fine of ten thousand pounds. What disgusted her, though, was the fact that he had that much in his account when Jackie was living in a rented bungalow. It would have been more acceptable if he had been living in his own house and had to put it up for sale to pay the fine. Now she felt he should serve the full term, and Jackie should do everything to improve her life, reject the marriage and forget the brute. He was a mistake in her life.

She left Jackie at eleven-thirty. Heading for London in the morning, she would probably see Jackie later in the evening. Living next door with her four-year-old daughter, she would be alone for the next two weeks. Then she would join her husband on the Spanish coast where he was working in a partnership, preparing a hotel for the coming holiday season.

Jackie went to bed without giving a second thought to Penman. She first looked on the two girls, saw that they were sound asleep, then closed the door gently and went to her room. Standing back from the mirror of her dressing table now, she peered at herself, concerned, and then sighed hopelessly before removing her clothes. Then she was back in front of the mirror for a closer look at her neglected body. The laced brassière exposed much of her breasts, but the cups held them firm. She quickly released the center knot and saw the cups separated and fall under her arms. The suspended breasts were suddenly disappointing. They sagged a little. Their powerful size made her shrieked. She retied the brassière, this time pulling them tight so that the two breasts contracted. She them looked at herself and felt better. There was less of her flesh overhanging the edges.

Since Pascoe's absence she had neglected herself. Two weeks ago she had decided to do something about her body. It was then that she had started the struggle to get back to her former shape.

Now she was losing a little weight, but clearly saw that it would take months of hard struggle to get down to the trim figure she was years ago. Her waist and hips would have to go down another three inches, and heaven knows how much effort would be needed to take the same amount off the top. Still the girdle, drawn tight, offered some consolation. She stepped back and abandoned herself on the wide double bed. Slightly drunk, it was not long before she was asleep, uncovered, the central heating was good, and besides, it was a warm evening.

But she woke in the middle of the night. The light on and, feeling a little chilly, she was surprised to find herself in such a state. Sitting up, she glanced at the clock. It was barely two-thirty. She pulled on a nightie and got under the bedclothes.

The rest of night was spent huddled against the pillow. In the blazing light she had quickly lost the heavy drowsiness and, despite switching it off, the hours to daylight were long and tormenting. For weeks now, sleeping had been difficult. The two tablets had lost their effectiveness. Afraid to increase the dose, she had taken to the Martini, having discovered its usefulness only a week ago when she had arrived back from the party very late and very drunk. Since then it had been a good idea to treat herself well before going to bed. Now she was putting away half a bottle to get the desired effect. The little bar, neglected during Pascoe's absence, was well supplied with Vermouth, sherry and other wines.

Chapter Two

It was pointless lying in bed and not being able to sleep. She was up at six, made coffee and lingered over it. Later she gave Diane breakfast. The child was just six, having been born eight months into the marriage.

Diane spent most days with a middle-aged teacher living further up the drive. Only recently married, she was a doctor's wife who had ruled out the possibility of giving birth. Stern and with a dislike for pets, she was unable to suppress the maternal instinct and had developed a liking for the child, especially since detecting that Diane was promising to develop into a very bright girl.

The younger child, another healthy girl, was two years old. After sending Diane off to the teacher, Jackie occupied herself with the baby, propping her up in the tiny chair and giving her the dish and spoon. A little chair had been fixed to the rear seat of the car for her. This made it easy for the mother to seat her in safely.

The morning was promising, with the sun already high. Watching the clock carefully, Jackie rushed to the dressing room and threw off the housecoat and nightie. She ran her hands firmly down the curves of her body. She had neglected the exercises this morning.

Slipping into a dress and clipping on two matching earrings, she brushed her hair and quickly put on make-up. Then working her feet into casual shoes, she turned to the mirror for a final inspection, collected her purse with only fifty shillings in it, and went back into the kitchen.

Moments later she was backing the car out of the garage and onto the front terrace, then harnessing the child into the little bucket fixture on the rear seat. She kissed her motherly and drove off. At the bottom of the driveway the Jaguar turned right and made off along the A20.

But she was in no hurry. The child was being very good in the back. Yes, the child was enjoying the ride. Her little eyes, quite curious, stared at the passing scenes. She actually looked forward to these little trips with her mother. Ever since the child's first birthday the little chair had been fixed onto the back seat so that whenever Jackie needed to go out there was no problem; little trips were easily taken, the child was invariable silent, yet had always enjoyed the cruise. She was even beginning to make exciting cries, especially when driving past a field with cows and sheep. Fascinated, she would gasp and sigh cheerfully, and drew Jackie's attention, to make her explain.

Then, with the child almost hidden in the back, passing motorists sometimes got the impression that the black-haired girl, spectacularly poised in the super car was actually giving them the eye. It was not a rare thing for Jackie to be taken at face value. Why, only a week ago one motorist, after passing the Jaguar, caught the persistent smile in his driving mirror. He took up what he thought to be an invitation and allowed himself to drop back so as to follow. Then travelling behind and returning the smiles, encouraged by the movements of Jackie's lips, he actually slowed and turned off the main road behind the Jaguar. When at last she finally drove into the gates to the bungalow, the car pulled up at the front and waited for the final beckoning, only to be seriously disappointed when the mother and child got out of the car.

Now even the little toddler was destined to lose the pleasure of the car, and wouldn't understand the situation when it was no longer available.

Heavy black hair piled at the nape and held by the broad ribbon level with the ear, the eyes interesting, her brows thick and natural, Jackie was strikingly attractive, with a small straight nose. A slightly broad mouth would sometime curl into a smile, and even more exotic was something of 'Eastern promise' enhanced by her dark complexion. In a smile her cheeks would flush and the narrow contours added more interest to an artist's impression; then they would smooth out to give a modest appearance. This would at once hide a coquettish nature. Well built, with shapely curves, Jackie was by no means delicate. With aggressiveness she would be a good match for the effeminate male.

A little way along the A20, she took the Canterbury road. Travelling slowly, she soon found herself on a divided road leading to the historical town. On the outskirts of Canterbury she spotted the sign she was looking for. It was outside a large showroom, saying 'NEW AND USED CARS,' also the 'SHELL' sign for petrol.

She signaled her intention and turned off the road, slowing right down, she drove passed the glass-fronted showroom with new cars, and pulled up in an extended area displaying used cars. Getting out of the car, she straightened her dress and smiled at the child.

A salesman met her promptly with the usual, "Can I help you?"

She smiled. "Will you take a look at my car? I'm hoping you'll buy it."

The salesman followed her out of the showroom with interest, his eyes close-set and respectful. He folded his arms and looked at the white Jaguar. Then he spotted the child in the rear seat and curled his features into a friendly smile. Jaguar sports, unmarked, excellent condition throughout. What was it like mechanically?

She had no idea how they judged cars, but she didn't think there was anything wrong with it. Then he was in fact apologetic. Of course, it was only three years old. There couldn't be much wrong, if anything. He opened the door and sat in the driving seat. Had she owned it from new?

Yes.

He got out and closed the door gently. It was a beautiful car, delightful to own, fascinating to drive.

Yes, she would miss it very much.

It was good. It should fetch top price. Would she like to exchange it, take out something smaller for instance?

Jackie shook her head regretfully.

"You're getting ride of it completely?"

"Yes, unfortunately."

His smile was not conclusive. Could he not interest her in a smaller car, something less elaborate, but very convenient, perhaps?

Again she shook her head.

"You have a second car? I see. There's already one in the family?"

Yes, there was another.

Well, as he had said, the Jaguar was as good as new. Had she advertised it privately?

No. she hadn't thought of it.

Oh, but it's the best way to sell these things. It should fetch one hundred pounds more than he could offer. An admirer wouldn't hesitate.

Jackie was impressed. She nodded and thanked him for the advice. But she was still curious to know what he thought it was worth. It would be a sort of guide when quoting a price.

"Yes, of course. Well, I would offer fifteen hundred for it. Was that the sort of money you're expecting?"

She didn't realy know. It was attractive, though; she would advertise it and hope to do better.

He opened the door for her. Pleased with himself, he watched the car out of sight.

Back at the bungalow, Jackie hurried to get the particulars into the local newspaper for the following day. It was imperative. Not only was she in dire need of the cash, the car was a burden, especially now that her purse was empty.

She ignored the baby and rang the newspaper office, stated her purpose and was asked to hold the line, then, with the return of the voice; she gave the particulars of the car and was asked to mail the fee. Five minutes later she remembered there was only fifty shillings in her purse. The cost of the advertisement was over twenty-five shillings.

Added to the disappointment was the fact that Mary was away in London for the day. She was unable to borrow even a modest two Pounds.

It took an hour to remember that the bank manager ought to be a reasonable chap. Armed with that idea; she went out to the car and switched on the ignition. There was scarcely a gallon of petrol in the tank. That settled it; the car would remain in the garage until it was sold, even if it took a year! At this point it was either her or the car, and she must keep her head! Since Pascoe's imprisonment, the damn car had eaten up most of her money with the terrific expense of insurance and everything else. Each time she drove it out of the garage she was spending on it. At times she was even buying oil. Always the attendant would ask if the oil was all right. How the hell should she know whether it needed oil? Pascoe had taught her to drive the car; he had never once warned her that one day it would become a burden.

She stormed back into the living room and sat down, chin in hand, on the side of the settee, deep in thought; even the cheerful sound of the child failed to distract her.

Suddenly she drew the telephone to her, contacted the bank, gave her name and asked to be put through to the manager. She explained the situation, that she was intent on selling the car and how much it would fetch.

All at once it wasn't so bad after all. The manager was agreeable, delighted. The amount of her overdraft was one hundred and twenty pounds, outstanding for four months. She was not even aware of this. It was news to her. The situation was definitely promising. Cheques for the next two weeks would be honoured.

Well then, with that settled she could relax; things were much better than expected and it had taken only a moment to sort out. The car would fetch a good price. It would be entirely hers. Why hadn't she thought of it before? Delighted with her new situation, she rushed to her daughter and playfully hoisted her. Later she enclosed a cheque, along with the particulars of the car in a stamped envelope. She would have to mail it right away. There was a post box forty yards up the drive.

Before her marriage to Pascoe she had been an exciting young girl, accustomed to taking her pleasure on her own terms. Born in Bedfordshire, she was acquainted with the London scene very early. A journey of less than one hour on the commuter train, most weekends she would lose herself in the big city. Her good schooling and stern parents had taught her proper conduct. Nevertheless, as a young girl, in love with life, she had conceived exciting ideas even before leaving school.

Then she had walked straight into a job in the Strand, working in a large cosmetics store. It held fascinating prospects for a young girl. In two years she had learnt to do the best with her appearance, having served some highly poised women, millionaires, actresses; she had even exchanged smiles with the so-called nobility. Her secret joy was taking special pleasure in advising the men who often approached her at the beauty counter about what to buy for their wives. With her generous smile and courteous poise, she would listen carefully to descriptions of their wives and sweethearts, their fancy girls or casual friends or women they hardly knew but wished to send presents. She would then decide exactly what was suitable for the settled wife, or the girl friend who would immediately rush into bed, or even the unknown girl who would be eager to meet her secret admirer after receiving a seductive present.

Jackie had made many acquaintances at the counter, foreigners of all types. She had even learned to sort them out according to their romantic undertones.

In the evening she took dancing lessons. Then, tired from being on her feet all day, she would go straight to bed.

She had spent a full two years at the cosmetic store, by which time she had got to know the place inside out. Then, with an outgoing personality to enhance her gift for making the largest takings at her stall, she was on the brink of promotion to assistant manageress.

But she has other ideas and soon left for a more exciting job, something that paid more. It was spectacular and well suited to a young beauty with a great zest for life. This was in a night club, as an entertaining hostess. The school of dancing had prepared her for this. It was here that she met Mary.

The club was exclusive, providing entertainment for members who thought nothing of parting with unlimited sums. Duty kept her until the early hours of the morning, and she was available for not more than two consecutive dances to any guest who had come alone, not to spend too long at the table with any one guest, and restricted to one drink with a guest, but allowed to take dinner at his invitation during the final hour before closing.

At this job she had met men of high positions, she had listened to their troubles, their intimate problems. Some were the loneliest of men, even with their high positions. She quickly gained knowledge and insight into them, and naturally, unknown to the club, had even gone to bed with one or two.

Mary had been more lavish. She had set herself up for every chance, available for a few hours a day to businessmen, diplomats or professionals visiting London from every corner of the earth. Her scheme had been to confine herself to foreigners, as they were temporary and offered little danger of becoming persistent. She preferred to call them admirers. Vowing never to go to bed with an admirer after duty, she would sleep off the night in her apartment. Then she would spend two or three hours in his hotel room the following afternoon. She had often collected generous gifts for the long hours of pleasure. The majority were generous men, and even if they were not, after a sessions with Mary in which an admirer would have her completely to himself, his delights would induce unbelievable generosity.

She had cured many problems with her special technique. Four years older than Jackie, less striking, but very graceful, she was a handsome catch for any man. With her friendly personality and her ability to hold conversation with the best of them, she was conquellish and self assured. She had prided herself in making full use of her life.

Meanwhile, Jackie would confine herself to more emotional affairs, between which there were periods of recuperation, occasions when she would reconsider and sum up her experiences. She sometimes pondered over what would become of her.

Her last affair before the marriage to Pascoe was significant. It had lasted six months, with weekly meetings when she would completely let her hair down. It was demanding for her, for the doctor had taken to her, body and soul. It began when she had

21

visited his surgery. The middle-aged doctor had been a member of the night club and had often gone there without his wife. Jackie knew him well and, as she was the last patient of the evening, her visit immediately developed into a friendly chat. They were well at ease, so that when he suggested they might have dinner together she was apparently amused. His elegant moustache and receding hair fascinated her. He had humorous eyes and a distinct authoritative pose. And he had made it clear that her qualities easily brought out the best in him.

A month after they had dined together he turned up at the club one Saturday night, cheerful and delighted to see her. He had a brilliant idea that they should spend two weeks in France. They were happy together; she had never once considered his family. She readily agreed.

Jackie enjoyed the two weeks, stopping in the best hotel, dining well and seeing the best shows. The fortnight took the pattern of a honeymoon, and she might have been a virgin, for he had not made love to her before.

But when they were back in London it was not so convenient. The agreement then was to meet only on Sundays when it was ideal for them to slip out of the city and rest for the day in Brighton or Southend. But by Monday, less than a day after they were back, he would positively feel that the week was dragging. Jackie had been far less absorbed. The affair had seemed more like a game which only excited her on rare occasions, yet she was punctual without ever looking forward to a single meeting.

The whole thing took a dramatic turn when, a day after they were back from Brighton, the telephone rang in Jackie's apartment. It was the doctor, very distressed and had to see her right away. When he came to her he was almost in tears. His wife had discovered his secret and, in fear of losing a husband at her age, had threatened drastic measures. Jackie saw the situation for what it was: why shouldn't she expose him if it were the only way to keep him?

By then she was already accustomed to Pascoe's serious words on the dance floor. He was not bad looking, but had nothing for her except admirable eyes. In fact, she had been uncomfortable in his arms at first, but bound by the rules of the club to entertain all guests respectfully, she had thought very little of being on the floor on his arm. He was constantly discussing his business. On the other hand, he was affectionate. But she had paid little interest. His outspoken expression of his great love for her, at first bored her to tears. There was even a time when she dreaded the thought of dancing with him. However, someone must have briefed him on how to get through to her, for dancing one evening he was suddenly a different man; acting, of course. But she appreciated the changed since he had obviously made the effort to reach her. Then, in order to get her to himself, he had been persistent and she had casually accepted. After all, he was not a stranger. On the other hand, she had considered herself perfectly free.

Pascoe was soon getting difficult. With their rooted friendship, he was bent on getting her into bed. She had never considered this. Her interested in him had never gone that far. But he was visiting the club nightly, mainly to dine with her and to see her nicely tucked in after closing time. He was clever that way. Within a few days she discovered he was making plans.

Then, exactly a week after her last moments with the doctor, she was manoeuvered into going to Brighton with Pascoe. He was spending Sunday with a rich friend and had insisted that they needed her to add real beauty to the place. She had nothing better to do and simply seated herself in the chauffeur-driven car.

Back in London the following day she had no regrets. Pascoe was acceptable after all. He had got her into bed, but only after she had carefully considered it. And he was so jolly afterwards that it actually pleased her. From then on she was getting fresh flowers each morning, specially selected by Pascoe. And only three days later, he proposed to her and promptly told the club manager that she was leaving in a week.

He wanted the marriage right away. Neither she nor Mary had actually understood why a man of his hardness should have suddenly become so infatuated. Yet the feeling was genuine. And while Jackie took the whole thing as a joke, Mary had thought him mad to expect so much of her.

However, one joke was enough. Within a few days Jackie had detected symptoms of something brewing inside her. Her stomach had been upset, and she felt certain of having eaten something violently disagreeable. But on second thought, after carefully reviewing the symptoms, she decided she was pregnant. How could that be? Retracing her steps was certainly not difficult. Pascoe was the last man she had gone to bed with. That was scarcely a week ago. It was impossible! She had been well protected. But a week before that was her last Sunday with the doctor. She had felt protected then, but retracing it now left her with some doubt. After a whole morning of being sick, she was forced to accept the possibility.

After another sleepless night she was certain of her condition. What she felt was hardly conclusive at the early stages, but there was no other explanation. Quickly she decided that Pascoe's eagerness to marry her and impress his friends had to be taken seriously. Within days, when she had taken everything into consideration, her life up till then and the fool Pascoe was making of himself, she decided to take things easy. If he insisted on marrying her, she would silently consent.

Despite herself, abortion was out of the question. The possibility existed, naturally, but not for her. No one was going to tamper with her in that way.

The next bunch of flowers was accompanied by a note explaining that Pascoe would call for her within the hour; they were going to the register office to make the declaration.

After the marriage, when she had told him of the child, he readily admitted that the weekend in Brighton had been the time of his life. He saw nothing but the most ideal woman in her. Then without delay, he had taken over the bungalow at Lenham, a snug little village off the A20 in Kent.

Mary had never understood why Jackie had settled everything with Pascoe. She had never liked him herself. They had chatted on the dance floor; she had even dined with him. On the other hand, he was somewhat distasteful. And though she would willingly have gone to bed with him, she insisted that he would have been too much to live with. A year later when she herself had married and moved down to that part of the country, she was puzzled to find that Jackie had totally confined herself to him.

Chapter Three

Pascoe was a Londoner, born in the harsh districts, and grew up hard. At the time he met Jackie, he had just launched a new business: a mail order firm with head offices in Charing Cross Road. It was immediately successful and the break soon went to his head. With Jackie's refinement, he had to establish that money was no problem-his mail order business sold everything from babies' push chairs to transistor radios. Having reached the nation by newspaper   advertisement, the orders came in at fifty a day.

He had extravagant tastes. The night clubs and roulette tables were part of his existence. On Saturdays he would rush off to Newbury, for he also had investments in a couple of racehorses. He had to establish an image. He honoured his bookmakers and never kept his debts outstanding for more than a week. In fact, Pascoe had always been uneasy when in debt and would readily clear himself to keep in good faith. But the amounts were enormous and his tastes were such that he thought nothing of it.

This was the basis of his troubles. It was proved that although he had sent his share holders regular statements and expressed fully that the greater amount of profits was pumped back into the business for expansion, the firm's account had hardly risen. And when the whole thing went into liquidation he was scarcely able to pay back five shillings in the pound.

At first when he was imprisoned, Jackie had paid regular visits. Once a month she would drive up to Brixton, leave the child in the nursery and trot off to the reception area where, behind bars, Pascoe would be looking out anxiously. They would exchange pleasantries. Jackie would be sweet and cheerful, and always he would ask how she was making out, how the car was running. He had given her the Jaguar on the third anniversary of their marriage.

Then he would insist that she should let him know when she was out of cash. He had a few thousand pounds safely tucked away. But after a time the visits dwindled. Jackie had lost interest, spoke less, and there was now a two month gap since her last visit. Now that she had decided to rid herself of the car and had sent off the advertisement, she felt eager to see him, since the convenience of the car would be short lived. She brooded over this for a whole day, telling herself that she would put in the last few gallons of petrol and make the journey. But another mind insisted that the damn car had cost her enough. It must not be allowed to suck her dry, especially now that she was broke. Then, before she had made up her mind one way or another, the telephone rang.

The caller was interested in the white 'Jaguar two-seater' advertised at that address. The paper said it was nearly new.

Yes, she was sure he would agree once he had set eyes on it.

Would she settle for sixteen hundred?

No. That was out of the question; nothing less than the stated figure.

There was hesitation. Did she not think that seventeen hundred was a little high?

Not at all.

He would come and see it tomorrow afternoon. Yes, she would expect him at two o'clock.

So the advertisement had brought immediate response. She was wise to state seventeen hundred pounds after all. That would give her a great deal more than the salesman had quoted. Now all she had to do was to sit back and wait.

There was still time to visit Pascoe after all. She could be in Brixton by six, despite the traffic. It was worth the effort, since she would hardly feel like visiting him again for months.

Having just left the bath and wandering about the house in a gown, she went to the bedroom to find a dress.

Leaving the house, she first took her daughter to Mary who was happy to keep her for the few hours.

In a white jumper and a lavishly long skirt, she pulled into the first filling station on the A20, paid by cheque, something she was accustomed to do at the station, and headed for London.

It was fifteen minutes into visiting time when she arrived at the prison. In the lobby there were a number of people chatting through the rails to relatives, but the cubicle where she expected to find Pascoe was empty. Apparently he had been there exactly on the hour, like the previous months, but had found no one to talk to and had gone back to his cell.

A warder, recognizing Mrs. Pascoe and throwing her a friendly smile, rang for Pascoe. Meanwhile, Jackie stood in wait for Pascoe. She soon caught the warder throwing the occasional glance at her and it set her wondering what was going on in his mind. He was tall, with a massive frame that was probably necessary for this job. Clean shaven with a fat and flabby chin, the warder could not help but force a smile at the mature woman in pink skirt with the refined pose. It seemed out of reality that she should be waiting for a prisoner. It puzzled him that a girl of such refinement should have got mixed up with Pascoe's sort. In his own mind he recalled that such women only came to visit prisoners who were in for political reasons. Yes, political prisoners were usually good sorts.

When Pascoe appeared in the cubicle behind the iron rails his face was hard. For the first time Jackie had seen him without a smile. Seated now, he said: "Well, three months exactly, and I've been coming here every week. What's the excuse? Were you sick?"

"No…"

"Then what kept you?"

"Oh, the children, circumstances; I had always thought of coming but the hours just slipped by somehow."

Pascoe saw nothing in that sort of excuse. "In this place a man counts the hours, even the blasted minutes. Believe me, every hour is like a day. It's hell! You even forgot that they deliver letters once in a while to this god forsaken place! You can write, can't you?"

It hadn't occurred to her. As she had said, she had been intending to come.

Pascoe looked at this wife suspiciously through the iron rails. He felt a strong urge to taste her lips, but there was little chance. Most women visiting their husbands did not mind thrusting their lips between the rails, but Jackie was not the sort. Even that kind of simple affection would be repulsive to her.

"Well, you still look like my wife, anyway, attractive as ever. You won't forget yourself, will you?"

"I can wait."

"You're very comforting." His expression softened.

Pascoe was in a dark blue open-necked shirt and thick flannel trousers. It didn't look too bad for a prisoner's uniform. He seemed quite free in it. His hair was cropped short and the usual heavy flop over the forehead had gone. At the sides where the shears had been held low, were signs of greying and his face, usually firm, was rough. He was evidently worrying; the three months without seeing her had damaged him. He was pale, and his eyes tired. Now that he smiled a little, there was some colour. She did well to come, after all.

"How are the children? Is the little one chatting yet?"

"Trying to. She's two now. And she's very lively."

The baby was only fourteen months when he left.

"She's running about the house, with a lively personality."

Jackie was being charming. "I think she takes after you."

"That's good. And how is Diane?"

"She's getting on well with her tutor. She's developing into an intelligent little girl. Very lady like. You should see her."

"She's a lot like you, I guess. Well, she couldn't have chosen a sweeter mother."

Jackie's face broadened into a mile which revived Pascoe's image. His eye flicked sideways and caught those of the warder who quickly smartened himself with sudden awareness.

Pascoe's eyes came back to his wife. "Listen, Jackie; I heard some good news a few weeks back that in spite of what the judge said, I might still get twelve months' remission."

"But he did say…"

"I know what he said, but the news source is reliable. They haven't told me officially, but I feel certain it's in the making."

"Oh, if it's true, then it would be good. It would mean you only have three more to do."

"Less than that. Two years nine months."

She would look forward to it.

"How are you making out? I find it hard to believe you're still holding out on what you had."

She was all right. But she might run short in a few weeks. She would let him know.

"I still have a few friends, you know." Pascoe was proud of this. "There's money tucked away that I want you to have until I get out. It's a good amount and you could live on it."

Again he caught the eye of the warder, but this time the situation was clear. Their time was up. In fact, all the other cubicles were empty. It was the warder's generosity that had allowed them the extra minutes, since the lady was late getting there.

Leaving the jail, Jackie drove quickly through the busy streets. What was the matter with her? Was she not inviting trouble? If not from the police, it would be from men who would dislike the idea of being overtaken in dense traffic, and less so by a dashing female.

Seeing Pascoee, even after three months, had done nothing much for her. He had not revived a single emotional chord in her. His gloominess and evident deterioration had actually reduced the enthusiasm she had when going there. Now, instead of going back to the bungalow, she was heading towards the West End without knowing where she was going, merely driving along familiar streets, manoeuvring the car from lane to lane.

It soon struck her that she might visit her old night club. Why not? It was years since she'd left and she had never once gone back there. Quite a shame, she thought. For the proprietor had been a great admirer. Who knows, it might even have changed ownership. But it suddenly occurred to her that she could not walk into the club without an escort. The doorman would simply refuse to admit her.

On reaching Westminster via Waterloo Bridge, she drove on up Whitehall, stopped in front of the theatre, and reconsidered. It was not easy to decide where to go. Since Pascoe was put away, she had neglected her friends. It had been difficult to face them for they had always considered him a bad choice.

She drove off, took a sharp left turn and went up Buckingham Palace Road. Entering the Ring Road, she manoeuvered cutely and got well to the inside; sped around and up the hill, turning left to join the sea of traffic in Park Lane. She thought she might go down to Bayswater, but indecisively allowed herself to be carried round the island in the stream of traffic. Straightening up now, she was already in Oxford Street and heading east, knowing she would have to turn back. Pulling up sharply at the red light she was next to an Alfa Romeo. Jackie glanced at the driver, quite absent-mindedly. Their eyes met but the curt smile on the rather handsome face made no impression on her. When the green light appeared, the Jaguar darted ahead, turned right and drove back along a parallel street to get back onto Park Lane. She had decided against going to Bayswater.

Well, never again would she allow herself to get confused. It was a terrible state of mind. One could get up to anything with indecision. She was severely depressed, her mind congested. How she despised Pascoe! Not because he was in jail and her life uninteresting and dull. Maybe it was inevitable that she should have come to this. Pascoe had been exciting to begin with, in a crude sort of way. He had amended his habits directly after the marriage and had made a big effort to fall in with her. But the refinements of her personality had been too much for him. Then he had reverted to his former self long before he was put away. Their love had dwindled. She had even found herself embarrassed at times when Pascoe was at ease and laughing at his own jokes. Apart from dancing and the night clubs, what else did they have in common? Conversations had been few; he had no taste for the theatre, the clubs he visited after midnight were distasteful. Yet it was his jokes and the lush atmosphere at the Brighton party that had carried her only because she was already pregnant. And the strange thing about it all was that, throughout their six years together, she had never taken him seriously.

Their incompatibility was reflected in bed. When she should have been totally at ease and letting herself be carried off, she had often recoiled. This was a reflection of how she had felt on the weekend at Brighton. It was even true to say that on that occasion she had given way to circumstances rather than to a genuine feeling. And this indifference had undoubtedly persisted throughout the marriage, when always she had given way to circumstances, and had never really abandoned herself to him. Then, of course, under such strain, she was forced to limit the occasions.

Well, he was counting on getting out a year early. She would not begrudge him that. After all, there was no hatred, she was merely indifferent. But where would they start? Pascoe had money, enough to keep her comfortable for the next three years. Even that had found her unresponsive. It hadn't registered even in such destitution. This was her last drive in the Jaguar and she hadn't told him. It was not that she had forgotten, simply that she was unable to accept that it mattered. She was cold even to Pascoe's generous proposals.

Arriving home, she garaged the car and went straight to Mary's bungalow, collected the child and put her to bed. When she was eventually settled in the living room, Mary joined her.

"How's Pascoe? Was he furious?" She helped herself to a martini and took a chair.

"Oh, he wasn't as furious as I had expected. He had some good news and I think that overshadowed it."

"It figures. All of three months… I daresay that was quite an insult to him. Didn't he ask what you were up to?"

"He was hinting at it." She smiled. "I think I managed to set his mind at ease."

"What was his good news?"

Jackie told Mary about the twelve months' remission. "I can't see it myself, but he is confident."

"It's doubtful, but it gives him something to look forward to."

"But think of the shock it will give him if three years from now he finds that he still has twelve months to do!"

"Oh, it will be a shock. But he will survive. In any case, if he finds that he has to do it all, the last twelve months will go quickly after four years in there."

"You're probably right. After all, a lot of men have survived twenty of more years in prison and still come out alive and well."

There was a hint of weariness in Jackie's voice. It was a good sign. Mary emptied her glass. Sitting back now she looked at Jackie with interest. "What will happen when he gets out?"

Jackie shrugged. She was not sure. "I don't really know. I suppose I'll decide one way or another by then."

"Is the drift serious?"

"I think so."

"You can't just hang on by yourself until be comes out before deciding whether there's anything left. If you keep yourself strictly to yourself for long, there certainly won't be much of you left."

"I'm already conscious of that. I had plenty of time to reason things out on the way back. You know that I was prepared to wait for him like a good wife. But after this visit, I'm confused. He looks bad, and he might get a lot worse over the years. You may be right that I need to pick myself up."

"You've improved a little. The last party improved things a bit."

Jackie was a little surprised. She did enjoy the party but she had felt that she was slowly drifting back into the confined space. She wrestled with her mind.

"You're blaming yourself," said Mary.

"There's no one else to blame. It would be unfair to blame Pascoe. He has never really been a part of me. I was day-dreaming long before he went inside."

Jackie rushed to the kitchen. She came back presently with cherries and cocktail sticks. She put three small fruits in each glass and topped them with Martini, pushed one towards Mary and reclaimed her chair.

Mary started on the cherries. "Why don't we throw a party? It would open up one or two doors."

"Not a bad idea," Jackie admitted. "But where would we make it?"

Mary considered. Yes, it was rather inconvenient. Jackie could not have it there for obvious reasons. They could not have it in Mary's bungalow before Bill's return, not for a few months. Nevertheless, they would think about it.

Mary was in casual shirt and slacks. She was graceful, with a large comfortable body. Full bosomed and round shouldered, she kept her short hair permanently curled at the top; a full auburn, there was a time when she had it bleached to blend with her complexion, which sometimes changed to a white luster in extreme cold. At thirty-six she was a fine woman, outward looking, and wearing a grand smile for all. Her full cheeks and wide smile with even teeth made her look ravishing. Without the reservation of a woman fixed in her ways, the personality was cheerful enough to lend her a look or permanent excitement and a flair for adventure . She loved men and took pleasure in being herself, while at the same time attaching great value to the security offered by an ambitious husband. Bill was a responsible man, a father figure with whom to discuss problems. He would also be vital in later years when her life would take its turn. She firmly believed that women should live according to their demands. They should not be confined when the inner self demanded otherwise. Life was too short to deny oneself available excitement.

Chapter Four

Mary had only a few yards to go before arriving on the steps of her bungalow. It was a modern home bought by her husband two weeks before the marriage, and separated from Jackie's by a wide area of unkempt grass; a new road passed thirty yards in front. This was an eight thousand pound present, snugly set, with trees to the rear for quarter of a mile before dwindling into rich farmlands. The house was almost square, the two front rooms being prominent, while between them another section enclosed the main glass doors which opened out onto a small patio. The large living room ran the full length of the house, to the left was the garage, while on the right were the dining room and kitchen. Then there were the two large bedrooms, one with a well appointed boudoir.

She entered the bungalow quietly; her four year-old daughter, Margaret, was asleep. She hummed a tune in her bedroom and slowly removed her blouse and got herself into a short nightie. Then she added expert touches to her appearance. She was expecting a visitor, a new admirer, perhaps.

For a week now she hadn't been so excited at that time of night. Apart from the child she was alone. The domestic help had already been laid off, as Mary would be leaving for Spain in a week. She carefully put on a dressing gown and worked her feet into light slippers. Another glance at the clock and she went out into the living-room.

There were three paintings and three photographs on the walls. One photograph showed her and Bill, a very recent picture. This was the one nearest to the front door, on the wall next to the dining room. The middle photograph showed them in married bliss, cutting the cake at the reception. She was excited, while he, with only a modest smile, was being careful to have the knife made a clean cut. The picture at the other end was a portrait of herself, six months after she had given birth to the child. On the opposite wall were three paintings. All done by an unknown artist from a small village in Wales. Two captured the full bloom of a village near Cardiff, showing clusters of spring roses against a hillside and two sheep cropping the fresh grass. The third picture was of the sea with two small boats through overhanging branches in Lantwit Major, another village in South Wales. They were collected for their beauty and bright traces of nature in brilliant colours.

There was a brief knock at the door. She glanced at the clock on the far wall; it was eleven-thirty. In her long open-fronted gown she went briskly to welcome her visitor. Penman strolled in and was immediately taken in by the spaciousness and grandeur of the living room.

"Make yourself comfortable," she smiled, showing him to the table at the far end.

He was hesitant. "It is very late…" He gazed at the room, the pictures. The atmosphere suited him.

Mary rushed to him and planted a kiss on his lips. Penman held her firmly and returned the pleasure.

"You must sit down while I get you something to drink. You're tired. How far have you walked?"

"There's a lay-by close to the turning. I left my car there."

"On the main road?"

"Yes. As you said, I only had to turn in and the lights would flood the place." He sat on the sofa and took out a cigar.

Mary watched with friendly eyes. "What would you like: coffee, gin?"

He settled for gin. The small bar was in the corner, opposite Penman. He watched her keenly, his eyes descending to her feet, the soft slippers on the carpet. He relaxed as she handed him the drink. Then, for herself, she poured half a glass form the same bottle and stirred in three small spoonfuls of honey.

So, that was how she kept her complexion. It certainly looked like a lady's drink.

She laughed. "You ought to try it sometime. It's a nice concoction, it stimulates the appetite."

But he preferred it on the rocks, to calm his nerves. After the long walk she agreed, but nevertheless insisted.

His eyes challenged her. "As you wish," he said.

Mary put her glass next to his. She attended to the candles, transferred the candlesticks form the mantle-piece to the middle of the table. "You must light them for me," she said, and trotted off to the other end of the room where, standing by the light switch until he had lit them, she put out the main lights. Now, with one end of the large room in utter darkness, and the other end showing only a moderate light from the two candles, she said, "That's better, much better. Now we can improve on this by lighting another candle."

And she brought in another from the dining room

"Here we are." She held it to a flame and then placed it at the

34

other end of the table. From the mantle-piece she took the three orange shades and fixed them to the candlesticks. "What do you think?"

Penman smiled. She read his thoughts. "I'm getting to like it."

"Good. Have you made love in this kind of light before?" He gave no comment, but his smiling eyes gazed at her, captivated.

"You'll find it thrilling. Have you drank much?"

"Two brandies."

"Well, one more gin should be enough. Come, you must help me with the chairs. We will fix them in a circle, so that we leave the middle open, with the table on the outside."

They brought up the three wide sofas, very close, end to end, and remained in the middle. She would bring up a single piece to close the gap before they were settled. The room was deliciously warm.

Penman had expected a late night, but nothing so elaborate. At fifty-five he could hardly believe he hadn't yet had the time of his life. But Mary, with gay unselfishness, had triggered off new vigour. He swallowed the last of the gin and she quickly refilled the glass.

They sat close. She assisted him in the 'simple pose.' Penman was already dizzy, almost in a trance. He laughed. She touched him. His coat already off, she removed his shirt, worked her hands to his chest and rubbed his false breasts, squeezing and rubbing them amidst whispers. Then, with sudden urgency, he bared himself. His large frame, over six foot, was fat, soft and sagging at the waist. She abandoned herself briefly, paused abruptly, then took her glass and fed him a strong dose of the concoction.

"What do you think of it?" she murmured.

He grunted agreeably.

They were on the carpet with everything around them. Mary worked herself out of the gown; her complexion a lustrous pink under the orange shades.

Penman was boiling inside. He was in full view of her bared thighs, large and inviting as his eyes moved upwards.

Throwing off the gown, she drew close and pressed him back. His body stiffened. Then he stirred a little. She pressed her body to him, circled him and they soon slumped to the carpet clumsily. She held him tight and the excitement began surging through him. He murmured as she massaged his chest and stomach, continuing down to other parts. Soon he became restless, the beast inside him raging.

She laid back as he took command. The candles showed her face in ecstatic joy, the layer of gin and honey reflecting the soft glow of her lips.

Penman's wild stroking excited her. Soon she was frantic. Then all at once she held fast, sighed and relaxed. Penman maintained his pace, blubbering occasionally, and planting sweet kisses on her lips and cheeks. He cuddled her with all his strength and raged on furiously under the dull orange light. Then at last he found a pause. She took the final moments as a treat, curled her body against him and happily returned his soft kisses. She smiled into the half-closed eyes under the coloured light and the cool whisper of her voice brought him round. He forced a smile, but she put a finger to his lips, pressed them together and kissed them.

"I thought you were married."

He confirmed it tiredly.

"Well, you were starved. Are you separated?"

"She's busy with the children!"

Their lips met, yet again, and the honey was delicious.

"She's hard at work," he murmured.

"An important career? I see. What happened to your mistress? Someone married her?"

"Not much luck," he said. "difficult to find a woman who will draw up a contract."

Mary was not convinced. "You denied your wife the vital thing," she proclaimed.

"Impossible."

She sucked at his lips. "It's mad to keep it back; it's shameful."

"Not true," he said.

"You pay too much attention to the impression you make on women. You behaved badly at the party, always making lovely gestures. Too generous. When we were alone you steered clear. All those compliments, never an advance! That was terrible."

Penman objected, saying that they'd only met once before. But she was having none of it.

"The party was the right place to be intimate," She insisted. She loosened the ribbon at her neck and put a full breast to his lips. "You were subtle and caressing, but only to one woman."

He sucked at it furiously. Then he turned on to her, swept an arm over her shoulder and pressed hard. He closed his eyes so that the soft flesh caressed his mind. Then, buried in this luxurious serenity, he soon arrived at his original pitch. She kissed him wildly. Their mad thirst already extinguished, they went on easily now, steadily, until alleviated, they gradually withered into drowsiness.

Penman would be rushing back to London in the early hours of the morning. He was an investor striving to keep a large capital above a bad market. Mary had chatted to him in London the day before. They had dined together and she had invited him down for this grand occasion.

An hour later she rose under the candles. Penman had passed out, sleeping soundly. Smiling fondly, she collected her clothes and slipped quietly into the dining room in almost total darkness. Instinct guided her to the bedroom where she bedded herself in cool comfort.

At six o'clock in the morning dawn was already apparent. Normally she would have stayed in bed until the child came in and woke her. They would lie together late into the morning. But now, wide awake, Penman came to mind. She went to the bathroom, and then slipped into a casual gown.

In the living room, the candles burned wearily, almost to the little brass sticks. The two half-empty bottles were still on the table. Penman was sound asleep in his birthday suit. His heavy breathing made her smile. Trousers slung over a chair, tie across the table, he was lying on his shirt, with part of his clothes slung in one corner against the couch. She laughed silently. He was not a bad sight after all!

Form her room she fetched a dressing gown and spread it over his nakedness, then listened to his heavy breathing for a time before gently shaking him.

Penman stirred, his drowsiness the undeniable sign of a deep slumber. He threw back his arm and gazed wildly before coming to. With a smile, she remained cool so as not to embarrass him.

He rose suddenly and found protection in the silk gown, his face changing to a triumphant smile as he let out a forceful yawn.

"I ought to compliment you on your selection of carpet. It was comfortable."

"Have you slept on many?" she asked.

"Not since my old college days."

She glanced at the floor, and back to him. "It is comfortable, yes. But you hardly had time to notice. You could have slept anywhere. It would have made no difference."

"Well, I haven't got a backache. It's as good as the bed at

Buckingham Place, I'm sure!"

"You may drop the credit," she said seriously. "You slept half the night on me."

She turned and blew out the candles, thus creating an opportunity for him to rise. After putting   away the bottles, she came back to him. Penman had not stirred an inch. His eyes had been following her.

"Do you know the time?"

"It is late," he admitted.

"Then let me help you."

And with a little help Penman was on his feet. He got his hands through the sleeves of the silk gown. It was four inches short at the ankles and sleeves.

"Come," she said, "you must use the bathroom. And you will have to be quick. It's nearly eight o'clock."

The bathroom was finished in blue, with two low wattage bulbs shining through pale, half-round shades. He fancied a bath. She turned on both taps and showed him the soap and towel. There was a spare toothbrush, still new in its packet, which she handed him. She kissed his cheeks. "I'll have breakfast ready in fifteen minutes." And without waiting for gratitude, she closed the door behind her.

After a moment in the kitchen she was soon rushing to the living room to tidy the place: she opened the curtains and struggled with the sofas, putting them back in their respective places. She took his clothes to her room and whispered at the bathroom door that she had done so. Then, rushing back to the kitchen she made haste with the breakfast. He must be got out of the house without delay. It would be unwise to have him there when the child woke up. A strange man would be a shock to her little mind. In a few years she would be learning the facts of life, and might easily recall the strange man in her mother's bedroom.

The breakfast was smoked bacon, eggs and a pot of coffee. Penman showed himself into the dining room fresh with enthusiasm. "I don't suppose your husband has a spare shaving kit?"

There was an electric razor. She went off to get it. Then he was instructed to use it in the living room so that the noise would not wake the child. On his return, clean and ready, she relieved him of the razor and handed him a small bottle of Arden after-shave lotion. He patted his cheeks, contracted his face and quickly went back to

38

the bathroom to rinse his hands. He was soon back at the table.

"How do you like coffee?"

"Is it strong?"

"Rather."

"That's fine."

He ate and glanced at his wrist occasionally. "When can I expect you back in London?"

"You mustn't," she said briefly.

Delighted with himself, he was disappointed by the negative reply. "You mean we can't have a sort of understanding?"

"You mustn't expect me whenever you wish."

"Is there no possibility of agreeing on something?"

She had never formed more than a casual liaison with an admirer. "We mustn't allow that to happen," she said calmly, "but on the other hand, we could leave it open and see how things develop."

Penman glanced at his watch again.

"How are you doing for time?" she asked.

"Not bad. I should be in by nine-thirty."

"What time do you usually make the office?"

"Nine-thirty. Sometimes earlier."

"Will you miss much?"

"No. Most mornings I merely keep an eye on movements. That's one of the things about the money market: you don't always make up your mind over small variations."

"Can I expect to spend much when I get your tip?"

"Difficult to say." He allowed her to pour his coffee. "Keep about five thousand ready. I might advise you to collect anything from two thousand pounds' worth."

Five minutes later Penman was ready to leave. In the passageway she slipped into his arms for a final kiss. It was friendly and warm, without involvement, not the spectacular sweetness with which she had greeted him last night. "You didn't come to stay," she reminded him, "but you did well. It's eight-thirty." She secured the top button on his single-breasted jacket. "I thought you usually carry an umbrella and hat."

"They're in the car."

She laughed as he went through the door.

For a moment Mary held her breath. Outside the bungalow the wide open area welcomed Penman. He was terribly conspicuous. The neighbours knew her husband was away. And Jackie! What would she think, seeing Penman emerging? Well, it was too early for Jackie. The others could assume what they liked.

Penman hustled along the unfamiliar road. The calm residential area with open fields made him conscious of being a long way from his own area and, the two women apart, no one knew him. To hell with it! He had had a high night with a handsome girl. Damn it all! This was a time when even a man of his stature must forget high-minded compunctions and credit himself for a good achievement.

The walk seemed longer than last night. It was a good half mile, but when he had gone to the bungalow in the darkness, there had been no reason to count his steps. Now it took ten minutes to reach the lay-by. He got into the Rolls Royce, wiped the sweat from his face then drove off.

At a steady fifty he switched on the radio and pressed the pre-selector button. There was good classical music, calm and serene on a brilliant morning. He pressed in the cigar lighter and fumbled with a box of cigars. Getting one between his teeth and lighting up, he sat back and enjoyed the mild flavour. In one hour he would hit the heavy traffic. Damn it!

Chapter Five

Jackie was awake in the early hours, tossing and turning since three o'clock. Like so many of her recent nights, last night was restless. She hadn't slept more than two hours. Throughout the night, her mind ran over a thousand things, not including the financial problem. That could solve itself! It was suddenly the least of her troubles. She needed a man, a constant companion, one with whom she could release herself and return to the gay life. It was sad to be alone, more so during the night.

For a time she was occupied with thoughts of Pascoe, how to be rid of him: once out of jail he would be a nuisance. Pascoe would once more become part of her, an intolerable burden, the plague. The marriage was stale and her feelings for him long dead. Pascoe had taken the best years of her life, he had made nothing of it. While the early months had produced some excitements, they were brief, for she was forced into confinement, with the pressures of pregnancy. Yet that was hardly the reason for the unhappy years. Pascoe's scope for recreation was limited: he lacked refinement, living only in the casinos and the bookmakers, nursing the one idea of uplifting his image and striving with a great passion to prove himself hard and aggressive. She despised him.

After hours of restlessness, worrying and burdening her mind with trivialities, her head was congested. Jackie sensed the danger and knew she would have to pull herself together. She had lost a little weight but was still a long way from a respectable shape. Months ago she had wanted to get down to work, but somehow had been unable to free her mind and gain the enthusiasm. Lying in bed now, and brooding over all the unwanted fat, she suddenly arrived at a firm decision that she would get down to work on the exercise bicycle and the belt master at least twice a day.

Then getting up, she spent an hour with the children; sent Diane off to the teacher, and contented herself with the two year-old for company.

After working herself into the nylon swimsuit she was appalled at the bulges at her hips and waist. The girdle had kept all this well hidden, it had made her look neat, so that she had taken little note of the scales. Now all the unwanted fat simply bulged out like interlocking spurs on a mountainside; she stepped onto the scales and was quite shocked. She would need to shed twenty pounds.

In the children's room she carefully shifted the bed to one corner and brought in the devices. Straight away she clipped on the broad tone belt, designed to reduce the hip and waist. There would be no need to remove it until she had done all the exercises. Bending at the knees and sitting back on her heels, she placed the tensile between her knees and pulled laboriously at the tension spring to work the muscle groups isometrically and reduce flab. The bosom would be firmer and smaller in a month or two. Ten minutes later she rested and kissed the child, pouting her lips playfully. The child giggled and imitated her mother.

Next, Jackie got out the slimming wheel, knelt over it and worked at it for ten minutes with occasional rests. The sagging at the stomach would go before long. This was the easiest part of the body to reduce. Even if she did no exercise, the abdominal section would go smaller simply by dieting. She was soon on the machine she preferred best: the cycle. On it she could remain seated even while catching a breath. It made her feel thirteen again, when she had had a bicycle of her own and had often ridden aimlessly with friends. Those were carefree days. This cycle did not go anywhere, but she adjusted the gears to a moderately hard and fast ride, got hold of the thick leather-covered bar which came up from the forward stretching stays, and started pedaling. The child joined in by sitting on her own little tricycle, enjoying the similarity. After a time Jackie removed the broad tone belt from her waist and got onto the belt master. Then, with its nylon belt hugging her hips, she braced her stomach against its soft section, stood on tiptoes and switched on the agitator. This was hard work. Occasionally she would rest   from exhaustion, for the contraption threatened to shake the very life out of her. It would unwind kinks, stimulate circulation and after a time relieve tension. Effectively it would tone the stomach, thighs and other parts of the body. Enough of this now, she was back on the bicycle for a last ride.

For two hours Jackie was hard at these exercises, then, exhausted, decided that she had done well. She would spend another hour at it later before going to bed. It would clear her head and make sleep easier.

In the bathroom she peeled off the clinging swimsuit and got under the shower; it was cool, a perfect refreshment after two hours of hard work. She breathed comfortably, turned off the water and reached down for the soap. She lathered the large sponge and transferred the lather to her face and ears. Now with eyes closed, she felt for the tap and held up her face to the raining water. After a time she glanced down at her tired body and told herself the exercises were already effective, that she had already lost inches form the vital sections.

Amidst great enthusiasm, there was a certain buoyancy. It was interesting, for she now felt she was preparing for a new venture, a new life. Back in her room she sat at the dressing table and mopped her hair, abandoning the hairdryer for the time being.

It was past midday. The sun was brilliant. An idea came to mind. She could go to Mary's bungalow and give her body to the sun, yes, why not? The rays would dry out her hair. She lifted the child and planted her in the middle of the bed while she hastily got dressed.

In the bottom drawer of her bureau she found a bikini, something she had not worn for years. Holding it up, she quickly decided that it would do. But it was quite inadequate, much too snall. Her flesh was already over the waist; she would never get the top on. She turned out the drawer. There was another bikini, an attractive turquoise which had been worn only once. This was perfect: she pulled on a short chemise dress over it.

Putting the child in her little chair, Jackie trotted off to the kitchen. The exercises had brought a pain to her stomach, hunger pain. In the middle of quick meal, the door bell rang. A man was expected to call. It would be him.

He was slightly built, and wore a tweed single-breasted suit. He removed his dark glasses smartly and adjusted his eyes to the sun. Then his eyes lit up. Somewhere around thirty-five years old, he was answering the advertisement for the car and took it that she was the person he had spoken to on the telephone. The car was in the garage. If he would wait a moment, she would get the keys.

She rushed back into the house and on the way out she summoned the child to be good and not to make a fuss. But the child gave no acknowledgement, for she was busy with a dish and spoon.

Thus, in the ridiculously short dress, Jackie took the few steps ahead of the caller and opened the garage door.

"By the way," she said, "I am Jacqueline."

"He smiled. "I'm Coleman, Graham Coleman."

Then he saw the white Jaguar. A thin film of dust on the car was hardly noticeable under the shade. The spokes wheels were non-corrosive being made of stainless steel. He was naturally impressed. In her short dress and no stockings, Jackie decided not to sit in it. It would be something of a struggle.

Would he care to drive it out? He could release the brakes and push it back. It was quite easy. He did the latter and the car rolled freely back. Now under the brilliance of sun, he said yet again:

"Yes, it is remarkably clean. Quite superb." He opened the door and got in behind the wheel, composed himself as if traveling at high speed and pushed the pedals down to feel the pressure. He inspected the interior and, leaning back in the seat, the top of his hat touched the curve of the hood. He took off his hat and tossed it out onto the lawn; got out, closed the door, and kept his eye on the car.

"Well, I'm interested." He hoisted the telescopic aerial and pushed it down again. He was about to raise the bonnet when she reminded him that the release was inside the car.

Of course he'd forgotten.

He went back inside and found it, then proceeded to inspect the engine compartment. That, too, was clean; no excess oil or grease. He was undoubtedly impressed by the massive engine and surrounding components. He seemed to know something about cars, but realized it would be useless to discuss things with her. Jackie assured him of its regular service, that he would find the history in a large envelope in the back. He smiled understandably, saying that in any case they would only be routine services. These engines were good for a hundred thousand miles, before showing any sign of wear. And he slammed the bonnet shut.

"Well, I think I can just afford seventeen hundred. You would want it in cash, I suppose?"

It was not necessary. She hadn't forgotten that it might be inconvenient.

He was pleased to hear that. He had just taken over a director's seat. The previous director had retired.

Jackie congratulated him. She thought he fitted the image well, and she wished him success.

"Thank you," he said, spiritedly. It was the best one he'd had. He looked beyond the bungalow and commented on the absolute quietness of the area.

Jackie explained that she had driven into the area some years ago and had fallen in love with it. The hills beyond were particularly attractive.

Yes, he wouldn't mind settling there himself. But the new director was digesting very inch of her. Jackie was unaware. This enabled him to view her with ease. The short chemise dress was no more than an inch below the bikini paths. And what fascinated him most was the smooth texture of her skin, particularly her thighs. Then there was the long black hair, soft and wet, flowing to her shoulder and below. His pulses stirred and in a short while there were other things on his mind along with the business of the car. For her attitude was almost childlike, completely unaware of the tremendous sexual signals she was radiating. At length he found his voice and said:

"We'd, better settle the deal. I must make out a cheque."

She naturally invited him to do it over a cup of coffee. He was automatically drawn to her as she made off. And from behind he had an uninterrupted view of her firmness and felt out of place by her casual perfection. Another woman might have tried desperately to pull herself together. But so far Jackie had shown no awareness of the situation. She certainly hadn't noticed him any further than the interest he was taking in the car.

She invited him to sit in an armchair and pulled up a small table in front of him. Then she was off to the kitchen and was soon back with the coffee tray.

He had already made out the cheque for seventeen hundred pounds.

"You're very generous, "he said with compliments. "They don't give this kind of service at the showroom."

She accepted the compliment. "My friend next door has a saying, that business is best done in comfortable surroundings."

"I will cherish that advice for the future," he said, as he poured the milk into his coffee and stirred in two sugars. He began sipping as she stooped to her knees to attend to the child who seemed to have a dry cough.

Her attention was soon back to him.

"About this cheque," he said. "I would like very much to drive the car back to my office. But of course, you will want some sort of security; like making sure the cheque is worth what it says. If I date it back to yesterday, it will be cashed in three days. On the other hand I don't suppose it would be quite enough, since you will still have until Monday to worry about whether it is genuine." But he dated it and tore it out, inspected it and added his name and address on the back, also the name of his company. He also signed it again. Then there was the embarrassing matter of a guarantee, only a formality, of course, but after all it was a lot of money.

Yes he would accept a lady's agreement for a month. It was a point he wanted to be over with. And Jackie would keep the particulars of the car until the cheque was through. While he waited, however, she picked up the telephone and dialled his bank in London, checked on the name and account number and got a clarification that there was enough money on balance to clear the cheque.

Throughout the time they had discussed the matter he had kept a straight face, not daring to let his eye drop below her bosom. She, on her part, seemed so innocent in her manner that it would have been shameful to show anything but the best intention.

After a second cup of coffee, he sighed. "Well, it seems a satisfactory way of relieving each other of our worldly goods." And he thanked her for everything, in particular her sweet generosity. She was entertaining.

Jackie watched as he made off in the car. It slowed at the gate, turned left and headed down the drive to the main road. She sighed openly. That was the end of it! Heaven knows when she would own another!

Quickly she ran to the baby, hoisted her and kissed her lovingly.

Chapter Six

Five minutes later Jackie was dressed. Leaving the bungalow with the child, she rang the door bell at Mary's. She rang a second time, wondering if Mary had gone out without letting her know. After the third ring she heard movements and felt better.

Mary opened the door. She had been under the sun bed.

Jackie smiled. Yes, she had thought about coming over, but she had had a visitor. They were in the living room now, a larger room than Jackie's, with expensive furniture, and another glass door opening onto the rear terrace. Mary was sympathetic at the news that Jackie had sold the car. Taking everything into consideration, it seemed necessary after all. Jackie could use hers for the time being.

The garage was already open. She got into the Ford Capri and drove out. It was almost as comfortable as the car she had been used to, but with lighter controls. She adapted herself to them with caution, having driven it only once before, nearly a year ago when Mary had just taken delivery of it.

In Ashford she was lucky enough to find a vacant space in front of the bank. Parking the car, she rushed in and asked to see the manager.

The clerk conveyed the information to another clerk who disappeared through a private door. Coming back, she directed her through a door which led to the manager's office. She knocked gently and a voice welcomed her.

"Mrs. Pascoe, Yes; good afternoon."

"Good afternoon," she returned.

There was a smile, an apology. "Well, it's not too bad, a modest amount, indeed. If you should see some of our customers' accounts, you would agree with me that you're very fortunate. It's the first time you've had an overdraft in six years; absolutely nothing to lose sleep over. We hardly take note of rare occasions like this, you know. Sometimes they're cleared up before we are even wise to them."

She thanked him for being understanding on the telephone. The little chat had been reassuring. Then she handed him the cheque.

"Very quick," he commented with a smile.

Yes, she had had an immediate response.

"And your instruction is to credit you account with the total sum?"

"Wouldn't you like to invest a portion of it?"

There were no plans at present, but she would certainly consider it.

He drew a slip of paper from a tray, credited the cheque to her account and handed it to her for signature.

When Jackie left the bank she was delighted with herself. She called at a flower shop in Hawthorn Road and bought two lots of fresh flowers. Arriving home she presented one to Mary, put hers in water and arranged them in the living-room and dining room then quickly got back into her bikini to catch the last hour of the sun.

The next two weeks were hard. She worked at her exercises in the morning and when the sun was up, she and Mary spent the time sunbathing at Mary's bungalow, catching the sun and listening to music from the extensive stereo system in the living room

Mary was soon off to Spain to join her husband, and was not due back until November. Before leaving, she had made Jackie promise to join them later for a couple of weeks. In fact, when it was first suggested, Jackie admitted the change would be good and agreed to consider it.

Now she was alone with the two children, bored, contemplating her bank account. Already a substantial sum had gone out of it. She had paid six weeks' back rent, plus two weeks' in advance. Then the grocer and the butcher were paid up to date, and all other outstanding bills were cleared up. She had telephoned the flower shop in Ashford and instructed them to deliver fresh flowers every three days to her address.

Engrossed with the two children, her problems were light during the day, but at nights, when they were in bed, it was a different matter. Physically, Jackie was in excellent health. She was losing weight fast, and this was her passionate desire for the time being.

She worked hard at the bicycle and the belt master for two hours each day. Two inches had gone from the hips and even the girdle was already showing slackness at the waist and could not be taken in. In a month she would have no need of it. Furthermore, constant exercising had left her buoyant and healthy. But the nightly rest was more difficult. For all her physical activities during the day, Jackie was drinking more and more at night. And already she was going off to bed with the bottle. Despite it all, she was waking early and only resting her eyes while the night dragged on. Her complexion showed the strain, for the eyes were severely tired in the mornings. It worried her too. The only remedy for insomnia was sleep. She had already frowned at tablets, since it was dangerous to take more than the stated dose, and it was a fact that the nerves eventually relied on them for calm. But with a mere hour's sleep at nights, the restlessness was driving her mad. Once awake, her mind would race with trivial scenes. She even wondered why it was that she was unable to control her own mind, night after night, in utter loneliness, she would make efforts to concentrate constructively; but quickly, without being able to hold for long, such thoughts would vanish, only to be replaced by ridiculous scenes. She would see herself making amusing signs at the children, sometimes feeding them; or with a man escorting her to the theatre or the opera house. Often she would visualize an actor with a handsome smile making advances to her, sending her presents and insisting that she became his mistress. She even saw herself making love with unknown faces. This would make her furious, especially now that she seemed to enjoy these visions, for always, in her sleeplessness, she would be smiling as her mind took on these visions.

Even the day-dreams were more frequent. Kneeling over the slimming wheel, she was often preoccupied with visions of herself massaging a robust male who had just made love to her. She even saw herself as the woman of three different men, each making love to her one after another, while she presented herself playfully and in control. During these revolting visions her face would be smiling and appearing to be enjoying something blissful.

The loneliness was terrible. The visions were in fact a refuge. Some were quite delightful day-dreams, especially those with her children. She pictured them grown up at a time when she was old but graceful. They were beautiful girls. The elder one, Diane, was a successful actress of tremendous grandeur, who preferred to remain chaste and radiant. The younger daughter, Connie, was a doctor at an international health center, making important decisions. Both girls were famous, and she, their mother, and old woman with graceful lines, was comfortably retired in a large country mansion, and was enjoying visits from famous people.

She was still their idol and directing their lives morally. And so for their male companions, she would test each one for his suitability before allowing him to have anything to do with her daughter.

Jackie lived calmly with these dreams, some soothing and

pleasurable. In others, she was shocked that her mind had a power to dream up such foulness. Whenever she was aware of taking delight in sexual dreams, she would rebuke herself sternly with much shame. Yet, in all these dreams, she had never once been involved with Pascoe. He had taken no part in these unconscious delights, and this was true evidence that she had rejected him. Pascoe had ceased to play a useful part in her life.

The better part of the summer had passed. Engrossed in her mad dreams, Jackie's only activity was the slimming wheel. But she was already shaking without knowing why. On occasions at the table her hands shook madly, even when feeding the two-year old. The elder girl once asked her mother the reason for this, but Jackie had been unable to answer the child, insisting that her innocence should not be corrupted by a logical explanation. Yet stung by this sudden awareness, she was suddenly fearful of the difficulties ahead.

Confined to the house, the shopping was done by post, and each time the grocery list was accompanied by a cheque. The door was opened only to take in boxes and parcels. Such parcels would come from the butcher. And the only other occasions when the door was opened would be to let Diane in and out of the bungalow, or to take in the milk.

One day in the middle of September the telephone rang. It was late evening and it startled her. None of her friends had communicated with her since the disheartening news of Pascoe's imprisonment. The voice was distant, it rang no bells.

"It's Penman, Karl Penman."

She smiled into the telephone and apologized.

But no harm was done. "After all," he commented, "it's a long time."

"Yes. Indeed. All of four months and some weeks. But I don't remember giving you this number. How did you get it?"

"From Mary, of course. I met her some months ago. Did she not tell you?"

"No."

How forgetful. Perhaps he should apologize for the surprise.

"No, no, it's not necessary."

"Then you don't mind speaking to me?"

"Not at all," she said cheerfully.

"Good. How are you; still as tantalizing, as I seem to remember?"

The tone surprised Jackie. "Well, I don't quite know. But I'm very well. You sound very much like the man at the party, complimentary, very generous."

"Thank you. I should like to think that I haven't changed at all. My health is good and I am making the best of the fine weather. I remember you danced well. In fact it was quite a pleasure for me, looking back. I wonder if I could invite you to a private gathering a couple of weeks from now."

"You mean a party?"

"Yes. It should be quite good. The best band. There'll be a formal invitation."

"I have to postpone my decision until later."

"Yes," he said with some confidence. "I will look forward to seeing you, all the same." And he added: "It's a pity about Mary; she's off to the Mediterranean."

"Yes. She usually goes for the summer."

"By thy way, I would like to see a little more of you, if I may. I'm sure you come into London sometimes; might we have dinner together on one of these occasions?"

"Whenever I'm up there I am always restricted. I usually have the children with me."

Perhaps he could arrange a nanny for an hour or two?

She was afraid that would not do. She could not leave them with a stranger.

"Hm, pity. And I don't suppose you ever go out otherwise, except with your husband?"

"Very rarely," she admitted.

Oh, but he would very much like to meet her, to talk with her a little. She was something quite above the ordinary.

Well if she were to accept the invitation, it would be a golden opportunity for him.

"Yes, of course. So, until then good-bye."

She replaced the telephone.

So, Penman was still interested in her; more now that ever, it seemed. Something must have inspired him; he was trying his utmost to get her to himself. What made him think she was that easy? She could not have given him that impression at the party. With her strict formality, she could never have led any man to suppose that she was an easy lay. The only conclusion was that Penman knew something about her–that her husband was doing time, as they called it! That she was broke and destitute. The fact

51

that she needed a man was too obvious.

It was a Saturday evening; throughout the week, apart from saying 'thank you' to the delivery boy, it had been the first time Jackie had spoken to anyone except the children. Locked in the house all week her only moments of calm were with the two children. She had resigned herself to solitude, taking delight in more passionate day-dreams and at times feeling the worst as she reflected upon her marriage.

By now she was a trim figure, living on only one meal a day. She had developed a firm, neat shape which the best connoisseur would have easily described as sumptuously exquisite. The exercise had not shaped her precisely as a sculptor would, but the fine details were now obvious under the thin chemise dress. Yes, she was due for a completely new wardrobe; her clothes no longer fitted the new figure, they merely hung from the shoulder like shawls and saris. But for the time being a new wardrobe was unimportant. She had not been out of the house since the day Mary had flown off. And there was no desire to. The day-dreams were a real comfort.

She had entered a new phase and now saw herself in only the most delicious scenes, in attractive colours, in neat dresses, in the best places. Her favourite scene was that of a young girl, innocent and vivacious, on the tennis court. She wore a white, flare-skirted dress, hip length, with a richly embroidered blouse. Her movements were particularly attractive. She played to large crowds and in these scenes she was the envy of all the woman. Each time she made to return the ball the action would lift the short skirt to reveal frilly underwear. And occasionally she would notice the smile on the men's faces while the women on their arms gave horrid looks of conceited envy.

For weeks Jackie advanced these scenes, filling in little details. Dressed alluringly in the same white outfit, she pictured herself as the only girl among a team of cricketers. She was a sort of hostess, serving their needs. In the middle of a game they would pause for five minutes while she paraded the field with soft drinks, moving purposefully from one to the other, doling out a glass to each. Then she would go round again in the same order to collect the empties. This was a good scene. Cameras clicked from all angles and, dressed as she was, all eyes were centred on her. This and the scene when she played tennis were comforting, even inspiring. They made her feel free and particularly gay.

So embedded were these visions in her mind that it was

difficult to concentrate on anything else. They had brought her to a point where she was incapable of even realizing her real actions. Under the shower or relaxing in the bath, she would picture the rough face of a man soaping her and touching her in place which made her curl with pleasure. There was even a man close by whenever she rode the slimming wheel. The same face appeared daily, noting her progress, allowing his hands to linger here and there while insisting she worked at this or that part of her body, so as to lose another inch. Perhaps this man was her greatest love, since he always showed the most interest in her, and was constantly with her when she got out the slimming wheel. He often rode the bicycle with her, sitting behind with hands on her shoulders, sometimes slipping down to her waist and occasionally sliding up to cup her breasts. She wore a stretch swimsuit and her man always appeared in boxer shorts. He would pull her to him, but was gentle with his hands. Then, at the end of each set of exercises, he would kiss her by way of encouragement. In his arms Jackie was like a child, innocent and desiring to be instructed.

This man was much better than the one in her bath, the former being ugly and rugged, with huge limbs, hairy all over, and rough with his hands. He would treat her as though she were some beast with a hide he needed for winter. At times she would actually ask herself if she really preferred this man to the more refined romantic who helped her with her slimming.

But her hands were already shaking. Day and night, her head congested with fantastic scenes that changed form time to time. There were times when her hands would shake, gently at first, but now more profound. She was aware of this and becoming troubled. Her worry was bringing on moments of depression. In the home she hardly knew whether she was coming or going. Preoccupied with these fantasies, the children were inevitably feeling the effects.

Incapable of understanding why her mother was continually grim, the elder girl was quite alarmed when, one morning at the breakfast table, her mother's hands shook so terribly that she was unable to eat. Jackie held the toast but each attempt to put it to her mouth resulted in the intolerable shacking of her hand. It appeared even worse when she tried to lift the cup, for this time it rattled in the saucer. Amused at this, the two-year-old giggled with excitement and insisted on Mamma doing it again. But Diane was frightened by the look on her mother's face.

Once when Jackie had retreated to the kitchen out of despair, the child followed anxiously. Finding her mother seated at the window, she wanted to feed her, to help. She had brought the toast and now held it so that Jackie could eat. But Jackie was astonished. Why did Diane want to feed her? She was not a child. She was grown up.

"I want to help," said the child.

And when Jackie saw the immense comfort it would give the young thing, she bit off a piece of the toast that was held for her.

"Now you must have the rest," said Jackie. "You're going to school and you won't have anything before lunch."

But the child had had hers, and pleaded still further, insisting that she never got hungry at school anyway.

Then to clam her and free her from the fear that her mother was terribly ill, Jackie ate the rest of the toast. The child embraced her and pressed her cheek to hers. Later that day, when Jackie was tidying the living-room, she came upon a card; it was the invitation card from Penman. She had picked it up weeks ago and had forgotten it. Well, it was too bad! The date of the ball had long past. She had never even replied to the card. It was surprising that the telephone had not rung. Perhaps he had given her up completely, since there had been no encouragement. It was a shame really that there had never been a generous word from her. She gazed at the card, unable to decide whether to lament one way or the other. She could have decline the invitation in the proper manner.

Next to the card was a letter from Brixton. She knew no one in Brixton except Pascoe. She had no desire to hear from him, she had completely forgotten him. The children had not once mentioned him. His absence meant nothing to them. There were no preparations for his home-coming! Pascoe could go to hell! Without opening the letter she kept it with the card, collected a match, and went out onto the terrace where she set fire to them. Holding the papers in her hand, she gazed at the flames and was thrilled. Yes, there was a distinct sensation. Was it the look of the yellow flames under the sun? Was it that she was burning a letter from Pascoe? As the flames crept closer to her finger and the burnt paper curled into white ashes and then to nothing, she came up with the answer: she hated men! Yes, she was burning them both; so that was it. She could live without them. Had she not survived two years without a man? It was more than that. She had refused Pascoe long before the birth of the last child, for on finding herself pregnant, she had reproached herself and promptly decided to have separate beds. She had gone cold and had later decided not to have him touch her. So in fact three years of frustration had piled up inside her, only to be released on imaginary occasions when she would let in a man powerful enough to reject her fine qualities. She would visualize these things and take delight in them, no longer rebuking herself for concocting such wild fantasies. But once confronted with reality, she was unapproachable. The dresses she now wore made even the delivery boy fancy his chances, especially when she smiled and gave out a word of greeting, but her fantastic naivety pushed her out on a limb along which few men would advance, since it seemed clear that they would fail before reaching the fruit.

Her slender fingers were hot with the flames. She released the paper and watched it burn to the last. Then, rushing back into the bungalow, she gathered all the papers she could find, most of them old letters from friends who had rejected her since her marriage. Looking at their handwriting now, there was satisfaction as she burned each letter in turn, feeling certain that she was ridding her mind of them and thus leaving it vacant for more powerful dreams.

Chapter Seven

Weeks later, when Jackie had recovered her peace of mind, she promptly resolved to change her present existence. It was madness to assume that she could carry on in this state, living with herself and taking delight in such ill-fated dreams. Intense preoccupation had brought about the collapse of her mind and who knew the next time she might go out on the rampage! A whole bottle of wine was ineffective at night. It seemed the only alternative was to start on the tablets which she had been holding out against, for at times she woke with red eyes, and there were moments when they were even waterlogged. Diane was sticking close to her, plagued with anxiety, aware that her mother was seriously ill. And the little one was scarcely getting the necessary attention.

Jackie had ceased doing the exercises, not merely because she was now the trim figure of her former self, but frankly she was afraid of the man who entered her mind the moment she was on the bicycle. The caveman was in the bath no more, he had simply confined himself to her bed, and she was in full harmony with his nightly visits. These fantasies gave her immense pleasure, and for the occasional fight to maintain her peace of mind, she was forced to take on particular tasks, to listen attentively to some sort of music so that her mind would no longer escape into old dreams. Yet it puzzled her that there were times when it would be completely out of control, when it would rush off, leaving her unaware but delighted with some sexual scene whereby she was the main attraction, the centre of interest.

Resolving now to turn over a new leaf, she emptied her wardrobe onto the bed and got on with the task of sorting out her dresses. The ridiculous part of it, however, was that every single one of these dresses was too large. Rejecting them one by one and tossing them to the floor, she was eventually left with only two that were capable of being taken up without having to release all the stitching. Then it was a question of what to do with the others. The thought of burning them scared her. She threw them aside and sighed at the final decision that only two were worth salvaging.

Where would she start? One was needed right away: she would have to go into Ashford for a decent dress to wear to London. She had never altered a dress in her life; there had been too many good dresses on the market for her to bother herself with needle and thread. All the children's clothes had been bought. Never had she made as much as a scarf with her own hands. It seemed unfair now that she should have grown into a woman without ever having held a needle.

The children also needed new outfits; she had bought noting for them in the past twelve months. She would take a good look at Diane as soon as the child was back from school. Her dress was certain to be too small.

True enough, Jackie was right. Diane had grown in height, but had maintained her slimness. All the same, the dress was tight, and although the child had not complained of any discomfort, it was quite obvious. Nevertheless, short dresses were the style nowadays.

The big problem was with herself. Jackie was hardly the type to go out looking as though she was too small for her dress. While almost anything looked reasonably attractive on her, a badly fitted dress was easily noticeable.

Next day, when Diane was off at school, she rang for a taxi. There was no holding back. Despite a slight headache she was more concerned with the state of things. Choosing between the two skirts now, she slipped on the blue cotton one with wide pleats and broad belt, along with a blouse. Pulling the belt tight, the crumpling at the waist seemed to fall in with the pleats. In time past she would never have gone through the door in a dress too large for her. But the blouse and skirt gave her a dash of youth and seemed attractive enough.

When the taxi arrived, she collected the child and was off. Connie sat with arms folded in exactly the same pose as her mother. Jackie smiled at the early traits of herself.

Out of the house for the first time in weeks, one might have thought the mother and daughter were strangers revisiting a place the mother had left as a child, for they simply sat back and peered out at the passing scenes. Selling the Jaguar had in fact contributed largely to the long weeks of solitude. There was even a moment when, on reflection, Jackie reconstructed some of the cruises she had made down the A20 with the child harnessed in the back seat. There were even vivid memories of occasions when, chatting to the child, motorists had dilly-dallied behind, thinking that she had been making suggestions to them. She smiled at these reminiscences.

Coming into Ashford now she viewed the shops with keen interest. There were changes. For where a furniture store had been, the window now had a notice 'To Let,' and traffic lights were under construction at a crossroad; even an old fish shop she once knew was now a respectable boutique. How strange. On the whole, she was delighted with the fresh air, the pleasure of seeing real life. She was undoubtedly inspired.

She gazed at the window of a large dress shop, as if going in was a great challenge, an exciting venture. Yes, she was buying a dress much smaller than last time. Her statistics were perfectly respectable now. She guided the child out of the taxi, and in they went. A middle-aged woman, smartly clad in a two-piece dress, first smiled at the child, then asked the mother if she could help.

Nothing in the window suited Jackie. On the other hand, she was not going to be particularly selective. A simple dress of the correct size would do. Among the first few she was shown, there seemed nothing of interest, all summer wear which would not do for the cold spell that was already in full force. Next she was shown a selection of frocks. Jackie eyed them with indifference, quite uncertain of what she really fancied; looking at them seemed to turn her of. Their quality more than anything else was disappointing. There was also a display of buttoned two-piece dresses that did nothing for her.

At last she handled a selection of cardigan suits with more attention and finally decided on a simple beige two-piece, in crimpling. Hardly satisfied, she choose it all the same and handed over a cheque for twenty guineas. It seemed the best of a bad stock; she settled for it only to ease the weariness, after the woman had painfully unfolded every single dress in the shop.

Back in the bungalow, she quickly got into the suit. It fitted well and with its smooth rich texture, was reasonably alluring. The short jacket settled nicely at her waist. She kept it on so as to get used to it. Then she would be confident of her appearance when making for London.

Meanwhile her head had become cloudy with the long confusion in the store and the noise of the traffic. On top of it all the weather was dull with heavy clouds, and worst still was the fact the there was no one to talk to.

Outside, the air was nippy and as the evening drew in, it brought with it a slight wind. Still in the new dress, Jackie opened the door to the terrace and suddenly drew back quickly. The slight wind was hardly apparent, but it swept through the dress. Really, it wasn't funny; she shivered and in that instant felt quite naked. Apparently the dress material was ideal for hot weather, when it would let in the air and keep the body cool. It did the same now, only the cold was severe, and she felt it to the bones.

Well, it had been her choice; the woman in the store had no reason to suppose that a girl of her standing was uncertain of herself. Jackie was furious; she had bought something quite unsuitable after all the fuss. Oh, she might have gone to a decent store in the first place.

Next day the sun was brilliant, quite warm, without wind. She woke with a new feeling. Being Saturday she would take the children shopping. They would all come back with new wardrobes.

The pleated blue skirt had become appropriate; with the pink jumper it was not a bad combination and, having worn it the day before, she was confident now.

At Charing station they waited for the train whilst, further along the platform a gentleman flashed a casual smile at the younger child. Connie had caught his eye and, still holding on to Jackie's skirt, flicked her eyes back and fore at the gentleman, even after he had ceased to be concerned with her. However, with the arrival of the train, he found himself directly in front of a door and courteously stood back for madam and the children to go in first. Connie hesitated, but as Jackie was about to hoist her, the introduction came:

"May I help?" he said. "It seems a lot for you."

She stood back as he lifted the child.

"Come on, my dear, you're getting to heavy for your mamma, you know."

Jackie and Diane followed him into a compartment where he seated the child. He himself sat opposite, at the window. Jackie seated herself near the door, next to Connie.

Looking on he assumed some pleasure at the tremendous set, so colourful were they, the two girls, rather dainty. Then, leaning against her mother, Connie's gaze was still curious. Inspired by the children, he smiled amicably. His hair, freshly cut, was thin at the top. He had a brilliant smile, with firm cheeks and widely-spaced eyes. When Connie caught his smile, she huddled against her mother, hiding her face to conceal amusement.

"Perhaps you will tell me your name?" he said, looking on.

And Diane, who was getting out her coloured pencils to start on a new book of drawings, looked across politely and said, "Her name is Connie."

"And yours?" he asked.

"I am Diane."

His eyes were now on Jackie.

"Any more girls?" he asked sweetly.

She softened and shook her head. "No."

Then glancing form one child to the other, he said conversationally: "Remarkable very beautiful. I can't remember seeing a pair looking so lovely."

He introduced himself as Phillip Russell, then added conversationally that he had been catching the occasional train from Charing station for the last twenty years. How odd that they had not met before. He could not imagine that he had failed to notice her.

As for Jackie, the little chat was good. Really, had he been travelling from Charing station in all those years?"

He nodded. And somehow, it seemed like yesterday. But he sometimes did the journey by car.

A conversation was maintained. It was in fact her first occasion by train, she mentioned, in almost seven years in the area. He explained the railway situation from his own experience, that there were frequent delays, inconveniences, terrible at times and then asked if she had her car at the station.

No, she had got there by taxi. And she explained about her car, having got rid of it a few months back.

Really, perhaps she did not support the view that a motor car was part of a family nowadays.

Oh, it is convenient, on the whole. But in her case it was bloodsucking, and besides, there was no use for it at the time.

"That is admirable," he commented. "It is surprising how many people this reasoning applies to. But, of course, they would not dream of admitting it."

Connie left her mother's side and went to her sister, attracted by the drawing.

"Have you missed it terribly?"

She did not regret selling it. In all that time she had not gone to London once, simply because there had been no need to. On the other hand, had it been sitting in the garage she would have found some reason to go up there.

"Yes, you're right. Visiting?"

"Shopping."

"Then you won't be staying long," he presumed.

Oh, she did not know exactly. The children needed new things. They had outgrown all they had.

"That should take an hour, perhaps?"

More like two, she admitted.

It was good news. They might have dinner together.

Jackie glanced at the children; she could not possibly leave them anywhere. Oh, but he would not dream of asking her to.

"Then what do you suggest?" she asked.

They would book a table for four, including two special chairs.

But wouldn't that be too much trouble for him?

Not at all. He could not think of a more beautiful family to dine with.

The train had slowed, approaching Victoria.

"Are you going to a particular store?" he asked quickly.

No. she might get to Mayfair, but first she would go to the Strand.

"Then you must let me help. You need the convenience of a car."

Taking Connie in his arms, he guided Jackie and Diane out of the station, ignored the taxi and made towards a black Humber Imperial, by which a uniformed chauffeur stood. It occurred to Jackie that it was a staff car of some sort. She got in all the same. Men's generosities were things she had lived with in her earlier years. They seemed to go out of their way quite extraordinarily to please her.

Phillip Russell put the child gently down and directed her into the car. Diane followed, and then he closed the door, said something to the chauffeur, and came back to her.

"It is the Strand first, isn't it?"

"Yes, if you please."

"Good. My chauffeur is entirely at your deposal. When you've completed you shopping he will let me know and I will join you for lunch."

The car drove off. What surprised Jackie was that he had stayed behind, to make his own way to his destination. The little chat had done her good. It had cleared her head. Months of solitude. Really, it wouldn't do to remain tied up within herself. She accepted the blame for the emotional set-back, but took some credit for picking up the pieces when on the brink of being rushed off to the institution.

With a handkerchief she patted Connie's brow: yes, even the children enjoyed the new air.

"Who was that man, Mamma?" asked Connie, already three. It

suddenly dawned on Jackie that she knew not what to say, how to explain.

"His name is Phillip," answered Diane when her mother remained silent.

The child echoed the name in her own imperfect tongue.

Jackie directed the chauffeur to the Civil Service stores. When they had pulled up, he rushed round to the passenger side and held the door open.

The store was the ideal choice. Jackie knew it well; the assortment of stock suited her. During her early days in London she had worked a few doors away, in a large cosmetics store. It was not surprising that, after so long, instinct should have guided her back to this vicinity.

In the children's department it was no trouble finding what was needed. Without paying much concern to her new school uniform, Diane took immediate liking to a dress she found quite exciting. Though in and out of the changing-room with the large stock being taken for her, she paid little attention to anything but the one she called her favourite: it was a printed silk dress with full-length sleeves. With a sash and plain neck, the skirt above her knee, it made her look twice her age.

Jackie was shocked when the child came out of the changing room into the bright lights. The transformation was too much. But the child was well taken in, which made her smile. Diane was quite tall, her seven years completely disguised.

In all, Jackie took a large stock for the two girls. Dresses, shoes, socks, coats, a small hand bag for Diane were made into two parcels and taken out to the car which had returned after an hour to see if madam was ready.

Madam would go elsewhere for her own things. Had she maintained the spirit in which she had left the bungalow, she would have done her own shopping there. But the excitement so far, the sudden change, chatting to Phillip Russell, and seeing the city so brilliant with people, had all inspired her. Now it seems she's quickly shedding the last seven years in order to resume her old life.

She instructed the chauffeur to take her to Brook Street where she spent another hour selecting three dresses; one in ivory wool with a broad neck, long sleeves, and belt. Another was beige, double-knitted, with high collar. The third was a two-piece dress with pleated skirt and three-quarter sleeves, acetate and viscose, the most costly of the set. She liked its quality and texture, but was hardly impressed by the fitting. Perhaps it needed altering. She was uncertain. The total cost, however, soon decided for her. It was promptly returned and, settling for the first two, she handed over a cheque for sixty-eight pounds.

Back in the car Jackie experienced the full pleasure of Phillip Russell's generosity when she sat back and relaxed with a smile.

Diane, who was also ecstatically pleased, turned to her mother: "I like your white dress," she said. "It is different from the others."

"Well, the others are too large, darling. All too large."

"Will you lose any more weight?"

Jackie laughed. "I hope not. Why?"

"Well, " said the child, "You're much prettier now."

"Really, Diane, you should have said it at home."

"I didn't want to."

"Why not, darling?"

"Because you weren't well. You were ill."

Jackie considered. "Did I look ill?"

"Yes. Every day."

"I'm better now?"

"Oh, yes. Everything's much nicer."

Again Jackie mused that the child should have mentioned her new attractiveness at home: it would have given her confidence. But it hardly mattered. She would not get sick again. Diane was a little replica of her. For a while Jackie was reminded of Pascoe, she immediately dismissed the thought. Sitting up now, she gazed into the busy street.

"Will we meet Philip Russell again?" asked Diane. She herself was looking forward to it. The child's face had taken on a new glow.

"Yes. He's meeting us again in a moment."

It was difficult to assess Diane's reaction. She sat back and gazed ahead with folded arms.

"Don't you like him?" asked her mother.

But Diane kept a straight face. "I am thinking of my new dress," she said.

"You have several new dresses," Jackie reminded her. "Is there one you like best?"

"Yes. The blue and white one. I want to know when I am going to wear it."

"Oh, we'll think of something."

"Will it be soon?"

"I don't know. We will think about it at home."

The chauffeur was young, twenty-five at the most, tall and athletically built, with a lot of hair. He was polite and seemed proud of his job. There was a moment when Jackie was prompted to ask about Phillip Russell. But she suddenly thought differently. It could wait. He looked genuine enough; there could be little doubt of his real status.

They were already in Maiden Lane. The car drew up outside a restaurant and Phillip Russell appeared. He opened the door for Diane, and then lifted Connie out. Jackie was surprised. It was evident that he had arranged everything privately while she was busy with the shopping. For a moment she was not sure she wanted to be manoeuvred like this, yet she went gracefully ahead into the restaurant, taking Connie, while he followed with Diane.

The table, already selected, was well situated. He had obviously been waiting for her. There were two special chairs, both higher than the others, for Diane and Connie. Jackie declared that he was very practical and hoped that she did not put him to too much trouble. The waiter took the order and disappeared.

The City and the arts took up most of the conversation. After the meal, over cups of coffee, he touched the main subject: that of her husband. Was he there in London?

"Yes."

And would she be seeing him before going back?

"No," she said with a secret smile.

"Good. Then we must travel back together. My business is finished for the time being."

On the train they talked in the same friendly manner, but this time the compartment was shared with a man who had buried himself in a newspaper. When they were off the train, it was the same generosity.

Had he mentioned that his car was at the station?

Yes, she seemed to remember. And he appreciated her own initiative when she said: "I know; with all my parcels, and these two, you would not dream of leaving us here."

The car was a new Jaguar. With Jackie and the children in the back, he stacked the boxes on the vacant front seat, and followed her instructions. As it happened, she was living a good way from him. His home was very much in the opposite direction, on a small country road between Charing and Westwell, quite remote. At least five miles separated the two homes. He assisted with the boxes, taking them to the living-room. Connie was tired and had fallen asleep in her mother's arms. Jackie took her to bed. Before going off, she had told Phillip to pour himself a drink, to make himself comfortable.

Getting back now, she found him chatting to Diane and sipping a large Martini with ice. Diane had played the hostess, fetching the ice and putting a cube in his glass, assuring him that Mamma said it was better with ice. Then, when he had taken the first sip, she looked on:

"Isn't it better now?" she asked.

"Yes, much better."

"Now you know," she remarked, "so next time you have Martini, you must have ice as well."

He smiled at the child's charming insistence. She was impressive for her age. "And what will you have to drink? You must be thirsty, too."

"I shall have blackcurrant and lemonade," said Diane.

"Will you have ice in it?"

"Oh, yes. I like it very cold. Sometimes I have milk, but don't fancy that now. There's no taste to it, and anyway I am fed-up with drinking milk."

"It is good for you. It will make you grow well."

The child frowned at this. "I still don't like it much. I think it is unfair to take milk from the cows and give it to people who can find other drinks. The poor calves can only drink water when there's no milk. I think someone ought to stop the farmers stealing milk from the cows and selling it."

"Do you?" asked Phillip Russell, surprised.

"Yes. And I think people should stop drinking milk, so that the farmers would not make any money from it, they would have to leave the cows alone and the little calves would get it all."

"That's a very good point; is that why you only drink it sometimes?"

"Well, that's one reason. The other is that I don't like it much. Mamma doesn't like it either, so I probably take after her. She doesn't drink it at all. That leaves Connie and me; but we don't even get through a full pint a day, so Mamma only takes one pint now. And Connie is already refusing hers, so very soon we won't be taking any milk. If everyone did the same, the farmers will have to leave the cows alone."

Phillip found it interesting. In fact, he was well taken in.

"Come now, you must forget about the cow for the time being. Milk is very good for you; it will make you grow into a beautiful lady, like Mamma."

"Oh, I will be as beautiful as Mamma anyway, because I am her daughter. But I mustn't grow too quickly, though, because all my dresses are already too small, and it's costing her a lot of money to buy me new ones."

"Is it so?" Phillip laughed. The little thing, with long chestnut hair, was quite serious. Already there were signs of her mother's qualities. Her cheeks, soft with the lustre of youth, and the little mouth had never once endeared a smile.

In walked Jackie to find him thoroughly amused.

"I see you two have made friends," she said.

"How else could we exist? She's quite a dish, you know, healthy, and bubbling with intelligence." And he turned to Diane: "My dear little girl, you have made my day."

"May I call you Phillip?" came the soft young voice.

"Of course. And I will call you Diane."

"Then perhaps I will see you again?"

Jackie looked on, but the child avoided her.

Chapter Eight

Mary was back from Spain and was hardly surprised that Jackie had not joined her for the short holiday. She had only half expected it. Jackie's new complexion, however, was undoubtedly marvelous; yet she was not to know that Jackie had actually got worse, even to the brink of a nervous collapse.

Mary herself was fresh and well tanned, bustling with health and vigorously buoyant. Her short hair, piled at the top, was recently bleached. For two days she talked only of the holiday resorts, the balconies overlooking the crowded beaches on the Costa Brava. Jackie listened with a smile, hardly regretting that she herself had not gone.

One hotel had actually collapsed. It was frightful. It was fully booked and people had only just escaped disaster. Then it was in all the papers and there was a big uproar too, with the management and contractors, even the travel agents. It had been handed over to the management only weeks before. Some say it was a rush job, quickly knocked up for the season. The government had rightfully taken the matter in hand. Someone will get the blame. It was very bad publicity.

All her husband's three hotels were packed, and still people were unable to find rooms. There was talk of some travel agents being only amateurs, even crooks, taking people's money without making proper hotel arrangement. It was disgraceful. Some were clearly to blame; it pays to be more careful with money. Too many were flocking for cheap holidays. It was no wonder they were let down.

The two women sat in the easy chairs, a bottle of sherry between them. The children were in bed. It was near midnight on the last Saturday of October. It seemed inevitable that they would be drunk in no time. Jackie needed it to find sleep; Mary was in high spirit. They were cheerful; they had missed each other. Now they happily caught up with the last few months, laughing and chatting about the children, the latest fashion. Yes, they were looking forward to the next fashion show.

In Spain Mary had hardly had time to consider dresses. She had spent most days in bikinis. But she had brought back something from Valentino's, a dress which had sent her in a daze when first she had tried it on

"But how did you get hold of it?"

"Well, you know what Bill's like. He spotted it, liked it, and then it didn't matter about me. I liked it in the end, though."

Valentino's designs usually left Jackie cold. They were shapeless and she often wondered whether women were really supposed to look sexy in them

Mary was keeping an eye open for Bellville's winter designs. She wanted to see what they were. Her blue wool crêpe was one of her best garments and it was an old Bellville's. And last year she had found a rather nice one: a brown two piece which she often wore without the jacket.

"I've gone off Dior's designs," said Jackie, who had not found a dress she liked in two years "I am disappointed in these top designers. Really, their styles are hardly exciting. They have no elegance at all, too much emphasis on low necklines and open back."

"Oh, but the man who looks for modesty in a woman is usually boring, to say the least," Mary maintained, falling back on a lifetime of experience. "They're only interesting to a certain point. They usually propose on the first date and waste no time in making in plain that you're their property. They will pour out their troubles and expect you to solve them. And have you noticed, my dear, they usually wear expensive suits? They study women down to their ankles, yet they never make the first move."

Mary emptied the bottle into both glasses, took a heavy gulp from hers, and raised her eyebrows.

"Interesting how you brought yourself down to this neatness. Whatever did you do? Resigned yourself to one meal a day?"

"Almost," said Jackie, cheerfully. "One meal a day, and lots of exercises."

"Exercises?"

"You know, the efficient way!"

"Well, it's certainly efficient. But where did you get the enthusiasm?"

"I had to find something to do. One morning I took a good look at myself and decided I was out of shape, then got out the equipment form the storeroom."

Mary had no idea there had been such equipment. Yes, they were Pascoe's, he had once used them to keep fit.

Well, Mary was pleased; but she would hardly dream of reducing herself. It would be hopeless. On the other hand, her shape

68

suited her. She was an exciting woman with a practical personality.

"Who do you suppose rang me yesterday?" she said.

Jackie had no idea.

"Karl Penman."

"Well, what did he want?"

Mary explained. He had asked about her holidays, and then he had said off-handedly that he had longed to see her. He did advise her on some shares, but she was certain they had not doubled their prices so soon.

"How did he sound?"

"Oh, delighted that I am back, happy that my hotel didn't collapse; he sounded as though he wanted to drop in one evening."

Jackie was curious to discover whether her name had been mentioned. It would please her if Mary were to touch the point without being asked.

"He was rather reserved," Mary went on. "I told him you had parted company with the car and had not left the house for some months. Then I had to assure him that you were not ill, just occupied with the two girls."

But Jackie was anxious to hear more, and she said quickly, "He didn't tell you that he had once sent me an invitation?"

"No, nothing of the sort."

"He was probably disappointed that I did nothing about it."

"You mean you turned it down?"

"Well, I am certainly not proud of it. But as it happened, I ignored it completely."

"What was it for?"

"One of his lavish parties, no doubt. He had rung first, and I delayed my decision. Then later, when the card arrived I read it, put it away, and had forgotten all about it. A month later when I found it, it was naturally too late. I am surprised he didn't mention it."

Mary resented this. She considered Penman quite amicable, deserving greater attention and affinity. Jackie, however, would not let up. He was over-generous, she declared, the type a woman must confine herself to, once involved. He was independent and self-possessed. He had suddenly caught up with himself and going all out to make up for lost time

"Oh, but it's ridiculous to think that of Penman. Perhaps he was withdrawn, reserved in his married life. A man was not to blame for admiring a woman; who knows, his wife might have recently turned into a bitch."

But Jackie was holding her point. Women did not rule men of his sort. Once involved she would be expected to shed all individual rights and conform to his likes and dislikes. She was indifferent, yes, and she had no plans to let Penman near her. Yet, had she searched her mind, she might have fallen back on the idea that he had too much money, that she was not impressed. At the party when they were first introduced, the women had emphasised the point of Penman's enormous wealth. They had openly implied that with such power and influence, he was to be admired. But the fact that he was going all out to get her did not go down well with Jackie either. He seemed to have lost his head and was infatuated. Had he proved himself the man who had first inspired her, she would have continued to respect him and might easily have fallen for him.

As the night drew on however, the old familiar restlessness crept back into her system. She had been drinking all evening, taking it slowly and chatting happily; but by the time twelve o'clock came, the sherry had worn off. An hour later she was wide awake, twisting and turning, and at times gazing steadfastly at the dim light that glowed by the bed. For a while she considered getting up and finding a book; it would be better than lying there thinking unhealthy thoughts. But switching on the main light was nerve-racking; the glare would be severe. Thus abandoning the idea, she was unable to contain herself and began taking refuge in the old fantasies It was almost dawn when sleep eventually rescued her.

Without doubt Jackie feared the loneliness. For months she had enjoyed these dreams, the mad fantasies, since the brief collapse, she had become cautious, knowing that a second attack might be severe. Now, whenever the mad scenes came back, there was a desperate struggle to abandon them. She would force herself to do vigorous tasks, at times even playing roughly with the children. But the nights were dreadfully dangerous.

Recently she had thought of Phillip Russell. Since the trip to London there had been one other meeting. Now he could be expected to drop in at any time.

One night at about four in the morning, when she had been throwing herself exhaustively about the bed, the idea that she might ring him crept into her mind. He would understand her problem, he would be a shoulder to lean on. But reaching the telephone, she suddenly drew back. Why, she was crazy! It was silly to invite a man into her house at that hour. Wouldn't it be obvious? God! What was becoming of her?

This was a new wave of fearful torment which had been attacking her for more than a month. Things were better during the days. With apparent dignity, correct and rosy with the lushness of her body, she was unapproachable. But if only she was able to sleep.

Jackie once thought of the good old days, exciting and carefree. The stories she had listened to over the counter in the Strand; she sometimes thought of the night-club and the gay life, she had met them all, and had chosen carefully. What was stopping her now? If a husband was absent there must be a substitute; when a man was ineffective there were other fish in the sea! Startled at this admission, she wondered if it would not have been better to remain unmarried. Yes, in the old days it had been her policy to slip from one man to the other and pay heed to her true nature. It was unthinkable now that marriage should have changed all that.

The union with Pascoe was a mistake. God knows what had come over her in that single week when she had let herself be dragged off to the register office. Her life had been ruined! The foetus inside her had numbed her senses. Was it not true that a pregnant woman went through hell? Yes, her stomach had been raging. She had even missed a few nights at the club.

Well then, she was not going to abandon herself forever, no, not yet. Pascoe was finished; he was in the past. She must pick up the pieces. Still attractive, she was probably more desirable now.

For a week she turned this over in her mind. Mary had never given up the life, no one could say she was anything but exciting.

All week the idea of taking the children to her mother in Bedfordshire clouded her mind. Then, on Friday night, when she was almost at a decision, the telephone rang. It was Mary.

"We have a visitor," she was saying.

It was Penman. He was passing and had suddenly decided to drop in. He had only just discovered that they were living so close to one another. "He wants to come and see you. You haven't gone to bed, I hope?"

No. not just yet.

"Good; then you don't mind if he calls?"

Jackie was not exactly dressed to receive a visitor. For Penman, she ought to be properly attired. It was already nine o'clock, however, and she quickly slipped into a nightie and pulled on a dressing-gown. In front of the mirror she made a final check of her appearance. Then, satisfied, she went to the living room, prepared a large Martini with ice, and waited in an armchair. It was her fifth glass of Martini in the last hour. The bottle was almost empty. Also in the cabinet were a bottle of Martell, one Hennessy, and a bottle of gin along with another of Heir Antique. They had been there for years, part of the stock Pascoe had kept to entertain his friends. Since she had had no visitor, apart from Phillip Russell, the hard drinks had never been touched. She herself was against the stronger stuff, inhibited by some senseless inner morality which forbade her to take anything but wine. The only explanation for this would have been far back in the days when she had worked as a dancer in the night club, and restricted to wines, as it was her duty to keep her head throughout the night.

When the door bell rang, she went to it briskly. Penman was his usual self, particularly polite, despite the past. She showed him the armchair opposite hers. He was in no hurry to accept it, however, but his eyes expressed admiration. He smiled discreetly and looked perfect in his worsted suit, but his manner was that of an old flame now calling on a mistress who had once given him up.

His thin lips and high nose opened out into a smile as he eyed the picture on the wall. He kept a hand in his pocket.

"What would you like?" she asked, gracefully. "It's always a problem knowing what to offer a millionaire; after all, they do have everything."

It was typical of Jackie. He disliked being told by a woman he adored that he had all he desired. It made him a little uncomfortable, it made him aware of himself.

"What are you having?" he said at long last.

"Martini."

It was an encouraging drink. He would have the same. She consented, but could hardly believe that Martini was his favorite. There was stronger stuff, if he preferred.

"These days it is not wise to over-do it. The law would prefer that I don't."

"You've already had a few, and you're driving back?"

"Precisely."

She presented him with a glass of dry Martini. "It is sweet of you to drop in. I was wondering when it would be."

"Seriously?"

Yes. She was certainly dreading it, one way or another.

Penman smiled knowingly. There were only two paintings and a large photograph of the children. He studied them.

So, he had not come to scold her.

Good Lord, no! He had been around long enough to understand women.

"Oh, then perhaps you don't need an apology?"

"That depends on how you see it. For example, do you regard it as carelessness on your part? Or simply a moment of despair?"

Jackie admitted it was carelessness.

"Then I can quite believe that you're annoyed with yourself. Prefer to allow you to correct you own mistake."

Jackie had followed him across the living room. She stood with folded arms, against the back of the sofa, watching him. He admired the paintings, he turned and was close to her. She caught the look of his eyes, close-set, almost grey, they looked at her with tremendous force, a secret cruelty. He was unpredictable. Was this not why she had misjudged him at their first meeting? She kept a smile to conceal her bewilderment when he extended an arm to her hair.

She was even more splendid that he had imagined her to be, he proclaimed. It was a long time since the first occasion; she must forgive him. He reclaimed his glass.

Jackie was back in her armchair. For a moment she felt that he would sit opposite her, to have the table between them; but he was in no hurry. Instead, he made towards the cabinet with his glass, attracted by a photograph of the children. He was a long time admiring them.

"What age are they?"

"Seven and three."

He marvelled at the elder girl's resemblance to her mother; but the three-year-old portrayed something which he could not quite recognize. Interesting, though; what was her name?

"Constance."

There was a mixture of the mother, and something wildly aggressive. There was hidden curiosity too, but of course, he had no knowledge of the father.

Did he wish to meet him?

Penman turned to her, almost serious. "Perhaps. After all, he's the man you love. It might help me to understand you better."

"By that you mean I'm rather concealed?"

"You're a charming woman at will. Extremely attractive, refined in your ways. But if I may say so, rather difficult to handle."

"I admire your frankness."

"One must know you thoroughly to get the better of you."

"And that is your aim?"

He came to her with the empty glass. "Hasn't it been obvious?"

"We sometimes assume these things, but we often need confirmation."

"Then I will be frank. I am utterly fascinated, perhaps because of your modesty, your difficult traits, your religious attitude. It seems to me that when you make a decision it is not to be neglected, or taken for granted.

With an encouraging smile, she said. "Tell me something about you wife."

Penman looked at her favourably. It was not a sensitive question. He seemed delighted that she should ask. It helped to reflect her exact mood and assured him that he was there for a friendly chat and would have to do better if they were going to be more than formal. But he wondered if she were not just making sure she knew what she was letting herself in for. He hesitated. "My wife is more exciting now than ever, for obvious reasons, of course. She's fifty."

"Quite an exciting fifty."

"Very much so."

"Is she demanding?"

"No. she's very civil."

"Of course; the wife of a millionaire has to be, or she'd be filing divorce suits every day. Would you say she's an interesting woman?'

"Certainly. But you know, at this stage, a woman of her thinking is consolidated. She's proud of the two boys and naturally devotes a great deal of attention to them."

"How old is the heir?"

"Twenty-four; he's a racing enthusiast. The younger boy is twenty; a law student."

"The older one reflects more of you?"

"Yes. Quite a coincidence, really, that between you and me, our elder children should reflect more of us than the others."

"It is a good point."

"Genetics are marvellous things. It's a pity we have so little control over them. It would be good to make a child the exact replica of ourselves."

"It's a thought."

"A tantalising thought, when you consider the possibilities."

Penman was more at ease now. He took out a handkerchief and dabbed at his lips, then straightened his jacket.

"You're not rushing to get back to London?"

"No, no, I hate the damn place. It's good to get away at the end of the day."

"I was under the impression you were heading that way."

"Good heavens, no! Didn't you read my card? My address was written on it."

"Yes, or course. It's on the coast. Sandgate, isn't it?"

"Quite right."

It was a good retreat. A rich part of the country with the sea close by. Had she gone to the party she would have discovered that the place was delightful in summer. She would have enjoyed the last of the warm nights on the balcony. She regretted it. Perhaps it would have been good to meet his wife after all.

"Where else do you retreat to, especially at this time of year?'

"Once in a while I take a quiet cruise. I am sailing for Jamaica in four weeks."

"That is the best thing I've heard in a long while."

"I often spend three to four months a year in the Caribbean."

Jackie was aware that Penman's yacht was fully oceangoing. She had learned that from the ladies at the party. On the other hand, she had never given it a second thought. Now that he was in front of her, enjoying a quiet drink, the whole thing seemed more interesting. He was an adventurer. It might even be a challenge for the woman who was lucky enough to find herself under his spell. It seemed obvious now that he was about to make some sort of proposition. After all, he could not have been seeking her out all this time without taking an interest in her welfare.

"So, the house at Sandgate is very convenient?"

"It is well situated. The yacht can be seen from the window. You must come down sometime."

"It that a challenge?"

He shook his large head, his grey eyes cooler now. He was being firm.

"No," he said with added warmth, "it's an invitation. I happen to be your most profound admirer, and under the circumstances, you would be doing me a great honour."

Jackie emptied her glass, refilled it from the new bottle, and sat back, legs crossed, with a finger to her chin. What did the invitation mean?

"The trip will take about a month," he added. "You will lack nothing. One or two months in Jamaica, and once I'm away from here I do my business by telephone. My time will be entirely yours. You have about three weeks to decide."

"I will consider it," she said, without conviction.

"In the meantime, you must let me escort you to a charity ball two weeks from now, Saturday night."

"Thank you. I am sure it will compensate for last time."

Suddenly Penman was calm and sincere. "Oh, we must forget that particular occasion. I understand perfectly. I don't suppose you're aware that I know a great deal about you?"

"No, to what extent?"

"I made it my duty."

"And was it difficult?'

"My informer was most cooperative; she thinks very highly of you."

Jackie wondered. Mary had mentioned it. She had spoken to him on one or two occasions. They had spent an afternoon together in London. Jackie could easily imagine what he had learned. She watched him with interest. Had he not spoken so admiringly to her on their first meeting, she would now have reason to think that his offers were made out of sympathy.

In his occasional movements, however, Penman finally settled behind the armchair, facing her. He disliked the idea of sitting. It would place him away from her and so deny him the authority common to his nature. Secretly though, he would have planted himself next to her, but on the other hand he was unable to regard her as a romantic. Her brownish-gold eyes had not once twinkled, instead, they were alert with awareness. And even with her luxurious pose, she was still not fully relaxed.

It was after midnight. Her glass was empty. Normally Jackie would have refilled it straightaway; but now it lingered between her fingers, a sign of weariness and induced patience. He took the hint; then, at the door, before she had turned the handle, he drew close and took the hand that had reached out to it.

At that moment Jackie suddenly switched herself on. First a smile, then with starlit eyes, her lips became luxurious and subtle. He simply kissed her cheeks and assured her he would call again one evening on his way down form London.

Jackie went back to the armchair and the empty living room

once more, in all its dreariness. She sat back and stared at the empty glass, eyes dazed. The long hours of drinking were talking toll. She had enjoyed the little chat. She was inspired. Suddenly there was the dreaded thought of going to bed, only to lapse back into her old self. What else was there to do? Why had he rushed off so early? They could have chatted all night. She had emptied her glass merely to stay sober and keep her head. Then his departure became obvious and she smiled at the thought: He was escaping back to Mary.

Sitting back now, with arms over the side of the chair, she was abandoned. In all her dreams she had never considered herself as Penman's mistress. Now she smiled at the thought. He was in love with her, and ready to lavish a great deal of wealth on her. He needed her to grace his bed, to flower his deck-chairs and his swimming pool, the final splendor to his Jamaican mansion. Well, it was not a bad idea; she could do with the change, it would get her out of this crippling confinement. The sea breeze would be good for her. It might keep her young and healthy; the warmth of the Caribbean air might be very good for her. She might even watch the carnival from his balcony in Jamaica; live on fresh fruits and vegetables. She would be escorted to the night-clubs where she would meet other millionaires, actors as well; was this not where many retired to, with their private beaches and treasure-hunting teams. She remembered reading somewhere that the film star, Errol Flynn, had a huge mansion in Jamaica, a fantastic retreat where he would go to rest after a swash-buckling episode. She could think of other names, too. Even in her semi-conscious state, as the pleasures of sleep was carrying her off, she felt as though she was already enjoying the adventure..

Chapter Nine

Convinced of better days to come, Jackie's head was temporarily at peace, the headache had gone, the severe congestion cleared for the time being. With a little sleep she was again full of enthusiasm. The pile of unsuitable clothes must be got rid of, and she would need three or four new dresses at once. Apart from two skirts and the odd blouse, there was not a single dress that would look decent on her. All old sizes, they were inches too wide in all direction. There were twenty dresses, all perfectly good and reasonably expensive, yet quite useless to her now. Had has been capable of holding a needle, she would have been able to alter one or two.

She was about to take the child to Mary when the doorbell rang. Who might that be? No delivery was expected. Perhaps it was Mary. She went to the door.

The caller was an old fellow in a smart blue suit and a stylish hat. With arms folded, he stood back form the door and, catching sight of Jackie, his eyes wondered. Behind him, in front of the garage door, was a bright yellow car of Italian origin. She glanced at it suspiciously.

The gentleman waved a hand and turned his attention to the car momentarily.

"I was instructed to deliver it to this address. Mrs. Pascoe?"

"Yes, who's instruction?"

"Mr. Karl Penman."

Jackie went slowly past him, leaving the door half-open. She folded her arms and peered down at it. It was a strange car; very few of them were on the English road.

He should have got there earlier, the gentleman was saying. But it took time to clock up the mileage. He had only just managed to run it in and the mechanic had to get through all the checks. He hoped they hadn't kept her waiting unduly.

"When were you instructed to deliver it?"

"Early, as soon as possible."

"That was Mr. Penman's instruction?"

Yes, but the car was only ordered the day before, with a demand that it should be carefully run in and delivered to this address. Now all that was needed was her signature to complete the transaction. He got back into the car briefly and unlocked the passenger door, then reached into the glove compartment and came out with some papers. He looked them over carefully and handed them to her.

Jackie was astonished. The car was brand new, two doors but with a small rear seat, the kind of lay-out with which she was familiar; with beige velvet upholstery. Still uncertain of the whole thing, however, she took the documents and studied them.

Yes, everything was in her name: purchasing order, guarantee agreement, insurance; all requiring only the final signature. When she was satisfied that it would be stupid to refuse, she signed, reluctantly.

The gentleman was grateful. "Should it need any kind of attention at all, you only have to ring us. The telephone number is at the bottom of the delivery forms. We will come and put it right, free of charge."

He left her there, looking at the car, wondering what to think of Penman and his extravagant gift. So, he was making sure she would not ignore his second invitation. Maybe this was to assure her of his tremendous admiration for her. Well, it would be easier to accept than to refuse. And besides, she needed a car. Was she not about to phone for a taxi?

The Fiat was a sporty looking car, with twin headlights and five forward gears; a portion of the roof was designed to fold back. Apparently the model was new, appearing only in the last two to three months. She would not have seen any on the roads. Perhaps it was just the name that she was familiar with.

Getting into it now, and closing the doors, she sat back. It was comfortable. The interior was neat, rather pretty. She turned the key and heard the gentle roar of the engine, then, sitting back and looking out ahead, she allowed it to idle. She fancied it would be more comfortable with the seat farther back. Finding the lever by the side of the seat, on the floor, she pressed it gently and the seat slid back to its farthest position. But suddenly it was too far back, she worked it forward a couple of notches and found the ideal position.

Oh, well, she took a final look at the car and went into the bungalow, collected her purse and came out with the child. Over at Mary's they chatted, and Connie made her way across the living room to her companion, Margaret. Then, leaving them for a time, the two women went out to the car.

At first Mary uttered a sigh of delight.

"It is nice. You must keep it."

"It's quite unbelievable."

Mary inspected it carefully, enthusiastically. "You can't possible send it back; after all, it is precisely what you need."

"No. I don't suppose I will, but he could have telephoned. He ought to have said something."

"It is intended as a surprise," said Mary.

She sat in it for a moment. "Yes, it is smart."

"Well, the least I can do is to drive it."

Mary watched the car of sight.

Jackie was heading for London. An hour or two was needed to acquaint herself with the car. Secretly she admired Penman for singling out this particular gift. Perhaps it was meant as a Christmas present and he wanted to seal the liaison without delay. Whatever the motive, she needed a car above everything else. It was good to be able to travel independently after so long.

In the heavy traffic at Westminster, she was particularly careful. The stopping and starting, edging forward, all demanded concentration. She made for Whitehall, then to Trafalgar Square, and soon she was at the Strand. It was not the best route, but she was beginning to like the car.

Phillip Russell was already waiting in the restaurant. He had a cheerful greeting for her when the waiter led her to his table. Since that memorable day on the train, he had only visited her once. A phone call had encouraged him to call one evening. But apart from admiration and one or two amusing remarks, they had remained uninvolved. She was getting to like him. He was practical, amusing at times, and the children loved him. Moreover, he was firm when necessary and seemed to understand her without showing sympathy.

He quickly positioned a chair for her, and complimented her on the new dress. He liked the refinements. In fact, it was the white ivory which Jackie had bought on the very day they had first met, a few weeks back. The exuberant black hair flowed loosely. Wearing it in this manner was unusual for her. Instead of her usual modest and careful appearance, she looked gay and adventurous, ready for anything.

"Have you eaten?" she asked.

"That was hardly why I came here."

"But it's a restaurant. It is appropriate."

"They'll have to see us as exceptions for the time being," he said, and he suddenly caught on. "Would you like something to eat?"

"No, no. I was only concerned about you."

"Perhaps I should order a drink."

He called the waiter and ordered a large Pimms for Madam.

Jackie studied him and sought his eye the moment they were alone.

"You look tired," she said.

"I am, but not physically. I needed the break, and having you here is precisely the right prescription."

The drink came, with plenty of ice. She sipped it slowly. "Come to think of it, I don't even know what your business is. You've never mentioned it."

"Research," he said. "At the moment I am investigating ultrasonic frequencies."

"You're a scientist?"

He nodded.

She raised her eyebrow. "I was under the impression you were a director of some sort. But a scientist!"

"Disappointed?"

"No. But I certainly would if you were working on something like a bomb."

"You're against that sort of thing?"

"Naturally."

"So am I. I don't take kindly to the mass destruction of people."

She made no comment.

"You doubt me?"

"No." Jackie's head shook with an inevitable smile.

Then it was the question of her husband. Did they have much in common?

"Unlikely."

"Why?"

"Well, knowing him thoroughly, and knowing a little about you, there's really no similarity."

"I see. He's in business?"

She shrugged the question.

"Am I sounding absurd?"

"Not quite. He's in Brixton prison, or somewhere else by now."

"You're getting your own back?"

"Hardly. He's already done two years." Jackie's expression was unchanged. She put away the glass, rested her elbows on the

81

table, and lowered her chin on bridged fingers.

He was puzzled. "Well, if I am to accept that, I might as well ask when he's expected out."

"In three years' time, perhaps. His sentence is a good one. The punishment fits the crime."

Phillip Russell could not guess. There could be a thousand things. But she told him briefly and waited for his comment.

"Interesting but regrettable," he said. "Was it difficult for you?"

Jackie spoke with a great deal of pride. Hardly the attitude of a wife with concern for her husband. But after two years it really did not matter. It was many months since she last visited Pascoe and she was certainly not brooding over his absence.

As expected, Phillip showed no sympathy. He was taken in by her cool detachment. Furthermore, he did not want to spoil the atmosphere by saying the wrong thing. His mind rushed back to their first meeting and lingered over the hours they had spent in each other's company. He recalled that the two girls showed no sign of missing their father. But he was undoubtedly disappointed at not having had the opportunity of going back to Newham with her. He'd been looking forward to it since the beginning of the week. Chatting to her had been a pleasure, nevertheless.

Jackie took the longer route to Oxford Street. She went under the archway and along Buckingham Palace Road, up Park Lane and into Oxford Street, driving hard whenever possible.

She was soon in Lewis's, where she spent two hours looking through catalogues and sorting out styles. Defying the new trend in calf-length dresses, she chose a style that were classical but apparently out-dated. This hardly concerned her, however. Her sole interest was in what she admired best, dresses that brought out the best in her, the refined look. The expense was secondary and she took no interest in designers, provided the styles were neat and the dresses suitably finished. One of the two dresses had a cut-away neck, exposing much of the bosom, and was even low at the back. The maker talked about the rough fittings as he took the measurements and even discussed jewellery to match the finished dress. This gave her something to think about. Apart form a string of pearls and a treasured diamond brooch, she had no jewellery. The brooch was an early present from Pascoe, while the pearls were the legacy of an American whose advances, some years back, had left her cold.

The dresses would be ready in three weeks, provided she called back in a fortnight for a first fitting. Before leaving the store, she selected another three dresses off the peg, all intricately designed and carefully chosen: one with sleeves and high neck embroidered at the front. Another was a v-neck open, with buttons to the waist and a narrow belt. In this she saw herself on deck with the wind lashing her hair. The third was a two-piece affair, quite attractive. It had not been on display, but was chosen from a new batch delivered only that morning. In fine silk and white print, it gave her a soft, young look and would make her glamorous in the Caribbean sun. The three dresses were a modest sixty pounds. The two on order would cost twice that amount. She bought other clothes, too, among them were two sets of bikinis, watery blue, with two sets of trims.

After two hours in the shop, she came out to join the congestion in the street, the traffic at a standstill. Stuck in a small side-street where her car had been parked, Jackie was unable to go forward. The main street ahead, Oxford Street, was jammed solid. There was no chance of getting onto it. It did, however, occur to her that she might reverse and take the back streets, but behind her the congestion in the narrow lane had made this impossible. She remained there, listening to the radio for half -an-hour, when the strain of waiting became unbearable. How stupid it was for everyone to be out on the road! There were too many cars. Something ought to be done to reduce the number. People should be made to use public transport. Why, it was no use sitting there without being able to move. Some cars were even old and needed clearing off the streets.

It was not until a police constable had taken charge at the junction where a traffic signal had failed that anyone was able to move. Then at last, edging out onto Oxford Street, Jackie turned left, drove onto high Holborn where she turned, crossed the bridge at Blackfriars, manoeuvered across Boron Street and into Great Dover Street. Here the traffic was again at a standstill. Already it was five o'clock. At this rate she would still be on the road at midnight.

Forging ahead slowly now, and looking on all sides, a particular shop caught her eye. It was a junk shop where the clothes on display interested her: jackets, suits, dresses. How could such rubbish be on sale? As the traffic was stationary, she kept a curious eye at the window and saw a woman enter. Before long the attendant was shifting some clothes and was soon replacing them. There was no doubt of it,: they were all for sale; the woman now came out with a parcel under her arm.

Jackie swung the car out of the line of traffic and parked in front of the shop. She would see! And she got out of the car, straightened her dress and went in. The interior was shabby. There was some old equipment on the floor: things like record players, old junk, even television sets. On the other side were rows upon rows of clothes, those she had seen from outside, evidently thrown out by people who had had enough of them.

The shopkeeper was a girl, attired roughly in a calf-length tweed dress and a brown jacket, which she would have done better without. Her white stockings disappeared up her skirt and made her look rather ancient. But the short curly hair and high cheeks were clear signs of healthy girlishness. The face showed certain firmness.

Jackie made out that she first thought it was a cleaner's shop, that she wasn't sure.

But the girl was apologetic. "No," she said, "I do have them cleaned, but not here." And she waved a hand towards the stock. "They're for sale."

"Do you really sell many?"

"Oh, it varies from time to time." She had only been open five weeks, and was still studying the demand in the area.

"But your customers, who are they?" Jackie was looking at the clothes, the majority in very bad shape.

"They will all go sooner or later, depending on how much a customer has to spend. The very good ones don't last long. Mind you, I don't get many. I could do with some more right now. "

"And your dress," said Jackie, "does it encourage customers?"

"Oh, yes. It's the trend nowadays."

An electric heater glowed in one corner of the shop. Two sewing machines were among the junk on the floor. Two chairs were still in wrapping paper; along with the only table that was in stock.

"I am sure I couldn't sell you anything," said the girl, confidently. "Are you trying to get rid of something, clothes perhaps?"

Jackie nodded. "I wouldn't mind."

"Old ones?"

"Mostly good ones…"

"I could do with some good things. They would lift the shop to new heights. At the moment I couldn't hope to get more than a pound for anything here. And, as you say, some are pretty awful." She eyed Jackie. "Are they anything like what you're wearing?"

"One or two. They're all very good dresses."

"Oh, I'm sure I could do with that sort."

"I am not sure when I could bring them in."

"Well, I wouldn't want to wait too long. As you can see, I really need them." She went to the display window. "As you can see, some of these are really down. I'm ashamed to show them, but I have to put something in the window." And she shifted them one by one, along the metal rail, while holding the skirts up to emphasize their bad quality.

"You could come and see them if it's not out of your way."

"Tomorrow, perhaps? I close for the afternoon, anyway; it wouldn't be any inconvenience."

Jackie wrote down her address.

"Are there many?" asked the girl.

"A dozen, maybe more."

"Oh, it is rather a lot. I might not be able to take them all. It's the outlay. I've only been open five weeks, with nothing practically."

"Well, come along, anyway. We'll see how it works out."

When Jackie left the shop the girl's eye followed her. She had apparently thought Jackie quite respectable and well dressed. Surprisingly so, since she herself was not the sort to be easily impressed by anyone. The very manner in which she was dressed showed that it mattered little to her what others thought. She watched Jackie drove off before applying the door latch and turned the sign round from 'open' to 'closed'.

Chapter Ten

The very next day Jackie was surprised by a knock at the door. She abandoned the Martini and went to it. "Oh, come in. you must forgive me, I had forgotten you."

The girl from the junk shop entered.

"Perhaps you would like a drink. Any preference?"

The girl was pleased. She found the yellow and gold living room very cosy, the carpet soft and luxurious. She was impressed by the ecstatic manner of the older girl, looking so graceful in a pale blue dress. She glanced at the bottles and consented.

She herself was dressed differently from the day before, in a green two-piece, tightly fitted. Jackie handed her the glass.

"Make yourself comfortable. I will see exactly what there is."

The room was deliciously warm, but the day was somewhat cold, with fog still on the high ground behind the bungalow.

The girl removed her cap and unbuttoned her jacket before taking an armchair. She was looking at the photograph of the children when Jackie reappeared.

Laying the dresses carefully on a sofa, she invited the girl to sort them out.

There were six dresses of various styles. The girl handled them one by one. Holding each one up for a careful inspection. The first was a cream dress, short sleeved, with low hipline, and pleated all round. Attractive cross stitching ran from the breast to the shoulders. The second was a two piece, not to be worn without the jacket. It was bluish white, while the jacket sported a broad collar and no buttons. A buckled belt linked the front.

In all, Jackie made three sorties, each time coming back with half dozen dresses. The girl, well absorbed, was scarcely articulate. This was even better than a fashion store, since the atmosphere was cozy and she could linger over them as much as she liked. Jackie asked her name and she had to repeat herself.

"I am Emily."

"What made you open such a shop?"

"There was nothing else to do." She held up a beige maxi with matching coat. "These are new, aren't they?"

Jackie looked at them. Yes, she had bought them only last spring. There was a reminiscent smile. She had never got round to wearing them.

But they were beautiful!

She had thought so too, at the time. But one soon got fed up with the style.

The girl held up another dress. "Oh, these won't last a week in the shop."

"What about the others? Will they be easy to sell?"

"Oh yes. All top quality, exactly what people expect to find in a second-hand shop: the things they couldn't afford to buy new."

She looked at a printed dress with flared skirt and no sleeves. It was well trimmed with lace. There was also one in black and white in the same style. In all there were about six summer dresses, all lavishly made. One was almost transparent and would have to be worn with special underwear.

Now that she had seen them all, she really didn't know how to choose. She would like to stock them all. They were just what were needed. Perhaps she could take some now, and collect the others some other time?

"No. If you can sell them, you must take them all."

But that would not be possible; she was unable to pay the money all at once.

Jackie had no idea of their value second-hand. She had seen prices on two or three in the shop and was sure the girl could not have paid much for them. But these were no comparison, the girl explained. These would fetch a reasonable price.

Well, she could have them all at the same price. How much was she able to pay?

"I have forty pound in hand."

"Then you must have them at a pound each."

"A pound? Really some are worth five pounds and more."

"Nevertheless, they're of no use to me. I wouldn't want them if they were altered. The only alternative is to give them away, and that is too much trouble. It is easier to sell them."

"You're doing me a favour, I'm sure."

"Where did you work before the shop?"

Emily smiled amicably. Her story was not very pleasant. She was in college for a time, and then there was nothing of interest to do. She had studied the classics and history. She must have wasted her time.

How long would she keep the shop going?

Heaven knows! The dresses would do marvellous things to it. She would now be able to choose her stock more carefully. Leaving the dresses for a while, she was back with the Martini. She planted herself in the armchair and sighed. Opening her handbag, she made out the cheque. She was aged about twenty-three and quite handsome, thought Jackie. But she could do a lot more for herself by wearing the right clothes. In her blue midi dress, however, she was vastly different form the girl of yesterday. Jackie knew the trend. It was modern yet only the good stuff looked right. The others made one look ancient and bedraggled. There were three or four more dresses in the wardrobe which she brought out, taking the opportunity to be rid of them all.

For Jackie it was not so much the money as being able to empty the wardrobe. She would no longer have to look at them. Having the cheque now gave her genuine reason to go into Ashford. The new car was still a novelty and any opportunity to drive was welcomed. Almost ready, however, it suddenly occurred to her that the bank was closed. It was four o'clock. Oh, well, tomorrow would do. Her nights were still restless, though less tormenting. Sleeping was slight and hardly more than two hours. The days were good. When bored she would visit Mary. The long hours of dinking were again evident, at times late into the night. Quite often she woke in the armchair and emptied the bottle.

When eventually she got into Ashford to credit the cheque to her account, Jackie asked for a statement out of curiosity. After all, she had not been keeping a check on her spending. The clerk soon fetched a large pink envelope which she opened in the car.

The balance was just over five hundred pounds. She was shocked. It was quite unbelievable. Almost collapsing, she lost herself for a time, quite dazed.

In five months her account had fallen from seventeen hundred pounds to some five hundred. At the time the cheque was lodged in the bank, there was an overdraft to be cleared up, then to her grocer, the butcher, the off-licence and the estate agents she had owed nearly two hundred pounds. With those bills out of the way, her spending had been extravagant. On top of that, over two hundred pounds had gone on new dresses for her and the children; and in all that time she had scarcely been out of the bungalow.

She quickly ran through the used cheques, but so many had been made out to the off-licence that she could scarcely see anything else. The reason was that the bills had to be squared immediately on delivery. And fifteen pounds a week had been a regular figure, whereas with the grocer and the butcher, they often mounted up before she would cover them with one cheque. Right now there were two weeks' rent outstanding, and one or two bills. After some quick calculation Jackie decided that there could hardly the more than four hundred pounds in balance. At this rate there would be nothing left by Christmas. Driving back and recovering from the shock, she studied the situation. There was not much she could do. The intake from the off-license could hardly be reduced, since it would mean sleepless nights, mad day-dreams, and congestion in her head. Oh, she wouldn't last a month! The alcohol was necessary. There would be no point in reducing the grocery bill. She was already down to one meal a day, and that was necessary to maintain her health. But with the two dresses to be collected from the store, another hundred pounds would go on them.

At the petrol station she filled the tank and decided that she shouldn't need any more for a week. The car was small. Two pounds a week would not alter things.

At eight o'clock the telephone rang. It was Penman. He was passing in an hour and would call on her. She welcomed the voice. After all, she was alone and dreaded the emptiness.

The first time Penman had called, Jackie was hardly dressed. Now she rushed to the dressing tale to start on her hair. Already washed and dried, she merely brushed it; then taking it in one handful, she wrapped it in a tight circle at the back. The style lent her face a high look, with eyes more alert. Now that all her neck was exposed, she went further by choosing the right dress, one without sleeves, and a cutaway neck, baring her bosom and exposing the shoulders. At the back the drop was deep. She drew the sash at the side. Meanwhile, slipping her feet into soft shoes before going back to the table to finish off her face. First a little cream which gave her cheeks a rich lustre, for she needed it now, since the restless night was evident, and furthermore, to tone down her complexion against the dress. Then the eyes had to be lightened. Finally she slipped on the pearl earrings and fastened on her necklace.

Penman was delighted. He wondered whether he had interrupted a special occasion.

"Certainly not," She exclaimed with a smile. The only special occasion was his visit. After all, it had been nearly a week.

"Maybe I should make amends."

"You've already done so. Quite extraordinarily, too. The car: it reminds me of you every minute of the day."

"Perhaps it is the perfect gift."

"It is wonderful. I shall drive it with care."

He too, was in white, a rare coincidence. His jacket was stylish, worn with white bow tie and tan shoes. His black and white hair was brushed forward and sideways, almost covering his high forehead. His smile showed even dentures.

Jackie escorted him to one of the armchairs and planted herself opposite, then leaned forward and poured the drinks.

"You don't have to tell me," she said. "Is it supposed to be a Christmas present?"

"Not at all. Something to seal a happy acquaintance."

"It's a grand way of showing appreciation, but I ought to have expected it. Millionaires do generous thing for women they admire."

"I'll go along with that. It's very well explained."

"But does it ever occur to you that one of the worst problem is knowing what to give in return?"

"My dear, you're missing the simple point."

There was a quick appraising glance.

His smile was perfect. "You should never make a gift simply because you receive one."

"But wouldn't that be showing gratitude?"

"Far from it. It shows that one is confused."

Suddenly she agreed. "I am confused."

"A present or a gift out of season suggests amity."

"And I'm not supposed to return the compliment?"

"Yes, of course, by all means."

She regarded him. "That is why I'm confused."

"You simply pay a compliment by accepting the present."

"And one must be content with doing just that?"

"Certainly, and making use of it, of course."

Jackie handed him a glass of Martini. "Have you a favourite drink?" she asked.

"Hardly. There are many with fine taste; this is one of them."

"And?"

"Well, Grand Marnier, Chartreuse–splendid liqueurs; Rickard, unique taste; Hine–very good refreshers. I may even settle for the popular labels. I sometimes make my own concoction, and even frown at the taste when it's not satisfactory."

Jackie was amused. I am terribly fond of peach wine."

Penman returned the glare.

"I was once addicted to it," she explained. "Oh, it was still delicious seven years ago. I must have taken to it at the age of eighteen."

"Hmm…at that age one is vulnerable. Peach wine has a rosy flavour. I'm not surprised."

"You like it yourself?'

"A sip of it now and then is welcomed. Much too sweet, though."

"Is it appropriate in fashionable places?'

"To a man who's meeting you for the first time, it might be interesting. But should you choose it now, I think your admirer would be delighted."

"Really."

"Individuality's a beautiful side of one's personality. And in any case, its delicate taste really suits you."

Jackie leaned back in the armchair. Time was irrelevant. She was drinking a light mixture of Dunbonnet and lime. By one o'clock there was a vague heaviness in Penman's voice. But he was perfectly relaxed in the armchair.

"Did you have a busy day?" she asked.

"Unusually busy."

"You did not come from Sandgate?"

"No. Straight from a conference."

"Routine?"

"Well, it was drawn up early for the convenience of one or two shareholders. Some of us go abroad for the winter, like some creatures hibernate. Winter in this country is rather depressing, snow and everything. It's not the kind of condition one likes to get used to."

"How about now; would you say it's terrible?" she was referring to the rain and wind which had been lashing the window for the past two hours.

"Yes, not intolerable, though. But it's good to know that the night is warmer elsewhere."

Penman went to the window, held the curtain back and peered out. It was not too bad. The wind was slight, with heavy rain. But the heavy condensation on the glass made the cold apparent.

"I fear this mess will go on all night," he said. "It is pointless waiting for it to clear."

"Perhaps you could use an umbrella."

She held the curtain back and watched him rush to the car. The

91

Rolls Royce was parked in front of the gate. Penman got the door open, lowered the umbrella and tucked himself in. just then the heavy shower turned to a light drizzle, and fresh winds took over.

For Jackie it was another night in the armchair. For all the new development in her life, she still dreaded the empty bed. Afraid of her own mind, she was staggered by what it would dream up. On the other hand, there were no regrets at being left alone. In company she was very much herself, but it had scarcely entered her head to delay him, yet she had given no thought to the emptiness that would follow. In fact, she was hardly aware of it now. She simply abandoned herself in the armchair and dropped off to sleep.

Chapter Eleven

A week later Jackie left the bungalow with the two children and made towards London. On the other side of the city she followed the signs to the motorway and headed north. In half an hour she was at the family home in Hockcliffe where she left the children with their grandparents and headed back to London. It was time the children were used to their grandparents! After all, in a little while she would be leaving them indefinitely. She was undecided on this, however, but as things were, she needed a few weeks of total freedom. There was the Caribbean cruise, quite promising. On the other hand, she was hardly happy to be rid of them, but it was impractical to leave them in the house for more than an hour, and in a matter of a month or so she might be out on the street with the furniture.

This situation had hitherto escaped her, but the possibility was certainly imminent. Thinking it over now, there seemed little doubt of it, unless she was ready to take up Pascoe's offer. Incidentally, Pascoe would be wondering what had become of her, what she was up to. The one letter he had written was put to the fire when she had lost her head.

In London she kept an appointment at a hairdresser's salon in Mayfair. Then, arriving back at the bungalow later, she quickly decided on a bath. While the water ran she poured a glass of Cockburn and laid out a Thai-silk dress along with a waist length jacket, before going to the mirror to see that her hair was neatly tucked in under the protective scarf.

Resting the glass on the edge of the bath, she hung up the rug and got into the thick foam, happily humming a tune. When the glass was empty she buried herself in the essence of the Pears' foam bath.

An hour later she put aside the sponge and reached for the rug, dried herself carefully and was soon out in the dressing room where she exchanged the rug for a towel and resumed the delicate task. Tossing the towel over a chair now, she planted herself before the mirror and gazed at her large firm breasts for a time before letting her hair down to set gently by itself. The style was a smooth flow down to her neck and, with her head high and straight, its great heavy tress settled snugly above her shoulders. Her complexion was right, but an extra smoothness was desirable.

Getting up she collected the rug and went off to the living room. Having rejected the glass in the bathroom, which was by now dripping with condensation, she took out a new glass, filled it with port, and went back to resume her toilette.

It was already dark. Without wind the November night was a rare treat warmer than usual. It was barely seven-thirty. Opening out her skirt, she planted herself on the edge of the bed. The dress was new, with only straps supporting the shoulders. It was perfect for summer, but with the little jacket, it now added glamour to the mild winter night.

From the bedroom window she saw the flood of headlights heading up the drive. Leaving the empty glass, Jackie made her way to the living room and opened the door, Penman walked in, planted a light kiss on her cheek, then stood back to devour her with his eyes.

"Without disrespect," he said. "I must promise myself to catch you just once when you're looking your worst. Really, I am almost convinced that your picture never changes."

"You saw me once when I least expected you," she reminded him.

But he shook his head.

"Yes, the very first time you came here," she explained. "I was wearing an old house coat that was too big for me."

"I remember it well. But perhaps you were not aware that you were remarkably well dressed?'

"Am I to believe that?"

"It's an honest confession."

Jackie led him across the room to the bottle of port. "Will you have one before we leave?'

"If you're taking my interest at heart," he said happily, "I will gladly give myself up."

But she was already pouring the drink.

He drank it quickly and returned the glass. Ten minutes later he was guiding her to the car.

At the end of the quite little road they turned left and headed for London. The Rolls Royce appealed to Jackie. Its cosiness welcomed her. The white upholstery was cool under the faint light of the dashboard. Sitting back with arms folded, she took on an expression of absolute calm.

Penman glanced sideways.

"How is your new car?" he asked. "Any teething trouble?"

"It's behaving extremely well."

"And you're adapted to it?"

"Certainly. It's a treat to drive. But tell me, how did you make the choice? What made you choose that particular car?"

"It is something new from Fiat, a brand new model. Sporty and suitable for a young mother with two youngsters. You can open the top to let in fresh air. And lots of space for luggage and children's things."

"So it was a personal choice? You did not just ring the showroom and have the salesman deliver a car to my address?"

"Good heavens, no! The very looks appealed to me, the colour so bright and refreshing."

That was what Jackie wanted to hear.

It took Penman an hour to get to Earls Court. Secretly it annoyed him. In the dense traffic there was no pleasure in manoeuvring the heavy car. On the other hand, however, with Jackie beside him, he remained fresh and complimentary.

It was not good for an honoured guest to be late, but Karl Penman was easily excused. The doorman was even apologetic.

"Ladies and gentlemen, our chief guest tonight, Mr. Karl Penman," he cocked an ear and Penman whispered the name, 'Miss Pascoe,' and with a smile and a flourish, the doorman announced Jackie.

The mansion was in a quiet mews, surrounded by trees and a narrow lawn at the front. The hall was interesting. A small stage held a group of musicians. One side of the hall was laced with white silk, while opposite, four sections of purple curtains were drawn back to reveal paintings. A cocktail bar occupied one corner, while two identical chandeliers graced the ceiling. The carpet was carefully layed, leaving an oval-shaped middle section for dancing.

The guests were an interesting mixture; all wealthy if not considerably rich, and apparently lavish. A table was reserved for Penman near the stage, on the right. Four people occupied the one next to it. Then there were two rows of tables on each side.

Cocktails were served to Jackie and Penman, whilst the music took on a kind of rumba tempo. When the piece ended, the chairman took the microphone and summoned the attention of his guests.

"Ladies and gentlemen, as you know, the proceeds of this grand affair will be a contribution to the relief of human suffering. It will go to those who are unfortunate in that they have lost, or have never been blessed with, the vital convenience of their sight. It is a pity that we cannot ourselves restore their sight, but in our capacity we can make it easier for those who are working towards that goal. As the night progresses, ladies and gentlemen, our distinguished guest , Mr Karl Penman, will be handing over the cheques for the amount we are donating, to Dr. Hislop, a representative of the society and a devoted worker himself. Thank you." Then, leaving the band to resume playing, he stepped down to greet Penman.

No stranger to Penman. Cimla was about forty-five, clean shaven, sporting a broad forehead and thick white hair. A graduate in economics, he had, like Penman, made his money on the stock exchange; he was also a prominent figure in the higher social spheres. Well known throughout the city, his wife was there too, enjoying the occasion. She was a doctor, also engaged in important work for the blind. Cimla decided to greet Penman personally. Needless to say, he had an interesting eye for the strange and adorable lady.

"I thought you'd never get here," he said to Penman, "but of course, you were excused the moment you showed up."

"Oh, why so quickly?"

"Madam, naturally." And he glanced at Jackie with a smile.

The compliment was accepted. Penman said: "Perhaps I'd better introduce her more cordially. You heard the doorman? Well, her name is Jacqueline."

Cimla gazed profoundly at Jackie. "I am delighted to know you."

"Thank you."

"My dear," said Penman, "This is David Cimla."

"Are you another gambler?" she asked.

"Yes. It's exciting you know; it keeps the mind in sharp contemplation of world affairs. I'm sure Karl explained."

"Naturally," said Penman.

"Only two months ago he created one of the biggest excitements in the market. I expect you know all about that?"

"No," said Jackie, curious, "I don't think so,"

Cimla went on to amuse her by telling how Penman had pounced on a new Australian nickel find within seconds of the announcement. At that time the two main countries supplying the world with nickel had closed up shop while they discussed between themselves a system to regulate their output. By throwing two million pounds into the new find, the shares rocketed to more than thirty times their original quote. It was a simple trick which had paid tremendous dividends. But the strength of it had been the headlong plunge, and the free atmosphere in which the whole thing had inflated. "Do you still hold any of those shares?" he asked Penman.

Jackie looked on, impressed.

Penman shook his head apologetically. "It's a pretty risk business, my dear," he said simply to Jackie.

"The proceeds are in other things?" she asked.

"Of course."

"It's best that way," Cimla added. "It keeps the economy rolling."

His attention was drawn to he other side of the hall. "Now you must excuse me, Miss Jacqueline, Karl, the night is still new so to speak." And he went off to join his wife across the room.

Penman looked at Jackie. "I think we should enjoy the music, don't you?"

Jackie wasted no time. She empted her glass and joined Penman in the oval. She had not forgotten any of her steps. Absorbed in the good atmosphere, she moved easily in Penman's arms. She had accepted him, dismissing the childlike inhibitions that had filled her head earlier. On the other hand his firm, almost impractical manner occasionally insisted that she kept her guard. She was actually aware of every move. So far, however, he presented no threat to her self-awareness, and it seemed unlikely that she would let her hair down completely. In short, Penman's attitude brought out the best in her.

When he was later absorbed in conversation with Cimla and others, Jackie chatted with Cimla's wife, an elegant woman, professional and extremely practical. She knew Penman well and, for the first time Jackie was faintly conscious of herself. Mrs. Cimla had assumed initially that Jackie was acquainted with Mrs. Penman, but on discovering that this was not so, she quickly dropped the subject.

"How long have you known him?" she asked.

"Frankly, we hardly know each other."

The doctor smiled. "Penman is a difficult one, much too pompous for my taste."

"You know him well?"

"Yes, over many years. I'm fascinated that you actually came here on his arm. He's usually a loner, you know. Oh, yes, he's hard to get into, provided you want to get into him, that is. He demands nothing but the best. Frankly, he's quite intolerant of imperfection."

Mrs. Cimla was in a silver-blue dress and wore a heart-shaped diamond brooch. She was blonde, not quite slim, and wore faint trances of cosmetic: orange lips and dark eyebrows. She smiled contentedly.

Jackie wondered: was Karl a regular one for this sort of thing? He seemed to frequent a good many of these charity balls.

"Ah, so you've noticed. This is your first, I take it?"

"Yes," she replied.

"Then he will probably invite you to many more. His only connection is the charitable one. He is a cheerful giver, my dear. They're all cheerful givers." There was a little flourish. "Don't be surprised that he gives away so much. Really, there isn't much choice. This is a respectable way of conning the Chancellor: he's the man who gets most of what is termed 'unearned income'; and the men you see in this hall, well, together they make more than the gross national income of some countries. As you can see, they're all practically over fifty, the majority are even past sixty. They love giving since they would lose it otherwise. This way they gain respect, they become known in many circles, and, of course, when money is of less importance, this is the kind of influence they crave. Even Al Capone used to do it."

Still sipping her cocktail, she continued filling the innocent Jackie with surprises.

"Take that gentleman over there, to the left of the door, in the dark suit; he's lighting a cigar."

Jackie observed.

"He's seventy-eight," said the doctor, "a veteran of heart attacks. He's very much alive, though." She smiled. "He was married pretty early in life. No heir and heaven knows what has happened to his wife! He's one of the richest men in the country, with good investments abroad. Quite recently he built a technical college in one of the African countries, and had it named after him. Now he's a proud old soul. Mind you, he's been living extravagantly all his life. He hasn't told me in plain words, but I'm sure he's looking for another institution to carry his name when he's gone. He might even build a completely new one, since he will want his name on the foundation stone. I think, too," said the dear lady, "that he's looking for something to influence people who will travel the world. Something to transport his name." She smiled. "They all get to this stage later in life, you know; they like to look back at what they've achieved, and if they are not satisfied, they crave the idea of doing something that will live on after them."

Jackie smiled pleasantly. "The afterthought!"

"Exactly. In a way, it is a wonderful afterthought. A lot of useful institutions would never have come into existence if left entirely to governments."

Penman and Cimla were making their way across. Dr. Cimla added: "Don't always remain cool, insist on having your dues. He can be quite selfish if you let him."

Penman and David Cimla went past with a gratifying smile. It was twelve o'clock. The hall, luxurious in purple and gold, was entrenched with Cinderella's. Men and women, well dressed, danced the rumba gently. The founder of this rhythm, on some remote West Indian island, had obviously meant it to be provocative and sexually appetizing, and could well have wondered whether these people were statues, unable to let go and float with the beat. However, it was a pretty movement, even in this grand manner. The women, in their flared skirts, rested their arms casually over their partners' shoulders; while the men, forgetting themselves after the long hours, sometimes allowed their hand to slip to the ladies' waists.

A whisper in the ear of the band leader by David Cimla calmed the music after a good number. It was a break everyone welcomed, as all hands now made for the glasses.

Penman took up a position in front of the musicians, facing the room. In his hand was a small folder.

"Friends, comrades, dear ladies, I am pleased to point out that we have reached the climax of this beautiful night, thanks to our superb musicians." The whole room fell to a quite hush as he waved a hand toward the band, "They've done well to take us all into this exciting phase. Well, I have been honoured by a request to make the presentation to Dr. Hislop, a devoted member of the institution to which we are giving our support tonight. Before you now, I am pleased to do just that." He paused while the doctor, a robust figure in brown suit and an old school tie, came forward.

A scientist himself, Hislop was engaged in work on the retina. Previously he had been studying its failure, but had recently been transferred to a more progressive section, concerned chiefly with grafting from the newly dead. A lot had been achieved in this field and results were reasonably satisfactory. Hislop was proud of his work, but amongst these men who would hardly appreciate a subject which did not involve financial dividend, he was to a great extent inarticulate.

Penman handed him the small folder of cheques and assured him that the total amounted to one hundred and seven thousand pounds. The scientist, with a slight quiver, took from his inside coat pocket, a small case which he opened, and carefully put on a pair of spectacles. Opening the folder now, he quickly sifted through the small pages. At last he removed his glasses and looked on.

"Mr. Penman, ladies and gentlemen," he commenced, "on behalf of the blind, my institute and my colleagues, I thank you all for this extremely generous gift of one hundred and seven thousand pounds. I must also stress that I'm honoured to be the recipient of this thoughtful donation. The institute is not only engaged in work for the blind, it is also concerned with those who are partially blind. In fact, our research is wholly involved with the eye, the failures which occur at all stages of life. It is difficult to separate total blindness from partial blindness, since one is the more advanced stage of the other. Thus, by studying the causes, we're automatically investigating the whole field.

"The institute is celebrating its twentieth anniversary and I am pleased to say that this is a milestone. From a stagnant position we are now able to thrust forward with enthusiasm and greater optimism. I thank you all, Mr. Penman, ladies and gentleman

With a few flourishing words, Penman finished off. David Cimla was already with his wife and Jackie. Penman joined them.

"The old boy look mighty pleased," said Cimla. "More than one hundred thousand pounds. That's a damn good figure."

"Indeed," Penman agreed, "there's no doubt about it. He's a likeable chap, too."

"Are you always so generous?" asked Jackie, surprised at the figure.

"Oh, it is probably a record for a mid-night collection. Eighty or ninety thousand has been a regular ceiling, though."

Jackie raised her brows.

"I told you, my dear, these people are generous givers," added Mrs. Cimla, "It gives them a great thrill."

Two more cocktails and half-an-hour later, Penman and Jackie were leaving. So were the Cimlas. They were living in Northwood. It was one o'clock when they finally dispersed.

Driving off, Penman and Jackie headed north and joined the ring road, then left it for the A20.

Was this the kind of party she was invited to some weeks ago?

"No," said Penman, "that was a genuine family affair."

"Why the surprise," asked Jackie, who noted the look on Penman's face.

"Well, I may have the convenience of comfortable accounts, but parties of that sort could hardly be held more than once a year. I couldn't afford it."

She watched the road for a time. At seventy miles an hour the Rolls Royce was traveling with little effort, cool as a gentle breeze, and the armchair comfort induced almost total relaxation.

"You said the previous party was a family affair."

"Yes, my son's birthday. It was very quiet. But I think he had something more lavish with his friends."

"I don't quite understand why I was invited."

Penman failed to comprehend.

"Well, you said it was a family affair, a private gathering," Jackie explained. 'I am a stranger. Surely your interest in me did not justify my being there?"

"I am sure I could introduce you to the household with sincerity. I hope you will not deny me some individuality."

"But surely there's an ethical point."

He threw her a sidelong glance accompanied by a smile.

"You're suggesting that the invitation might have been indiscreet?"

"Yes."

"Perhaps, but not entirely. You're an adorable woman. It would have been clearly understood."

"But your wife?"

"My wife is at the stage of life when conjugal activities are insignificant. She's an active woman, socially: president of an organization that meets regularly. And she's engaged in several others shall we say useful activities, between here and Australia. She's an independent woman."

The idea was suddenly clear to Jackie. Mrs. Penman was a working woman, influential, no doubt. Marriage was simply a status from which she could radiate. There was nothing unusual about it. Some of the world's best known women had progressed in that way. Born rich, instead of remaining elegant and charming and floating from one man to another, they had preferred to lend themselves to humanity to be admired from one generation to the next.

However, she was not dismissing the obvious assumption that

Penman was at the stage where his interest was automatically going out to a younger woman. Don't all men relish the idea?

"Do you suppose I could have enjoyed myself at the party with that in the air?"

"No question about it, my dear. My wife is a civilized woman. She would have been the first to make you feel at home."

"Really!"

"You would have found her in the kind of mood that would have made you forget yourself completely. She is, above all, a charming woman."

At this stage Penman forgot himself so far as to move his hand across the seat to find hers. Taking it, he squeezed her affectionately. Jackie lent herself to it, knowing very well that Penman was making a desperate effort. She was prepared to lengthen his stay. His steps were slow and cautious, quite uncertain on his part, then there could be no other way of reaching her, since she had previously disregarded him. The little acts of affection assured her now that he could be practical as well as intellectually passionate. He was an academic, a great lover of art, with a good knowledge of the classics. This she appreciated, though underneath she was very much a simpleton, knowing little about such things, but for which she had always maintained a curious admiration. And even with a certain simplicity, she kept a high standard, regarding dignity as a great virtue, and being extremely modest in order to make up for the other qualities which were scarce. Her beauty was a great asset, enhancing those qualities to a reasonable standard. Almost naïve, this showed an innocence which flattered her admirers. Penman was one of them. With his hand in hers now, he had unconsciously succeeded in making her forget even the difficult nights.

They were now on the quiet road to the bungalow.

"Well, here we are," she said.

Penman declared that he would stay long enough for a night cap. It was past two o'clock, he pointed out, and he wanted to start early in the morning.

Was he forgetting that the new day was Sunday?

Not at all. Unfortunately, he had certain commitments. He would be rather busy for the next two weeks, when he would sail for the Caribbean.

There was no moon and the street lamp was out of order. Jackie led the way, walking slowly and purposefully to the door, where she paused.

A dim light was on in the living-room. She threw the main switch, and soon abandoned herself in an armchair. Crossing her legs, she threw back her arms.

"Now what will you have to drink?"

Penman had decided to help himself. After all, he was not a complete stranger. But he paused with some uneasiness behind her; then, leaning forward, he stroked her hair and kissed her forehead. The act was accompanied by a little whisper, regretting he was unable to stay the night. He would make up for it on board the yacht.

He brought out a full bottle of Tia Maria and two glasses, handling them so that their long stems slid between his fingers. The rich flavour of the Blue Mountain coffee was distinct. Jackie had tasted it before, loved the flavour but had never followed it up. Now at this hour, after an active evening, it seemed perfect, with its strangely caressing taste.

"So, I am to accompany you on a cruise?"

"It would make me a thousand times richer. But I couldn't insist that your refusal would reduce my admiration for you."

"It's a grand opportunity that I wouldn't dare to miss, isn't that so?"

"I'd be disappointed if you were to refuse."

"Is my position vulnerable?"

"Hardly. I don't find myself in company with a different woman every day."

"And without admiration, you could not be sincere."

"The novelty would be gone in a day, and naturally, things would be irritating afterwards."

"Exactly how would I fit in?"

"Perfectly. The interest would be considerable. Your beauty would be something to wake up to one morning after another. You would be like someone rising out of the sea, especially to love me, to inspire me. How else should I express it?" Penman wondered. Her presence would make the stars unnecessary.

"How then would you navigate?" she asked with a smile.

"Oh, damn the navigation. The climax of it all would not depend on us arriving at any particular place."

"Not even Jamaica?"

He emptied his glass. "Jamaica is a place we can visit any time of the year."

The idea of drifting sounded good. Jackie was not adventurous, but after the pains and depression of the last few months, being at the mercy of the stars seemed far better, a sweet challenge.

Would there be many on board?

Six or so, including them.

This disappointed her a little. It sounded like a sacrificial cruise. He certainly wasn't an exciting playboy, neither was he anything like the rugged incorrigible caveman in her bath who subjected her, mindfully, to gruelling sensuous pleasures. It seemed above all that Penman was going to be boring. Despite herself, she was still dreaming of that brute, secretly welcoming him into her thoughts. Three years of chastity had imbedded into her mind that sensational image and it was silly to think that she would be rid of him overnight. She was actually on the last sip of the Tia Maria, while at the same time wishing that Phillip Russell was there with her. In this situation he would have been more demanding.

On the drive back to the bungalow, when she had held Penman's hand, there had been a slight moment of expectation that something would happen, that there would be an alternative to drinking herself stupid. But the thought was quickly lost in the conversation. Now, however, with the children away, tomorrow could be long and hard.

Chapter Twelve

Finding rest in the armchair was greater now than ever. Overriding this desire was an impetuous demand, quite insatiable. For a moment she slumped back while a thousand ideas rushed though her mind, among them the frustration of recent years, years that were empty, regrettable, almost tragic.

Relaxation was impossible, for the heat was fierce, coming in waves and proceeding at times, so that every now and then it seemed she was bent on wrecking the chair. Jackie was actually afraid of herself. Once, when a wave had subsided, she rushed quickly to her room out of fear of other attack. Then, throwing herself across the bed she pressed her breast fiercely into the pillow. This was a little act that had always given her a flush of relief. It had been her usual move when accommodating the incorrigible brute, but now, quite tense, she uttered a cry. And even when obliged to relax, there was no peace, the drink had worn off; she would remain in torment.

Numbed with despair, she faced the empty room, the bed ransacked, restless for a time, assessing the situation, the great distress now so unbearable. Suddenly a fantastic idea came to mind. Then, smiling passionately, she quickly threw back her hair, brushed and reset it, and complemented her cheeks with a smear of powder. Finding the evidence of her own tears, she rushed off to the bathroom. In a moment she was back, replenishing her cheeks. From a small phial she applied sparingly to her ears and neck little touches of the delicious Ma Griffe. But it certainly wouldn't do to look her best while the rich fragrance might be wise. She removed her dress and selected a less refined, more instyle calf-length skirt with a white lace blouse. Then she drew on a Cashmere sweater over her shoulders.

But the new appearance was still too much. It was necessary to come down a peg or two, to wear a simple dress. While none of the new ones would make her any less magnificent, it had to be an old dress. But surely the one or two wearable ones were all gone? With a mind to check, she threw open the wardrobe door. Ah, there was the blue skirt and pink blouse she had worn last. Hardly appropriate on a cold night, they would have to do. She would be driving and, once out of the car, the sweater would help.

She quickly got into them. The broad belt took care of the

slackness at the waist to lend her a neat appearance. Then in front of the mirror she ruffled her hair and felt better. A pair of high-healed shoes provided the finishing touches. She collected the Cashmere sweater and switched out the light.

It was two thirty in the morning, cold and unspeakably quiet. Where was she heading? One thing was certain; she would not remain in the house and go out of her mind. She got into the car and was out of the garage, headed through the gates and fast down the quiet drive, onto the A20, towards London.

Even now there was uneasiness. She consulted the radio and pressed each button for a good programme. There was no music: nothing but irritating crackles to break the monotony. The car gathered speed steadily, and she kept her wide eyes steadfast on the rushing white lines. They gave her a certain airiness, while on the other side she was well away from the kerb. The first time the car approached one hundred miles an hour. Despite having been used to a more powerful car, she was hardly accustomed to holding this speed, certainly not at night when vision was limited. The road, however, was almost deserted and endless.

Fifteen minutes later Jackie was hustling along Old Kent Road. Bearing left on to New Kent Road, she made across St. George's, over the river at Westminster, and headed for Belgrade, the night club where she had once worked. But there was no question of going in, especially if the old rules were still in force. Furthermore, her dress would hardly fit the occasion.

Approaching the club, however, and in sight of the neon lights, she slowed to a crawl, edged forward and sought a space to park. The Nightingale was still a grand place; at three in the morning there was still activity inside. When she had worked there, several years back, the outer walls were dirty black, with only a large window to the right of the door where coming attractions were displayed; There was even a time when her picture had been on display for a whole season. Now the outer walls were an appropriate reflection of its rich interior.

Twenty yards off she found a vacant space. Then, driving past and turning round, the Fiat came back to the spot, drove past and backed in. Then Jackie composed herself in the car and gazed hopefully at the closed doors. The thumping in her head wasn't so bad now, and as she became able to think clearly, it seemed like only yesterday that she had danced here, and chatted with one guest after another. Flirtation had been natural to her. What wonderful times, with one lover in the background to whom she would rush at least once a week. But then she had never felt such flames. How unfair that when she was surrounded by such wonderful people, she should have been so selective. Was this not how Mary had felt? Yes, she had often frowned at Mary, failing to comprehend how Mary had managed to throw herself at everything that had crossed her path. But really Mary had never been serious about her demands. There was certainly a difference between genuine want and simple adventure.

Something caught her eye; a tall figure in a dark suit came out of the club. Perhaps he would see her. She was the only person in a car out there. He had left the door open and was looking back. Presently a girl in furs rushed out and into his arms. Then a taxi pulled up and they were off.

Oh, well! It seemed as though she had been there for ages. But it was impossible to note the time. The nearest street lamp was a few yards away; but people were leaving the club now, and the car's light would attract undue attention.

All the men had woman on their arms. Perhaps it was different now from when she had worked there. In those days half the men were loners, mostly visitors from aboard, businessmen, diplomats, government officials, on quiet evenings with secret assignations. It had been grand. One got to know everyone. Perhaps the rules had changed. Maybe the facilities had altered and single men no longer flocked there.

The silence was nerve wrecking. She tried tuning the radio, insisting that there ought to be some foreign programme at least that she could listen to, even if the dialogue was senseless. It would ease the strain. When the tiny light appeared through the dial, she held her wrist low to check the time: it was twenty minutes past three.

Leaning back wearily, she gazed on, envious of the women who came out of the club hanging onto their men. Ah, there was one fellow walking off alone, heading towards her. He was black, an African official perhaps, robust, in a sort of flannel suit. He wore no overcoat and the front of his jacket swayed with every step. She peered anxiously, her eyes close to the screen. The white floral tie flew loosely with his sway. His face was round with prominent cheeks and a firm chin, his lips untraceable in the dark. But as he approached the car her eyes avoided him. There was no pause in his brisk steps. Perhaps he had failed to notice her. She listened to the footsteps disappearing behind her. They stopped abruptly. Seconds later a car door slammed. Jackie turned quickly in her seat and stared wildly. The Mercedes Benz coughed and drifted cautiously out from the line of cars. As it accelerated past, their eyes met. Suddenly she sighed. He could have offered a smile.

In the days when she had worked at the club, she had danced with the men, entertained them, and enjoyed their company. She had dined with them. Perhaps because of the rules they had remained intimately remote. On the other hand, she had known Mary to have found excellent lovers amongst them.

But seriously, it was useless to sit there like that. Jackie switched the radio to another wavelength and turned the knob until music broke the silence. There was even a spectacular air about it now. How silly to expect a man to introduce himself. She was not at the wheel of a taxi, and these men were not the sort to expect the unlikely when looking at a strange woman. Deciding now that her tactics were mad, she toyed with the idea of getting out of the car.

Five minutes later, when two men had gone by without a pause, she opened the door slightly. On the pavement now, and standing by the car, her sweater drawn about her shoulders shielded her from the cold; but scarcely, for with only a thin blouse under it, her lack of protection would be immediately oblivious. Then with arms folded in front of her and holding the sweater in place, she walked the pavement towards the club, but on the opposite side where the tall office block was in darkness. On this side, however, directly opposite the club, was a street lamp. Once under it, she would be conspicuous. But she stopped short, for the blue skirt and shapely legs, enhanced by the way she walked, exhibited too much firmness. And the long raven hair and firm lips were more than enough. Had she been in rags she might have stood a better chance. The whole thing was a disappointment when suddenly a young man, tall with long hair and bearded face, emerged from the club. He crossed the street with unsteady feet, quite merry after a drop too much. He spotted her ahead of him, but she turned in her tracks and walked on absentmindedly. When at last he was up behind her, she sensed his eyes looking for a glimpse of her face. But no sooner had she caught the expression than she saw the lips curl into a smile: "Good night, lovely."

Jackie would have liked to return the kind words, but her lips failed to break their seal, and as she moved slowly now with her elegant flair, her eyes followed him out of sight. Back in the car, she slammed the door shut and decided that the whole thing was hopeless.

Then, as if insulted by her very attitude, she started the car and drove contemptuously away form the club. She had a better idea, something that would be more productive. When she was held up at a traffic light, the deserted street yawned at her. Then, glancing at her watch told her that breaking the red light at this hour of night would hardly matter. In any case she wouldn't mind exchanging a few words with someone, a policeman, even; it would help her head. Thus, edging slowly to the middle of the junction, she darted up Grosvernor Place. In no time she was heading north-west, along Park Lane.

Severely depressed, she hadn't spoken a word for two hours. Fancy not being able to open her mouth when the young fellow had uttered 'good night' in his friendly tone. Now she was humming to the radio, merely to convince herself that her voice had not deserted her. It also eased the tension, helped her to relax, and brought on confidence. Now she would be more deliberate. Why not? No one would know her. She was a stranger to these parts.

Turning into an intersection, Jackie went from one lane to the other, before pulling up twenty yards from the Playboy Club. Exclusively new, the club had been open for only four years. It was unheard of during her days in London. However, in its first few months of establishment, Pascoe had taken her there one night. There were vague memories of its luxurious interior. But another thing bothered her: it was terribly late. There would be only a few men inside. On the other hand, things were better here, since they would be mostly without women.

Avoiding the direct vicinity, Jackie turned the car and drew up further down; then, sitting for a moment, she watched the neon light, quite intrigued now by the prospect.

Yes, it seemed livelier here, out of the ordinary, and better lit by the brighter lights. There was a misty hue about the street; at four in the morning the November cold had set in, the streets totally deserted. However, she was yet to feel the cold, for she had just left the car. Her tactics were different now. Walking the street she would approach the first male to leave the club. It was the only way. Being a woman was a staggering advantage. Her only flaw was her respectable appearance. This was one occasion when she could have done with being able to reduce herself to the typical street prowler, for even they were certain of themselves at this game

A car went by, a large black limousine. She kept a straight face. It was chauffeur driven, with a lone figure in the back.

Immediately it was out of sight, there came the sound of footsteps. Then, with arms folded and holding the sweater in place, Jackie turned automatically and spotted the figure that had just left the club. She straightened her head. By this time she had gone past the club on one of her strolls. The man was indeed alone, yet she remained absentminded, for another car was approaching. It pulled up outside the club, soon the door slammed and it was off. Turning now, and looking on, she could see only the two rear lights disappearing into the distance. Oh, well! The chance had hardly existed anyway.

But she hardly had time to retrace when, almost in front of her, two men rushed out of the building: One in a top hat carrying an umbrella and wearing leather gloves; the other, with both hands in his pocket, strode forward, ahead of her. They took little note of her, yet Jackie maintained her slow pace and watched them out of sight. Meanwhile, a girl and her escort had left the club, got into a car and had driven off.

Perhaps the whole thing was in vain after all. These people would notice no one! She might have been lying sick on the pavement, the attitude so far was clearly that no one would have taken the slightest interest.

Feeling the cold now, and nearly heart broken, Jackie was momentarily going back on her own stupid idea. Yes, she was back in the car, grief–stricken. No one had looked at her. It was the time of night when men had given up the chase.

When she had caught her breath, cleared her throat and felt the new rage inside her, it was time to try again. By then only two couples had left the club. Now she was back on the street, walking the pavement. A few paces and she would be right in front of the door.

With purposeful steps, she clung to the sweater, then before she was under the club lights, the door swung open and out came the doorman, blocking her path. He opened the door of a black limousine which drew up against the pavement and waited.

Out of the building came a tall figure in a blue sports jacket. Apparently in no hurry, he paused outside the door, lit a cigarette and observed the surroundings. Jackie lingered in front of the car with a fixed gaze across the street, knowing that his eye was on her. Then came the moment of truth, for he was going into the car. But he made a comment:

"Ah, the lady in the flat above? But of course. Perhaps we

could share the same car. Why not?"

Jackie turned her head apologetically. There was no smile, only a calm civil expression. He was mistaken. Yes, he would soon correct himself.

"No? Oh, but there's enough room for two. Besides, it's very late."

Without further encouragement she felt herself drawn to the car, hardly aware of herself. Then, with a mind clouded with desolation, she sidestepped the doorman and got into the car, right across the seat, to make room for him. When they were actually on the move, he turned to her:

"I am Michael," he said, "Michael Gordonstone. Oh, I must apologize for not introducing myself before, but I did notice you. I've watched you going in and out of your flat on countless occasions. But you know, I've only been there two weeks. And I have been so busy."

Glancing sideways, Jackie forced a smile. He had genuinely mistaken her for someone else.

"So, your friend is still at the club, eh?"

She shook her head wearily, hardly the way she had wanted to, but that was how it happened. She wasn't quite herself.

They had reached Grosvenor Square and had turned into Carlos Street. Now they were turning into High Mews. Perhaps this was where he lived. Yes, the car pulled up. The chauffeur held the door open. Her companion let himself out, then lead the way to the apartment. Still in her passive mood, she paused behind him as he opened his door and turned to her:

"Forgive me, but I don't know your name." He smiled. "I appreciate your living above me. It's pleasant watching you come and go, knowing that if I want assistance, I could easily call on you. Maybe, well, maybe we could talk quietly for a moment." And he stood aside. Jackie twisted her lips.

Suddenly she was aware of herself. The little talk had revived her, lifted her from the weary lamentation of the last few hours. Now she studied him, retraced his words and, without as much as a smile, went past him with an air of indifference, as though to inspect the place.

From the outer door she moved along a short passage, noting a large reproduction of a landscape on one side. Then she was struck by the confusion in the living room. The furniture disarranged, and he was already trying his best to set her at ease, to acquaint himself.

"May I offer you something to drink? Coffee, wine, anything?" she shook her head.

Oh, he would treat himself to a late Cusenier; it was perfect for the occasion.

It was the same carpet from the passage that was lavishly laid throughout the living room. A wide, circular divan embraced one side. It was new. So was the table with the under-shelf, made homely by a vase of artificial flowers. He had been there only two weeks, she recalled. Decorated no doubt before he had moved in. there was newness about it all. So were the pictures on the wall. She moved closer to one, hardly paying attention to him. Only aware of his eyes following her.

The picture was that of a man about thirty. It was him, taken about five years ago, playing tennis, performing a swift back-hander. His white outfit triggered memories of her past daydreams, when she had seen herself on the tennis court with crowds of onlookers. But the picture she gazed at now was that of a private court, portraying him in fast spectacular action. Knowing what her own daydreams had done to her, Jackie moved carefully to the other photograph.

This was a full picture of a cricket team in action. How strange that both pictures immediately revived memories of the old fantasies.

He was seated in the middle of the divan, arms flung back and legs outstretched. The glass was not far off. He had been watching her, studying her, with the air of a high priest of a nunnery without regulations. His blue single-breasted blazer opened at the front revealed a pink shirt and knitted tie. Quite affluent looking, to say the least, with well groomed hair. His high chin blended well with the sculptured cheeks, while his eyes were dark and close set. He was particularly refined, with all the privileges of a young aristocrat.

"Why not tell me your name," he said. "I'd love to be acquainted."

Jackie sat gently on the divan, two feet away from him; she pulled the sweater comfortably over her shoulders and folded her arms. His eye touched the skirt and stockings. Suddenly easing himself up, he tucked both hands in his pocket and brought out a piece of paper.

"You must look at this," he said extravagantly.

But she was uninterested.

"Oh, do come and see. It's interesting, especially at this time of night."

Jackie stirred a little and sidestepped his feet. The slip of paper was on the table. It was a cheque. She read the instructions: seven hundred and fifty pounds. But it made no impression on her.

"Not bad for a night's work, you must agree."

Her whole attitude puzzled him. Not a word was forthcoming, yet a certain sophistication made her, to say the least, intriguing. Her inadequate dress on such a cold night escaped his notice, yet he had no reason to doubt that she was coming from the club, she was living in the flat above, he had seen a lot of her, and there was no hurry to get her talking. But this absentmindedness threatened his prospects. He swallowed the remainder of the Cusonier and decided on a refill. When he was across the room, Jackie seated herself casually.

"I'd be happier if you were to have a drink," he said, calmly.

At last she gave her consent, not by a single word, but simply by offering no objection. He handed her a glass.

There was a certain cosiness about the place. Quite warm, with ample signs of extravagance, the deep pile carpet, velvet curtains, expensive wallpaper.

He again referred to the cheque. Did she want to know how long it had taken him to accumulate it? But she only looked at him with unpursed lips. He explained, nevertheless, that he had been at the tables since eleven, winning and losing, winning and losing! At one tine he was controlling over two thousand pounds, and he was actually worn out when finally he had decided to call it a night.

Now his glass was empty. It took only a few seconds, yet the liqueur was having little effect on him. Perhaps he'd been so busy at the club that he had hardly drunk much.

But putting the glass on the table now, he turned to her, quite flamboyantly: "I've watched you a thousand times in the past two weeks. "I'm sure it was inevitable that we would have got together before long."

Jackie was silent, childishly disinterested. She paid little attention, but showed no objection. He took the glass from her, placed it carefully on the table, then turned her cheek and planted a kiss on her wet lips. There was no response. But her head was against him, docile and feeble as a childs. He quickly relaxed her against the cushion and pulled himself closer; then, proceeding on a long encounter with her lips, he worked his way down to her neck and actually threatened to devour her, her own luxurious fragrance spurring him into her flesh.

When it seemed she was sick of the ordeal, this total stranger gnawing at her, she pushed him aside and escaped to the middle of the room. But he followed quickly and blocked her path, his face heightened with desire.

"Oh, you can't go now. In an hour it will be dawn. You might as well stay here." And he studied her for a moment, estimating his chances; then, convinced that it was now or never, he pleaded calmly and employed both hands to tidy her hair.

Before long she was again calm, and he started on her now, as though it was the final act before damnation. When Jackie abandoned the sweater, it fell to the floor, revealing her full breast against her blouse. Breathing heavily again, he coaxed her back to the cushion. She made a desperate attempt to seal off herself. But he sucked at her lips, her neck, sighing and groaning as he mauled her, all the time planting kisses to her face and breast. Quite subdued now, she felt an acute pain at her neck, and suddenly she tore herself from him, disturbed and concerned with the part for her neck where his teeth and sunk. But he rushed to her, half naked. And again, with some caution, he got her back. Working his way down with little murmurs, he was soon on his knees to kiss her legs, to soften her, to remove her stockings. Then kneeling before her, he pressed his head to her stomach and brought her to him. Jackie had not expected this. He was uncontrollable,

He heaved a great effort to cradle her and carried off to the bedroom. He laid her out and was quick to remove his clothing. She watched him in a sort of half dizziness: He was more than a silhouette in the darkness, for his white body was strange. Her own caveman was not like this. He was black, and in the darkness, would have been only traceable. Furthermore, he was rugged, fierce, and uncomplimentary. He would have thrown her onto the bed without gentleness. One thing puzzled her, though: in all his ungrateful acts, he had never once bitten her.

Lying back, she was right in the path of light from the half open door; and coming to her now, unclothed, he switched off the light and lingered by the bed, fumbling. She held her breath. There came the slick of rubber, for his hands were quite impatient to get the sheath on.

He rushed onto her in fierce eagerness, and had scarcely settled in when she felt the sensation. This was unfamiliar, due to her years of chastity, yet she could scarcely shut her mind off from the timid

114

pace, the great difference, the vast gap between him and her caveman. How ridiculous to be there with this stranger, and letting him into her. The feeling that had driven her there had touched a new peak. She had thrown her head back, giving part of her neck to him, exposing the sore patch that was the imprint of his teeth. In this state she had abandoned herself, indeed lost. At length when his strength had subsided, he calmly withdrew and was eternally grateful. His last kiss stung her to the quick, for it had left a flame still raging. She suddenly new the familiar feeling of neglect, unquenched when she had hoped for so much. She remained there, unmoved, thinking back. There had been moments of bitterness in the past, but never had she been inflamed so much. It was unbearable.

But he was hardly at rest for long when suddenly, he was making for her. Quite inert, she had not moved an inch and she was more luxurious now than ever. He started on her lips again and murmured all along how he had wanted her, how he had watched her movements in and out of the flat. Jackie heard it all without acknowledgment. He left the bed and disappeared briefly, emerging again and closing the door, plunging, the room into total darkness.

Suddenly he was back with her, kissing and stroking her body all over. For a while she remained totally resigned, but her feelings were soon stirred and for once she began to show some interest by fostering him. Amidst his sighs and groans, he went on, lasciviously devouring every inch of her body, her breasts, every contours, working his way down, even caressing and kissing her toes and feet. Then he began slowly to work his way back to her body, along her legs and thighs, squeezing and taking in mouthfuls of her flesh. Thrusting her skirt out of his way, his arms beneath her waist and, taking her body into a perfect embrace, he eagerly tucked his head between her thighs and began suckling her. Had he given her time to review this intent, she would have rejected him. But the sudden glow overwhelmed her, forcing her into an ardency that threw out all objections. The intense pleasure quickened her senses, summoning every nerve in her body to tremendous heights. For a while Jackie knew not where she was, only conscious of the immense pleasure surging through every corner of her body. The smacking of his lips deep in her thighs made her forget herself, enough to reach down a hand to caress him and attempting to take handfuls of his hair for keeps. But spurred on by the lush taste of her sap, he continued to drive her frantic. Then at long last he became conscious of her sighs and ecstic gushes which excited him on. He held her tight and went on a wild enjoyment, finding her so succulent. At length he felt his hair being tugged and pulled, and then he was happily aware, for she was soon uprooted by an explosion which sent incessant tremors to her head. It was only then that he had found a satisfying reason to relent, at last deciding that it was quite enough.

He released her and began to relax. But he kept his head there, pressed up against her lower parts, against her sensitive area. He felt in charge and could find no reason to let her go. He had fallen in love with her and wanted to keep her forever.

He considered her heavenly. But after a while, when he was dropping off to sleep, he felt his hair being stroked. And he knew she wanted to leave. Then he remembered: She only lived upstairs in the flat above. And he had never seen her with a man. He had once or twice tried to catch sight of her fingers, she wore only an eternity ring. Suddenly he felt certain she'd be back there in his bed by the end of the evening. Happy with that, he eased himself up and allowed her to recover herself.

The light in the living room still showed at the door crease. Jackie found her garments, but she threw the light switch all the same, for she had to see the room. He had got beneath the sheets as she left the bed, and was sitting up, covered to the waist. His features were as calm as the silver moon, so serene, so content. He blew her a kiss and whispered: "See you later." She felt her features softened and, for the first time, she gazed at him with a friendly eyes. She took the few steps back to the bedside and sat slightly on the edge. Then, for a brief moment she tidied his hair with elegant fingers. As she did so, he reached out a gentle hand to her knees and into her skirts, letting it rest across her thighs. Finally she kissed his forhead and stood up, slowly letting his hand fall from her. She moved backwards, quite slowly on the soft carpet. At the door she turned off the light, but only pulling it up far enough to cut the view between them.

In the living room she paused long enough to tidy herself. But it's compactness made her wonder what he was all about. There was a large book-rack. She glanced at the books which only indexed the names of artists, others were biographies. The name Michael Gordonstone was on a notebook on a small corner table; and also the cheque, as payee. It meant nothing to her. She'd never heard of him. She guessed he might be about forty, only a few years older than herself. On the other side of the room stood an easel and stool; a dirty sheet covered what was obviously unfinished work. Not bothering to ask herself why there were no paintings on the walls, she returned to the divan, found her shoes and got her feet into them.

In the bathroom a large mirror was situated above the wash basin. Her face looked tired, but she carefully avoided the soap and used only water. Even rejecting the comb and brush, she did her hair as best she could without them. Her blouse, creased, hardly mattered. It was Sunday, she would scarcely meet anyone at this hour.

Once outside she pulled the door to. Then, refusing to look back, she walked briskly across the street. At Upper Brook Street she turned left and five minutes later was getting into her car. It was after six, and without the street lamp, the morning was very dark.

Chapter Thirteen

The telephone rang. The extension to the bedroom was disconnected. Jackie had preferred it that way during her difficult months. Now in the bath, she readily rebuked herself for not being more tolerant. But the first tinkle had actually caught her in the process of getting out. Thus, without hurrying, she dried herself and was quickly in the bedroom to exchange the bath towel for a flowing peignoir.

Clutching the telephone now, she forgot the formalities and said spiritedly, "Yes, who is it?"

It was Mary. She had heard nothing from Jackie all day, and had decided to telephone. They chatted for a time. Yes, Jackie had only been up an hour, and would Mary believe it, she had been in the bath all that time. Well, when would Mary see her? Later perhaps, when she had had something to eat. By the way, had Jackie seen outside? No, not yet. Oh, she would congratulate herself for being in bed all day.

Mary was right. The snow which had been coming down all day was still falling even at this dark hour. But before breaking off, Mary was firm in her insistence that Jackie should not stay long in that house. It would be unbearable without Connie and Diane.

Putting the telephone down, she went out into the narrow hallway, switched on the rear terrace light and went back to the living room. With the whole terrace now under the floodlight, the snow was coming down heavily; she followed the flakes from the roofline to the terrace where they melted quickly. How beautiful, she thought.

All this seemed to provide the final word in a decision she was to make. It was a matter which was to be decided that very weekend. Now her mind was made up, and with a smile she went back to the hallway, put out the light, and was off to the kitchen.

What would she eat? The groceries were delivered yesterday morning and she had put them away. Now she was hungry and needing her one meal a day. What was it to be? In the refrigerator were some cutlets of fresh fish: three portions of hake, and salmon, all ready for cooking. And in the trays on the storage basket were vegetables: tomatoes, carrots, potatoes, cucumber, cabbage, lettuce and fruits. And there was still a bottle of milk outside the front door. She had vowed to avoid all meat since her firm conviction to lose weight and maintain a sumptuous figure.

In good spirit, Jackie was quickly back in her room where she exchanged the peignoir for a simple dress, then back again in the kitchen, where she was ready to do a quick meal.

First, she put a saucepan with water and salt on the stove, then peeled and cut two red potatoes and carrots into small pieces and put them in. Next, she put a frying pan with some vegetable oil on the stove. Then she chose one portion of salmon, which she would fry gently on both sides for three or four minutes. She also sprinkled in some dried seasoning from three vials of Schwartz condiments that she kept, her own parents had taught her several methods of cooking. Growing up, and in her early teenage years, she'd been made to help with the Sunday cooking before and after attending church. It had been a family tradition. And now, dishing out her quickly prepared meal, she put a small dish of fruit cocktail on the table and settled down to eat. While eating she was flicking through the pages of an American women's magazine: Cosmopolitan. It was Mary who'd introduced her to this magazine a year ago, and she was still passing on her monthly copies after she herself had read them.

Awake for more than an hour now, it was a constant fight to dismiss the little rendezvous of the early morning. Jackie was desperately trying to forget it, perhaps for fear of remorse, or even the possibility of taking delight in it. She was uncertain, but really, it must be kept under the surface. She'd slept soundly through the day and was satisfied with her state of mind for the time being; no need to persecute herself, for the few hours when she'd lost her head. But one thing was certain; she would pull herself together, abandon the bottle!

It was time to visit Mary. But first she would telephone her mother and father. The children were important.

Secretly, Jackie was beginning to accept Penman as a new interest: He was to be admired for his generosity and excellent taste. Pascoe was ineffectual, quite inadequate to her interests. Penman would flourish, he represented something enchanting and she needed what he was offering. He was established, self-made, maybe pompous even. But if he was infatuated with her, she would see.

The truth was that Penman had married the first woman he had never respected, and she had followed him to many parts of the world in his search for prospects. He had taken to combing the poorer countries for new opportunities. And always he would be the anonymous donor, the certain investor who preferred to remain unknown, but gradually now he was becoming more adaptable to life at sea. Obsessed with contempt for the state of modern cities, traffic problems, crowded streets, people behaving badly, reckless youngsters. He was in England only for a few months a year. He had taken up sailing as a hobby from the years of his early twenties, and had traveled as a volunteer deck-hand on small sailing crafts for the adventure and experience. It was from then that he had began to nurture a plan that one day he would have his own yacht. Over the years he had owned a few sailing and diesel engine boats, one after another, graduating now to a modern luxury craft.

A great deal of time was spent on his ocean-going yacht, with the ship to shore radio being well maintained, it would provide him the vital links to his stockbroker, and with the money markets of the countries where his investments flourished. Then two or three months would be lost in relaxation at his private hide-out in Jamaica, in the Blue Mountain region where he had an attractive villa. It was his favourite retreat.

Penman was now in his mid-fifties and had only recently woken up to the fact that he'd seriously neglected the many woman that had crossed his path throughout out his life. He's been much absorbed in one hobby after another from way back in his school days when he had decided that girls were difficult and often vengeful, and their minds were confined mostly to trivial things. An incident happened in his young days that had planted this idea in his mind, and he'd never forgotten it.

Back in his school days, when at the tender age of fifteen, he and his friends took pride in grooming themselves to impress the girls, always chatting with them, discussing music and the arts, among other topics. Then one day he was told by a couple of his friends that a certain girl, a year younger than himself, had a crush on him. He had no idea what to do, and in fact did nothing. However, the Monday morning after the school concert, the girl apparently arrived with her mother and reported him to her teacher for molestation. He was then called up before the head teacher and assistant head, and interrogated. The episode had left him in shame because he had to call in his two friends to help convince the heads that he had not met the girl at all on the evening of the concert, that he had never ever touched her in his life.

Many years later, when he was aged thirty-two, his elder sister arranged for him a birthday party, mainly to celebrate his wealth.

On the night she also introduced to him a very pleasant lady friend who flirted and took a deep interest in him. At first he had tried hard to keep some distance between them, engrossing himself in his life-long pursuit of money. But the sweet lady was of similar age and, though quiet by nature, was clever enough to take all the initiatives, and a year later they were married. In the bedroom she was rather delighted to discover that he had strangely neglected this most important side of his life to the extent that he had been totally without experience. Calmly and lovingly, she had helped him to recover much of his confidence. Over the past five years, however, the good lady had become socially absorbed and had little demand of him. And somewhat conveniently, it seemed to coincide with Penman's feeling of coming of age. He had been secretly trying to gain confidence in this area of romance, having decided that he ought to be taking advantage of some of the opportunities that seemed to be passing by.

It was clearly evident now that he intended to recoup. When he had spotted Jackie, it had been the incredible episode, love at first sight, despite himself. From then on, plagued by her image, he had fought vigorously to dismiss her as unimportant, a simpleton. But overriding this abhorrence was the fact that he had found himself picturing her at various places, holding on to him, being playful. She was surely taking him over. And he was beginnig to feel that she would be good for him. So beautiful and pleasing, she was like a butterfly, calm and gentle, incapable of creating problems. Most days her loveliness was clouding his thoughts. And he also found that, with these images, his body was also demanding her. As much as he tried to free his mind, the raven-haired damsel was drawing him closer with every passing hour.

Open minded now, as he had never before conceived of himself, he indulged his thoughts in great expectations. For a few years up until recently, he had even considered sex a dull subject, inhibited by a pretence that the act was undignified, a gross reduction of man's qualities, a true sacrifice that left him unthinking and less champion of himself. But caught by the sheer brilliance of Jackie's complexion, he had become obsessed, at night even kissing her image, and at times embracing her, wallowing in the warmth of her body which he had not yet seen. But he was sure of himself, and there was no reason to suppose that she was not soon to be his mistress. He had shown himself sincere, he had even kept himself from her when she had least expected it. Yes, it would give her time to realise that she needed him and would come to him eventually.

That night with Mary, when her dominance had excited him, the delicious encounter had brought considerable sensual ideas to him. It had been his best achievement. Following that up with Jackie would be the new climax of his life. She would be on board his yacht, to lie in wait night and day. He easily pictured himself enjoying the luxury of her company. And why not? At fifty-five he had long achieved his aim. Now he must divert his interest to more exact areas, it was damn silly to preserve oneself any longer. Who knows, in a little while he might be finished. Really, it mattered little what credit a man received after death. Was it not like saying things behind one's back, when he would be no wiser for that matter?

The mast of Penman's yacht was visible form the house at Sandgate, It was anchored in the bay less than half a mile from his house. A good set of binoculars would trace it's outline with good clarity. From the cold balcony which was sometimes lashed by strong offshore winds, he had lost himself on countless occasions while staring at the gentle calm of his pleasant retreat. When it rained he stayed indoors and peered out form behind closed windows through mist and clouds to make visual contact with the Grey Lady. He often uttered a cry of damnation, too, when the bad weather brought mist and clouds to rob him of a clear view. On this occasion however, personal instructions were issued to the crew. He would sail in two days. The voyage would be a special one.

Orders were given to his broker that small changes in the money market should not be communicated to him, he should only be contacted on important matters. He would also be listening to the BBC for daily announcements of the Financial Times Index, as well as one or two important company movements. It was customary for him to tune the Racal short wave radio to the BBC overseas broadcast from about five o'clock in the evening, local time. He would keep the station alive in the background for a few hours, as, approaching each hour, the Lilly Ballaro would alert him to the news. He often found his feet stumping to the very tune.

As for Jackie, it was a question of what had to be done before the departure. Her financial affairs needed attention; a decision was needed on the bungalow, the furniture, perhaps Mary would keep an eye on the place while Jackie might consider advancing a cheque to the agents. And there was the car. Mary could be persuaded to keep an eye on the home. Penman was already aware that the children were safe with their grand parents.

Chapter Fourteen

Jackie had waited out of breath. Four hours ago Penman had confirmed that he was on his way. He had telephoned from London saying he would call for her personally. It was one occasion when the chauffeur alone would not do. Anxiously wondering now how he could possibly be delayed all this time, she was back and forth at the window and keeping a sharp ear for the telephone. There ought to be an explanation. If Penman had left London after the call, he would have got to her within the hour. For the hundredth time she was at the window. Now in her yellow coat-dress, she dug into the pocket for a handkerchief, dabbed at the corner of her mouth and, when at last there was a flood of light approaching the bungalow, she turned quickly and rushed to the door.

The car reversed up the drive and halted on the terrace. When the door flew open Penman came out briskly. Jackie was vexed and in no mood for a jolly reception. She was actually expecting a telephone call after all the delay, having thought that she would hardly be sailing again before tomorrow. But Penman quickly defended his position by making it clear as he was the owner of a fully equipped ocean-going vessel, time was of little importance.

Jackie smiled with a hint of apology. The absolute convenience of his position had escaped her. He collected her stole and assisted her. But in fact, he had driven in feeling quite uneasy about his delay and was relieved to find her waiting. For her part, had it not been for the hours of waiting, she would have kissed him. That would have been appropriate. But now such a greeting must be overlooked. The atmosphere was not exactly right.

"Come, come." he said, calling her from her trance; they ought to be going.

In the car, as the chauffeur sought his way through the rain and slush, Penman invited Jackie to a large drink of Medallion export. Though she would have liked to refuse the drink, since she was in need of a good meal it was really not the occasion to exercise such discretion.

"How long would they be in Jamaica?" she asked.

"About three months. He had never managed to keep a precise schedule when at sea. And besides, in Jamaica one usually forget about the other side of the world." He refilled his glass. Four months would be a better estimate. They would allow the awful

English weather to clear up before coming back.

Jackie was thinking of the children. Would she send a letter to Pascoe, inform him of her new plans, explain herself? At the mention of the bungalow Penman assured her that he would see to it.

The car found the gap to the promenade, drove cautiously off the road and drew up in the parking lot. Penman guided Jackie along the sea front, two hundred yards out to the yacht, where its blue and white funnel was outlined by the light of the upper deck. The Grey Lady welcomed Jackie into its luxurious quarters.

She was hardly aware of what to expect, yet she stood on deck and locked back at the town where amber lights outlined the road she had just travelled. Before long a raw breeze threatening the yacht stung her with cold fury, and for protection she fled to the lounge where Penman waited.

The two main luxury berths were on the same deck. Penman led her to one. First she stood at the door, quite absorbed, in the same protective manner which she had adapted against the cold wind. This was no time to explore the cabin, but the bed was still fresh, with a flowered spread. She glanced curiously at the high edges that would keep her in, and wondered if she was really accustomed to tossing and turning in her sleep. Then the beauty of the interior brought back her smile. As she stepped inside the door, the steward appeared from behind and announced that dinner would be served in five minutes. Penman, having dismissed himself briefly, had gone to his quarters next door.

The steward was a Barbadian, a serious looking man dressed in white. Much to his approval, he caught her smile as she turned, and when later she appeared newly dressed, at the table, he held a chair for her before taking special delight in serving her. Penman uncapped a bottle of Gancia himself, and suddenly the drift was felt. He immediately glanced at his watch. They would clear British waters in about twenty-four hours. They were heading for the Channel and tomorrow they would head south. It would take a good day to clear the region.

"Come," he said, "I must show you the pilot's house."

Jackie was on her feet, obeying for the moment. But she would prefer to see it in daylight. Yes, it could wait. They went down to the lower deck and back to her quarters. Then, left alone to admire the place while Penman rushed off to the control room, she first noticed that her things had been removed from where she had left them. She checked the wardrobe and found that the dresses were neatly stored away. The suitcases had been removed; the drawers of the bureau were filled with her small things. Everything had been put away professionally. But by whom? Could there be a second steward handling her things? Penman had a valet, but he was not on board, and there was no mention of a chambermaid.

From the window the cluster of twinkling lights were some way behind. A mental picture of the area gave a rough idea of their position. The cluster of lights drifting behind the yacht would be Hythe. They had not been sailing long. The next town, already ahead would be New Romney. Already the trip was looking exceptionally interesting. Was this not what she had dreamed of? Life was really too short to remain in one place. She must see what was on the other side, enjoy whatever delights there were.

Her best years had gone, barren with the earlier prospects well neglected. She should never have left the dance floor. Confining herself had been a tragic mistake. She might have taken her admirers more seriously then, instead of listening to their proposals, their caressing words, and refusing to commit herself by quickly forgetting them. The years with Pascoe had been a great injustice, with nothing but solitude and uncertainty. She'd been mad, yet it had taken years to find out. Now she would offer gratitude to Penman for being persistent, for persuading her that living by herself was the worst thing a woman could do. It was impossible to be healthy in such confinement. Many great women had influenced the world with their feminine charm, using their individual splendour to set themselves up. Was she not blessed with some of these qualities? What was it Penman had said of her? Naïvety? Yes, he loved the air of naïvety about her. Perhaps his sincerety was due to the fact that he had picked her up from nothing, discovered her for himself.

And the men she had known before the marriage? They had been quiet men, undemanding, afraid; yet they had worshipped her with undue passion. And they had failed to discover her. Penman had lifted her out of the mire, opening up her life.

And there were those whose advance had been restricted by her marriage, even her two children. Men such as Phillip Russell who had lost himself in her presence. What was it that had kept him back? Penman knew of her crisis but had kept himself detached from it. It was of little importance. He wanted her and would have pushed anything out of the way. Wasn't that the sort of advance that made women? This was the recovery of her life. The pieces were being put back together: even the headache had gone.

The coastline moved swiftly now, dark, but outlined by rows of amber lights, and beyond was the twinkling of a million stars. She was looking at New Romney, its light waving goodbye. Jackie closed the curtains and looked at the bed. She was sleepy.

There were three switches on a narrow strip behind the pillows. She studied them. Pressing the first switch brought a faint hum as the side of the bed lowered to the level of the mattress. She sat down. In front of her was a small table with padded sides. There was a lamp with a blue reflector. She opened the small cupboard under the base, revealing glasses and a few bottles. She removed the bottle of champagne and sampled it. Perhaps she could be well asleep before Penman got back.

Chapter Fifteen

The luxury cruiser cut steadily through calm seas, its tiny mast-head, with flag and Arial, ineffective in the heavy mist. At half speed, commanded by Penman, the Grey Lady was heading south, its precise course to be set later. The radar, not quite ultra-modern, was being relied on to detect any imminent danger from other vessels Twelve knots, with constant supervision, was the role for now.

Jackie was in the wheelhouse, watching operations. Her presence, in calf length grey skirt, and white blouse, gave the control room a spectacular mode. She stood back form the console with folded arms in a grand manner. Penman was an enthusiast. His navigation skills were good, his knowledge of the yacht almost as thorough as if he had built it himself. His boating days went back a very long way, back to his early twenties. For after leaving university where he had studied History and Politics, but couldn't imagine himself being stuck in an office or in a lecturing hall, he had volunteered as a deckhand on two different voyages to the Caribbean on sailing yachts, just for the adventure. Then, ten years ago when he had first considered owning a yacht, he did take the opportunity to inspect two vessels in dry dock at Southampton. Now after seven years' ownership of the Grey Lady, and a wealth of experience, he was actually thinking along greater lines. His need was for a bigger yacht, preferably form the same builders. He had learnt to rely on their superb engineering, their careful and liberal taste for appointments. Already he was planning the new vessel, to be built to order. But negotiations were in the balance, the cost being unduly high. It was pointed out to the company, along with competitive figures from the Italians and Norwegians. The British builders were ridiculous! And force to overlook their so called engineering superiority, the new craft would probably come from a more generous builder.

The Grey Lady was gradually sailing into rough seas. Three days out and the approach to the Atlantic was far from calm. Jackie's tranquility was severely disturbed. Rough seas had brought on a mild uneasiness that gradually got worse. On the fourth day, even in brilliant sun the ocean was in turmoil, with huge white foam dispersing on the main deck. The yacht was unsteady, floating high one moment and dropping low the next, its floors shuddering under

127

Jackie's feet. Even the shortest walk was dangerous. Penman was anxious and could only look in on her on the odd occasion. He insisted that she remain in her quarters. He also instructed the stewardess to stay with her and hoped that the two would become friends.

Jackie was suffering an upset stomach and, apparently having a mild headache. The stewardess reported that for three days she'd been refusing all her meals, only eating fruits, bananas and pears, but enjoying all the different juices they have on board. Penman didn't feel too bad about that. He was aware that she knew how to look after herself and would know what's best for her. But he was a little concerned when told that Jackie would not take any tablets, not even for her headache, that she seemed to have a strong objection to tablets.

In fact it was on the fifth day that Jackie began to show clear improvement, so much that she started laughing and chatting with the stewardess. The girl was a young nurse with a friendly smile. Aged twenty-five, she had short straight blonde hair, a neat pointed nose and round features. She had in fact, confined herself to Jackie's needs, a mutual development rather than just following Penman's instructions. After all, they were the only two women on board.

In the bad weather Jackie was used to seeing her in white slacks and a white nurse's jacket, a precautionary outfit in case she fell while moving about. Entering Jackie's quarters on the fifth morning, she looked more casual in an off-white polymers dress. It sported buttons down the front and a narrow belt that showed off a neat waistline.

"Have you seen outside? She asked on entering. No, of course not. Shall I open the curtains, just a little?" Yes. And she parted them at one porthole.

In came a patch of sunlight to settle on the far wall. "It's peaceful out there; quite unbelievable, really."

Jackie had already guessed this. The yacht was steady. It was the first thing she had noticed on waking up. There was no rocking and rolling over perilous waves, lurching in and out of deep valleys. The feeling was hardly any more than one would experienced in a car driving along a country road. She smiled pleasantly. She looked at her nurse with friendly eyes:

"How long have you been traveling with Karl?"

"Two years and a month," she answered as she turned to face

Jackie, who was obviously poised to get up.

"Were you sick on the first voyage?"

She was somewhat amused. "For the first two weeks I was helpless, hardly knowing why I was on board."

"Why were you?"

"Oh, to get away from the hospital, the horror of the emergency cases, the strains of watching people die, young and old."

Jackie's comment was instinctive. "I would have thought you'd get used to that sort of thing."

"No, I'm the very opposite. I would have given up nursing if I hadn't found this job."

"How did it come about?"

An advertisement was in the Sunday Times. She had followed it up and was lucky.

Did she really like being at sea?

Yes, it was a pleasure to get away from the busy scene. The sea was a dream, with this changing climate, the blue skies and endless horizon.

They had something in common, after all, thought Jackie. Her name was Deidre. Jackie had learnt that from the first night on board.

"How did you escape from your boyfriend? You must have been courting at the time."

There was clear embarrassment in Deidre's smile, she'd been a little uncertain about Jackie, the long, well groomed raven hair, so much of it, and the casual way she restored her elegance. At first, Jackie's striking appearance had kept her at bay. It was comforting now to find that she's rather warm and receptive.

"I really didn't know anyone well enough to say he was my boyfriend. So it's fair to say I didn't have one."

"You've never been in love?" asked Jackie, in her casual voice.

Deidre suddenly seemed flushed with innocence. "I've never considered myself as courting at any time. But from seventeen to when I became nineteen, I did find myself with a steady boyfriend. It turned out he was not the marrying kind. He went off to a polytechnic college, and I went into training for a nursing career. I think we drifted apart while I was enjoying the clubs scenes, you know, the all night raves." She paused, then continued: "So, you see, there was really no one to hold me back. It's great to be free."

Jackie was already feeling better. Left alone, she pulled on a towel gown and went to the porthole. The sun was warm against the thick Perspex. The sea was calm. In the distance another vessel was heading in the opposite direction. She thought about the binoculars, but unfortunately they were left in the wheelhouse. Nevertheless, she could see it was a large passenger liner, probably one of the names that were familiar to her.

There was a knock at the door. Would it be Karl? He must not see her so soon, not until she was dressed and had something to eat. But the voice was distinct and confident. It was the nurse, Deidre. She had brought her breakfast.

"But this is ridiculous," Jackie pointed out. "I ought to be in the dining area."

Deidre disagreed. Jackie was only just recovering. It would be her first meal in three days. Mr. Penman would expect her to lunch, so she could have her shower at eleven.

Jackie intended having her shower right away. But it was too early, the nurse insisted. Jackie should allow herself time to recover, then she could take advantage of the good weather.

She was drawn to the try as soon as it was lowered to the folded out table. Lifting the lids one after the other, she was already sampling the scrambled eggs. Then, opening the curtains fully and letting in the light, she settled down with the tray. Finally, in front of the mirror, she looked quite pale. She rushed to the shower and ran the taps.

After bathing and refreshing herself under the shower, and two glasses of fruit juice, later, Jackie was back in front of the mirror and putting her hair in order. She smartened her face, streamlined her brows and lashes, tucked into her earlobes a pair of blue topaz drops and, finally moistening her lips and dabbed a little perfume under her arms.

By ten o'clock she was out on deck. The tiny yacht was insignificant in the vast expanse of water. There were no clouds. The breeze from the forward surging of the vessel was cool against her. Surprisingly, they were cutting along smoothly. Then, leaning back against the rails, she gazed up to the control room and caught Penman's wave. She waved back and thought she saw him leaving the controls to his pilot.

She turned again to admire the sea, the lovely clear view in front of her, the cold breeze against her face, even blowing her hair back from her neck and shoulders. Over a set of towel-look bikini, she had put on a matching blue knee-length beach jacket. They were very suitable for the outside air, shielding her now from the temperate breeze. Jackie was about to look down at her raised soft shoes when she heard him. She turned and he was almost with her. She heard her voice said, "Karl," and she skipped the two or three steps and he had no choice but to open his arms and suddenly folding them around her as she threw herself at him. She buried her head in his chest and remained there for a while. That they should become familiar was well overdue. His only choice was to embrace her and hold her tight, shielding her from what? He didn't know. But he felt particularly great, very much like he had landed on the moon after negotiating a hazardous journey through space. After what seemed a long while, she found her voice:

"I hope you're not disappointed in me."

"Why would I be?" He asked.

"We've been sailing for five days and I haven't been any help to you. I didn't know the sea could make me so ill."

"It's the rolling and weaving, my dear. We had bad weather, and it's your first time on a yacht. Most people get seasick on their first outing."

"Deidre said so, too."

"Very true," he picked up. "She was bad for almost two weeks."

Jackie held up her head and he was forced to fold back her hair from her face. Then he kissed her temple.

"You look lovely as always, I am very proud."

She opened her eyes and looked up into his face.

"I'm glad. I didn't want to let you down so badly."

"Not at all. Believe me, I'm very proud you're here. From now on, it will get better. According to the weather people, the worst is behind us. And it will get warmer day by day, I promise you."

She unfolded herself from his arms and flicked her hair back.

"I'm beginning to enjoy it now. I'm sure it will be everything you said."

"Good. I knew you were better, but I wasn't expecting you till later, in the afternoon."

"It was very tempting. I had to come out."

"You must be careful, you know. I don't want you getting under the weather again."

"I won't," she said seriously. "I'm fully recovered. Where are we?"

"We're just near the Azores."

She shook her head with a smiled; it meant nothing. Her geography had left her. And even if he had quoted latitude and longitude, it would have been equally vague.

He explained further. They'd been sailing for precisely five days. It would take twenty days to reach Jamaica; they were indeed a long way off.

"What about stopping?"

"Just once; we'll drop anchor off a small island in the Bahamas."

"Will we go ashore?"

"Hardly worth it, not much there. We're only stopping for fresh water and supplies."

She looked at the sea and the sky: "Will it be like this all the way?"

"Probably not," said Penman happily. It would get warmer, sometimes scorching. They were moving into better region all the time. And he planted a kiss on her forehead. "Come, you shouldn't be out here so soon. It's still a little cold. Tomorrow will be better."

They went back inside, entering at a side door, Karl opening it and letting her in first. From there they went to the lounge, a lavishly fitted, relaxing room in blue and white. It adjoined the wheel-house and extended the full width of the yacht. Further down was the small speedboat that would be a life craft in any emergency. At noon Karl escorted her back to her quarters to change into something suitable for lunch.

The air in her cabin had been drowsy and stale after she had had her shower. That was one reason for escaping out on deck. Even the bed was untidy; so was her dressing table. Now the place was respectable. She would have to compliment the nurse. Along with her charm, she was prompt and efficient.

He was dressed in casuals; white jersey-knit shirt, brown worsted trousers, with a towel about his neck. His hair was brushed forward and then sideways. For a moment he looked strange. The short sleeves had bared his arms; now they appeared long, with fine white hairs sloping evenly. His pale complexion had not yet caught the sun.

Jackie was looking forward to lunch and, they'd reached the table, the aroma rising from the galley told her she was going to enjoy it. The Barbadian steward was infect a very good cook. Claiming to have been trained as a chef, but had found it hard to settle in a Barbados hotel where the pay was well below expectations, he had really wanted to be a sportsman, being good at lawn tennis. But he had settled for a job that would take him across the Atlantic and didn't have him tied down. Moreover, being on board the yacht offered him real adventure. He was a man of forty-five and was particularly good at Caribbean cooking, the main reason why Penman had taken him on board.

He'd prepared fresh tuna stakes with a Caribbean flavour, serving it with brown stew sauce that was mildly spiced with various items, including a little curry powder. The whole thing was then left to marinate for a couple of hours before cooking. The dish was served with potatoes that were half boiled and baked in olive oil; also fried plantains. Jackie and Penman sat opposite each other, with Deidre next to Jackie; the steward looking on from the galley with a permanent smile on his face. In the end, Jackie had eaten more than she'd intended. The mild spices had got to her, opening her appetite and driving her on to finish the main course entirely. So did Penmen and Deidre. And they chatted while eating, Penman telling them about his early days on two different sailing yachts; how, in those days the term 'yachtsman' was commonly used, for it wasn't seen as romantic to be on board a diesel engine craft where a man was not required to know anything about sails. Deidre cleared the table quickly and helped the steward to bring on the sweets, which were wedged shaped cuts from a large cheese cake, dashed with grated almonds, part of the supplies they'd brought on board. They looked to Jackie for approval and she declared that it was delicious. It rounded off the meal. And while Penman and Deidre enjoyed a glass of port each at the end, Jackie seemed to have lost her taste for alcohol. She happily settled for a small glass of pure orange juice.

On leaving the table, Penman and Jackie went into the control room where Penman relieved his pilot, George, a man in his seventies who had found it hard to give up the sea. George had been a merchant ship's captain who had retired at aged sixty-five, and now relishing the chance to get back at the helm whenever the opportunity came up. He was glad to be relieved, for the aroma from the galley had also waken his appetite.

For an hour or more Jackie was completely absorbed with the intricacies of the control room. She kept close to Penman and was very much aware of his heightened feelings as he explained in details all the instruments and controls. They sat side by side at the console for a while, at one stage letting her steer so that she felt the full weight of the rushing seas against the rudder. Very much excited, she laughed playfully and insisted that he remained very close to her in case she found it difficult, even telling him she was never going to steer the vessel at any time without him at her side, that she would tie herself to him if he ever tried to leave her there. After a while, Penman locked the controls while he took pleasure in explaining the compass to her. She listened with interest, meanwhile, taking every opportunity to remain close to him. Some of her questions were designed to amuse him. Then as she asked about the compass, he sat himself down and appeared more leisurely. Still leaning against the console, she simply turned to face him, her eyes soft and friendly, her smiles tantalizing. His knees apart, their feet were touching when she pushed back her hair and asked why was a needle on the compass pointing behind them. As he was about to explain, she purposely stumbled forward, in between his knees. His very safe arms reached out automatically and seized her at her waist, her soft body bringing together all his delicate instincts. "Oops," she uttered, "yachts are never stable." Penman laughed and said cheerfully, "You're learning, my dear. You should never stand freestyle, always stay close to something for support." But Jackie was enjoying the play. With his chin pressed into her soft stomach, he was quite amused and looking up at her. Gently, she put both hands to Penman's cheeks, then, after looking down into his eyes for a moment, she lowered her head and kissed his temple. His hands then slid down to her hips in a loving embrace before letting go of her. She steadied herself and leaned back against the console. Then she was suddenly aware that he really wanted her. Good! Her playful act had worked well. She turned to face the sea while he explained the compass, that magnetic north was behind them, that wherever they were in the world, that particular needle would always point to true north. The other needle was showing the course they were sailing. A short while later, George, the main pilot, returned to take over his post. The couple happily made off to the lounge to sit in comfort.

But they separated briefly, in fact, for the best part of an hour, simply to freshen up. Back in her quarters, Jackie removed the warm beach shirt and tossed it aside. Standing in front of the mirror, she looked at herself in the bikini outfit. For a moment she bundled her hair and held it back from her face, the large meal she'd eaten had certainly put some life back into her. But it became clear that she'd lost some weight. Her cheeks had lost some of their roundness, and her waistline had gone in a little. She came on board at her ideal weight of eight stones and ten pounds, And with her height at five feet-seven, her bust and hips looking full and supple. Now she could tell that the few days of seasickness had left her two or three pounds lighter. And she remembered that it was in fact four whole days that she had eaten nothing but bananas and pears, and drank only fruit juice. But she felt fine, and the confidence that she would easily regain her weight in a week or two, made her performed a few ballet steps before skipping off to the shower.

First she tied the protective cap over her hair, and brushed her teeth before removing the bikini pants and bra. Then she turned on the taps and stepped under the shower. For more than five minutes she enjoyed the raining water, slightly tempered. And the aromatic soap was enough for her skin. By the time she'd dried herself thoroughly, she felt no need for body lotion, they were not really going out, the need was only to feel fresh and free for the evening.

Removing the protective cover, she allowed her hair complete freedom to dry out. Then she found some new clothes and began to get dressed. This was suddenly important, in case he ran out of patience and came looking for her. Reasonably secured in fresh underwear, she was back at the dressing table. Jackie applied just three burst of spray to her hair and began brushing it out. Noticing now that it flowed well below the back of her shoulders, she decided it was getting too long. She needed to have two inches off. Why had she not noticed that it needed cutting before coming on board? Her mind must have been in a state! She rebuked herself, knowing full well that it would get more unmanageable the longer it grew.

For a moment she contemplated whether Deidre would be handy with a pair of scissors. Then a thought came to her: She might get Penman to cut it. And why not? She needed him close to her, and the closer the better. Perhaps he might enjoy doing it, she would see. And she continued brushing it out, then letting it flow down the back of her shoulders.

Ready to dress, her first thought was of wearing a pair of stripy short pants and printed top. But it was too cold. And she remembered what Penman said, that it would be another two days before she could comfortably wear light skimpy things. Finally, she settled for a knee-length pleated skirt, in white with circular gold bands; and on top, she slipped her arms through a white woolen sweater, barely reaching her waist. But the knitting was wide and the sleeves quite short. Finally, in soft shoes, she was satisfied with her casual look. The evening would be just quiet and relaxing.

In the lounge he was waiting for her and she rushed to him with a happy smile. "How do I look?" she asked.

He gazed at her for a moment and then said, "Turn around." She did a little twirl.

"Lovely," he answered, holding out a hand for her, in case she stumbled.

"Are you sure?" she asked, taking his outstretched hand.

"You're looking very sweet, my dear."

She sat herself down, firming her skirt on one side. But on his side, part of the lavish skirt overlapped his knee. She did nothing about it, neither did he. Jackie simply shoved an arm through his bent elbow. Their eyes held each other and for a moment she thought he might have kissed her. But he didn't.

Penman was in khaki trousers and a pale blue T-shirt, a sailing yacht printed across his chest. They were the only two in the lounge, but he expected Deidre and Rayno to join them when the film show started.

Comfortably seated in the high backed lounge chair, Jackie kicked off her shoes, stretched out her legs and raised them up off the floor, bringing them up to the level of the seat.

"What do you think?" she asked, her smiles tantalizing.

He looked on, then, untangling his arm from her, he knelt next to her outstretched feet. He put an arm beneath them to take the weight; and very much like a sculpture, or an experienced connoisseur, he moved his free hand smoothly along the top of her legs, to her toes, cupping her feet. The same hand moved back along each calf, up to her knees.

"Absolutely lovely, he muttered, perfectly shaped."

"Are you sure?" she teased.

He was still on his knees. "If I were shaping a pair of ladies legs for souvenirs, I could not have shaped them any better. Somebody must have made you aware that they're lovely and very sweet looking."

She stretched out her hand, he took it and eased himself back into his seat next to her.

"It's been said to me once or twice." She mused. And she lowered her feet to the floor and sat comfortably back, against him. "I did something specially for you, in a little while, you might notice."

"I'll give myself five minutes to find out what it is. If I don't, then you'll have to tell me."

"I won't. But I'm sure you will soon notice."

Penman found himself gazing into her eyes, brownish blue, and twinkling; her head was innocently poised. The luster of her cheeks, her gold-pink complexion complimenting the lovely sheen of her hair, held him spellbound. "Jackie, my dear, you're not wearing any make up, none at all."

Her smiles were exuberant and the spell was broken. "There, it didn't take you long to notice. I decided it's time you saw me as my natural self."

"You're delightful in every way. I am very lucky. And I'm sure you must be thirsty. What are we going to have?"

She suddenly gave the subject of drinks a serious thought.

"Karl, I seemed to have lost the taste for anything with alcohol. Have you noticed?"

Penman got to his feet. "Yes." he said "Deidre told me you've gone all fruity."

It tickled Jackie and she bubbled with laughter.

"What will it be, Martini Rossi, Dubonnet, Cinzano?"

But it was to be Rayno's mixture. The steward had blended four different fruit juices and kept it in the refrigerator specially for her. "I hope you don't mind, Karl."

"I am rather intrigued. We're going where there's fresh fruits abound. You might well find yourself in the garden of Eden, I'm pleased to say>"

"Good; I'll be Eve, and you will be Adam."

They laughed merrily and he brought to her a full glass, with ice cubes. For himself, his glass contained a creamy yellow drink. Having put the two glasses in front of her, on the table with shallow cut-outs to stop them sliding off with the movement of the yacht, he went to the projector and began fiddling with some knobs.

"I've got a film show for you. What would you like to start with? Make your choice. We have delightful Disney, or Hitchcock's suspense, or Edgar Wallace's crime."

She was in the mood to decide promptly. "A light-hearted cartoon, please."

And he took pleasure in looking at her as she stretched the last words by showing a set of pretty teeth. Then he credited himself for having already made the right selection, and having it ready to roll.

Yes, he was beginning to predict her taste in most things.

He started the projector rolling and quickly went around the lounge closing the curtains. But it was almost seven pm. and already dark outside. As well as the screen, soft lighting at the back of the lounge provided a twilight atmosphere. He made his way back to his seat.

The Eastman colour film started rolling and the film music took over from the faint hum of the engine. Jackie took a few sips from her glass. Penman lifted his glass and looked at it purposely before taking two large sips.

Jackie took her eye off the screen for a brief moment, and looked at him, curiously. She was not familiar with the creamy yellow drink. It didn't look appetizing to her.

"What is it?" she asked.

He looked at her proudly. "It's a popular Dutch drink, Advocat."

"It looks rather sweet."

"It is indeed. Not exactly my taste, but it's recommended."

"By…" tongue in cheek.

"Rayno," he answered.

"Oh, perhaps he might be a medicine man," she exclaimed with a smile.

As the film started to break into a story line, Penman's glass was empty and he quickly refilled it. Whatever the taste, he was putting it away with pleasure.

Rayno and Deidre entered the lounge and sat apart, in other lounge seats behind them. Only George, the pilot, was left out. He preferred life in the control room where he made his own entertainment, reading books of sea stories, and also his stacks of 'Ships & Boats' magazines.

Every fifteen minutes Penman would get himself up and got busy changing the spool on the projector to continue the film. Four small dots on the bottom corner of the screen would tell when to prepare for the change. There was a time when he had considered training Rayno to do this. But he gave the steward the job of re-winding the spools and restacking them in order each day. Every third night when Penman took his turn in the control room, George would also make use of these films. And he was well capable of running them himself.

The hour-long cartoon was a lovely story for Jackie. It was about a young couple traveling to a distant country by car, across difficult terrain and some bandit territories, to attend a brother's wedding. They allowed themselves six days with overnight stops in hotels and guest houses. And made the journey after fighting fiercely, arriving just in time for the ceremony. Then the star gave a speech, stressing the point that nothing could have stopped them getting there. Jackie found herself clapping at the end.

While Penman prepared the projector for the next show, Rayno suggested that they might have a late snack right there in the lounge. They agreed and a few minutes later he brought in a tray for them. As they watched the new film, they also enjoyed the well prepared fritters and some fruit cocktail. Penman soon switched to a stronger drink, Jackie simply settled for another glass of mixed juice. All through the films, Jackie sat mostly detached from him, as he was having to get up so frequently to change the reel. It was, nevertheless, an absorbing evenings entertainment.

It was about eleven o'clock when they decided to retire. But Penman wanted to take a last look at the condition outside. Jackie took his outstretch hand and they made their way out on deck, stopping by the front rails. It was only darkness in every direction. They were cutting along smoothly, with just a narrow foam of water below the bow, the sea being gentle waves of blackness around them. Penman guided her to the west side and, by looking up, they spotted the quarter moon and lots of stars. It was slightly cold so they did not linger, they made their way to the control room where George greeted them, having been watching their movements.

"How goes it, George?" asked Penman.

"Steady as she goes," he answered. "If it gets any calmer, I might need a pulsing machine to keep me alert."

"Good, we deserve calm waters after the first five days."

"Sure do." said George. "And how is my good lady, now?"

Jackie had a very appreciative smile for him. "Couldn't be better," she said.

"Very true. You look well enough to take the controls."

"No, no." she joked, "I must leave that to you at all times."

Penman circled her shoulder with a playful arm. "She's a grand lady to have on board, George; she's divine inspiration."

"Well said, Boss."

Penman guided Jackie back to her quarters. He closed the door quickly behind him to keep out the cold. The cozy warmth of the interior caressed them, the luxury, so inviting.

Jackie sat at the dressing table and began folding her hair back, making sure all of herself was neatly in place. She felt fine, as though they'd just returned from a premier show at a grand theatre. Penman went about closing the curtains, despite the darkness outside. Then he came up behind her and, pushing much of her hair aside, he kissed her neck, very lovingly. He then straightened up and toyed with her hair, dressing it back the way it was.

Jackie liked it very much. She didn't expect it of him, but it told her something important. Still toying with herself, she focused on him through the mirror.

"Did you have someone else in mind if I hadn't accepted your invitation?"

He was seated on the bed behind her, admiring her, through the mirror and from behind. The question had caught him off guard. He hesitated, then said, "No, I suppose not."

"That cannot be true," she heard herself saying.

He took a deep breath, as if pondering. "The truth is, my dear, I would have been burying myself in the stock market. I would have made a few thousand pounds by now."

She did a cute little twist and stood up from the chair, then paused in front of him, quite shocked at what he had said. "But with all this, you must have had another lady friend."

His knees parted and his protective hands reached out to her, holding her waist to prevent her stumbling. Then he found himself looking up at her. Jackie was getting to like this stance, for it meant getting very close to him, and as much as he's having to caution her, she was going to do it very often.

"Your wife wouldn't have come?"

"No, no. She's occupied with her work."

"But you couldn't have sailed alone, in such a lovely yacht?"

"Indeed, yes. I'm not in the habit of taking ladies away from themselves."

Jackie thought about it, then smiled down at him. "And what would you've been doing now?"

"You really want to know?"

"Tell me," she said in a gentle voice.

"I would have been listening to the BBC broadcast, picking up news, ready to phone my broker tomorrow on the ship to shore radio."

She still did not believe him. But his arms tightened around her waist, and she lowered herself onto his knees, then rolling off on to the bed and laid back. Penman reclined a little, stopping short, and propping his head on one elbow.

"You know Mary very intimately, she said, but there must be another lady somewhere. You couldn't have become a millionaire without having lots of ladies around you, particularly when you're operating in the city."

His free hand fell to her stomach and her partly upturned skirt exposed most of her thighs. Her body appeared deliciously free. She twisted her head closer to him as she spoke. He had contemplated whether to kiss her for the first time, or make another comment. He put his free hand to her cheeks and toyed with her gently. Jackie looked up at him in silence, her lips slightly parted. Then he lowered his head slowly and their lips met, cautiously, softly, searchingly. Moments later, his tongue came forward and his first taste of her was the juices she'd been drinking. Her hand laid on the bed with fingers curled into her palm. She allowed herself to be kissed as much as he wanted. Their lips remained sealed to each other for a while before his tongue began to explore, even gliding over the smoothness of her teeth before he began sucking her lips. He savoured every moment and was suddenly compelled to ease up when a juicy sound issued from his mouth and he had to recover himself.

There was much more of her to be devoured and his heightened senses were urging him on. But he needed to make himself more comfortable. For a while Jackie laid still, her eyes closed. He even thought she might have fallen asleep. But then, her eyes opened slightly and her hand came up to touch his lips. He took her hand and moved the back of her fingers against his cheeks. It felt smooth and caressing. Then he put her small finger in his mouth, he needed to taste more of her. His tongue twirled around her finger and it felt good. He removed it and put another finger into his mouth, twirling his tongue around it in exactly the same manner. And he went on to savour each of her fingers, thoroughly. Finally, Penman kissed the back of her hand and lowered it to her stomach. Then he noticed her full breasts, rising and falling with her breathing. And he whispered, "Back in five minutes; must get out of these things." He raised himself from the bed and was off.

Jackie sat up and eased herself forward to lower her feet to the floor. She was dazed, but she quickly recovered and decided that she, too, needed a break. Getting to her feet, she took off the white sweater and stepped out of her skirt, hanging it up quickly on the clothes rail at one corner of the suite. She went off to brush her teeth and to prepare herself for bed. She was soon back. Then, quickly she removed the rest of her clothing and slipped into a short satin nightdress she'd collected for the occasion. Two ribbon straps secured the shoulders and could be easily undone. In front of the dressing table, she wet her index finger from a perfume bottle and smoothed her eyebrows. They were natural, for she'd never believed in plucking them out simply to follow the fashion. And that was all. Getting back into bed, she put out the main lights, leaving just the very dim orange light at the bedside. The fluffy sheets were folded half way down the bed. Sliding her legs down between them, she allowed herself to be covered only to the waist. Then she laid back luxuriously on the pillow and closed her eyes, breathing deeply, knowing that all her bosom down to the top half of her breasts, were on display.

Penman returned shortly as expected. He appeared in the dimly lit room, the orange bedside light showing only her head and bosom. He removed his short dressing gown to reveal bared chest down to his waist. But she hardly saw much of him in the darkened atmosphere.

As he climbed into bed, the sweet feminine scent enticed him even more. Then she smiled and he knew she was very much awake. He pressed a button next to the lamp and the faint hum of an electric motor was heard, the padded safety bar that was built into the outside edge of the bed, came up. Jackie uttered a little laugh.

"Can you guess what I thought when you first showed me that button and what it did?"

He was in sympathy with her. "You thought that I thought you might go sleep walking and probably fall into the sea."

She found that even more amusing, "Not as bad as sleep walking. But I thought you considered me a bad sleeper, likely to roll out of bed."

"Hmm," he murmured.

"It was afterwards that I realized you were protecting me from the raging sea."

He worked his feet down between the sheets and they were close together. "I have to, my dear," he assured her.

But the yacht was very steady. At fifteen knots, it's forward surge causing no uneasy moments. Jackie was steadily getting used to it.

He started on her hair, stroking it against the pillow. The

bouquet of her perfume was new and he was loving it. He rested an arm on the pillow behind her head, and her face, her body, her whole self, was being presented to him. So much luxury, his most private dreams had come true. His other hand was resting gently, partly on her breast, partly on the silky garment. He suddenly felt the velvet hardness of her breast as he caressed it. His face just over hers, he could kiss her at will, as much as he wanted.

"I have a confession to make," he declared.

"Tell me," she said softly.

"I never thought of getting you any perfume, it just never came to mind."

She thought it amusing and smiled prettily.

"I'm going to have plenty of catching up to do when we get back."

Jackie put two fingers across his lips and Penmen fell quiet while her friendly eyes searched his features. Then her hand extended to the back of his neck and he sensed the gentle pressure willing his lips to hers. They kissed and their lips sealed them together. After a while the tip of her tongue came to the front of her lips and he went on to enjoy the peachy texture of her tongue. Penman was on a long course of enjoyment, her warm breath breathing more and more life into him. It was a long while before he remembered that his hands were free, that there was much more of her to explore, to discover. Then, as his lips went on working on her mouth, her cheeks, her eyes, her whole face being showered with kisses, his hand began to pick up the feel of her breasts. When at length he drifted down to enjoy them, his lips could only slide smoothly over their fullness. After several attempts, his mouth each time only managing to gather in her nipple. Suddenly he became aware of Jackie's heavy breathing and he instinctively reacted. His hand wandered down her body, massaged her naval, and then further down, he found a surprise. The garment he intended to remove was not there, and he knew for sure that Jackie had prepared herself for him. He bathed her lips again with his, and his searching hand found the sweet center he'd longed for. He massaged her there, and a sudden eagerness reared up in his loins The Y-front Activity briefs he was still wearing, had released him once he'd got sufficiently excited. He felt the pulsation in his loins and, with his knees easing her thighs further apart, he slid sweetly into her without further guidance. He kissed her gratefully and his body moved on in ecstatic enjoyment. Soon, the passion in his loins

143

became intense, the sweetness of her body driving him on. He tried hard to keep control, to prolong the driving force, this was important to him. Penman was a cautious man at heart, his temperaments always under control. But he had been priming himself for this, and some strange instincts were getting the better of him, taking him over, driving him to work harder. He was not even aware of his grunting as he worked on in intense passion. Jackie's sweetness had taken control of him, spurring him on into ecstasy. He was loving every moment, and willing himself to go on forever.

Her arms came up around him, one circling his neck, the other in the middle of his back. She began to massage his flesh with some urgency. She felt him deep inside her and she allowed her feeling to reign free. Her breathing quickly heightened, almost panting, as she was taking short whiffs of air. She felt her body being carried away, across the sea, by someone she could live with. And he was going to keep her in captivity. She knew she would enjoy it, because he was a man she could love. Then suddenly all her nerves seemed to be rushing off in different directions. And she too, was murmuring, whispering involuntarily out of control. Her hand ran up and down his back, at times tried to steady him, while the other rubbed his neck, his ears, his hair. Then her nerves seemed to be rushing in from all directions, converging fast, and then suddenly, crashed. It seemed she'd fallen into the sea, for the gentle waves were flowing over her, she let go of him and her arms fell back on the soft pillow. Moments later she was smiling and gushing with happiness.

In a little while she remembered that Penman was right there with her, lying beside her, his head on the pillow, his body next to her. He'd released her only moments after she had experienced the crash. Having availed himself to the full, he had withdrawn from her and was lying there counting his blessings. Jackie turned herself to him, she snuggled close and kissed him.

Penman had fallen into a state of ecstatic drowsiness and was savouring the luxury of her presence, the magic of it all. After she'd kissed him, he barely managed to get a hand over her head and to let it rest quietly on the pillow. And it was about half an hour later when he began to show real signs of life. Then he discovered she was sound asleep. He could not hear her breathing, owing to the permanent whine of the yacht's machinery. But in the dim light he carefully observed the gentle rise and fall of her breasts. Quietly, he removed himself from the bed and carefully pulled the fluffy sheets up to her chin. He collected his dressing gown and made his way out.

The few paces to Penman's quarters were giant steps, he experienced a feeling of walking on the moon: He felt buoyant and powerful, much like he'd discovered the universe. Pleased with everything so far, he laid back in his bed and smiled proudly. Checking his watch, it was actually approaching three o'clock. He would need to put it back an hour in order to keep in the new zone. But there was no urgency.

Reaching to the bedside table, Penman opened the box of Havana cigars and put one in his mouth. Then, lifting the lighter, a large ornamental Ronson, he flicked it alight and suddenly had second-thoughts: The last time he smoked was the night before, in his quarters, a little over twenty-four hours ago. As usual, it had calmed his nerves and had helped him to relax. For a long time the Havana gems had become his regular night-cap. But he remembered suddenly that Jackie smoked nothing at all. Her breath was fresh and her lips very tasty; even her teeth, so pretty and smooth. The thought that she would be there for him in the morning when his own breath would still carry the taste of tobacco, made him reflect. He snapped the Ronson down and replaced the cigar in it's box. Then he smiled even more. For the rest of the voyage he would not be needing a cigar to sooth his mind. She would be much more than a night-cap.

Chapter Sixteen

The shower was raining full blast. Penman held up his face momentarily, so that the cool freshness quickly removed the early drowsiness. After about fifteen minutes he walked from under it, and dried himself, then drew on his robe. After combing his hair, he used the cologne liberally then, dressed in a red sports shirt which hung outside the cream shorts, he grabbed a towel and made for the door.

On the second deck, leaning against the rails outside the dining hall, he gazed at the new day. The sea was less calm now than the day before, with more traceable waves. A light breeze played cool against his neck. Already the day was hot. He noticed the position of the sun and glanced at his watch. It was quarter to nine. On other mornings he had woken earlier, but the reason for being late this morning was understandable.

He went into the dining hall but immediately had second thoughts. Tracing his steps to the lower deck, he went past his door and knocked softly at the next. There was no reply. He knocked again and entered. Jackie was still asleep, with the coverlets up to her arms. He decided not to wake her and went out again.

Back in the dining hall he helped himself to a large glass of pure orange juice from the refrigerator and went back out on deck, this time to the other side of the yacht. He downed the fruit juice in slow mouthfuls as he scanned the ocean. Visibility was excellent, the sky perfectly clear. He soon seated himself in a deck chair.

When Jackie joined him later she was wearing a blue beach jacket. There was a twinkle in her eyes, an exciting gleam.

"It's beautiful," she said.

"Quite a picture," he agreed.

The steward appeared with fruit juice for Jackie. She took it carefully and sat with her legs slightly sideways, the table between them exposing much of her thighs. He was not yet used to seeing her like this, but he would soon be taking her for granted.

"Slept well?" he asked, proudly.

"Very well," she admitted truthfully. She could not remember when she had slept so well.

Would they have breakfast? Yes, they were both starving; he summoned the steward and ordered breakfast. Meanwhile, Jackie studied him: it was not difficult to discover the effect she was having on him. The arrogance had gone. He had abandoned the haughtiness and seemed remarkably flexible, quite adaptable. Highlights of their moments in bed flashed through her mind. He was gentle and warm, she was undoubtedly accepting him. He could be made to suit her. They ate and chatted under the caressing sun.

"You've never considered a swimming pool?" she asked.

Yes, but only very recently. At first it had hardly seemed necessary, since he was in water all the time. He smiled proudly. "It hadn't occurred to me that I wouldn't be able to take a dive from the bow. It was after a year or so that the unreality of it caught on. It will definitely be on the next craft."

But he was holding back. He hadn't told her the initial truth that he was not the outdoor type. Reclining in the sun was all right, but the idea of swimming had not occurred to him. He had taken little or no interest in it at first.

The yacht was inadequate, he pointed out as he ate the last portion of deeply fried fish. The lounge was small, he had no projector room, and his screen was not ideally placed. In short, he was forced to get rid of it. There were only two main quarters. The new vessel would have four.

She flashed him an appraising glance. Did he not take a good look at it before buying it?

Indeed. But he was having to learn the sea, and it was absolutely necessary to learn something about yachts. This vessel was ideal for the purpose: it was good for quick manoeuvring, very simple to handle, and was designed for fast cruising.

The next few days were spent similarly, relaxing on deck, retreating to the lounge at night, rising late, breakfasting on scrambled eggs and fruit juice. He would escort her to her cabin at bedtime, later dismissing himself.

One morning when she was late, weary and unpleasant, he waited out of patience. Jackie had remained in bed, hardly at peace with herself, for she had been thinking or the two children, how she had planted them on their grandparents and had left without thinking seriously of their future. But there was soon to be a knock at the cabin door, and she invited Karl in. He was in shorts and white shirt, and was obviously pleased to find her awake.

"Another two days and we'll be stopping for a few hours," he said. "How do you like the sea now?"

She rushed to the window. It was beautiful: the surface rough and choppy, rugged with white foam where the waves creamed off.

There was nothing aggressive about it. The movement of the yacht reflected it. It floated high and cut evenly. She had never seen it so beautiful.

Karl studied her. "You won't find the sea in a more graceful mood, my dear. Very rarely have I seen it like this. It is something a man might fall in love with.

She looked round at him now, smiling. He was right. The sky was a soft blue, fading only on the horizon. There was a cargo vessel in the distance, heading in the same direction. She was unable to decide which of the two vessels was making faster time. She looked at Penman who was close beside her now, so that she was almost in his arms.

"Is it passing us?" she asked.

"Its water line was low, the tide it's creating at the bow is high, that means it's making full speed, my dear. It might get there two days ahead of us. It is the Jamaican planter, sailing form London." He had in fact, seen the ship form the control room earlier.

He guessed she might have had a restless night and felt like apologizing. It had been his turn to man the control room last night, so he had not spent any time with her. But he had religiously taken his two small glasses of Advocat in the evening and again in the early hours of the morning. Since leaving Sandgate, the drink had become his regular primer. It was recommended by his steward, Rayno, when Penman had asked him in a short man to man chat, for something that might help him keep up: He had heard it said that Caribbean fellows knew a thing or two about keeping up their strength. Rayno had suggested ginseng and the egg and brandy elixir, not terribly potent but absolutely legal. Ample supplies were therefore brought on board, and he was discreetly priming himself regularly. He planted a kiss on Jackie's forehead and rubbed his chin in her hair, carefully breathing in her feminine bouquet to which he was becoming addicted.

"We're already in the Caribbean," he pointed out. Then, stepping back a little, his eyes fell to her bosom and followed the dressing gown down to her waist. His mind contemplated whether there was much beneath it: a nightie, negligee, or perhaps her bikini. He had no idea how long she'd been awake. His arms circled her waist. His body stirred. He lowered his lips to her neck. Jackie was quick to offer her lips, which he took gratefully, meanwhile pressing her to him. After a while she recovered herself and rested her head against him, breathing softly. But the chant d' Aromas was getting to him, and he stammered:

"Have you had breakfast?"

"It's not important."

"You're not hungry?"

She shook her head and studied his face.

He guided her to the bed where she turned form him, but his arms still circled her. He unbuttoned her gown from behind, down to her waist where he gave a gentle pull at the sash and the whole thing came loose. He peeled it away from her, leaving her in just a pair of pink panties. He quickly threw off his clothes. She turned to him and her full breasts bubbled. He was more than impressed, for he slumped down on the bed, as though their feminine power had forced him there; or perhaps it was still to conceal himself. For she suddenly noticed that he was still in his briefs and already alert. She gushed a smile and he pulled her to him, between his knees, embracing her and burying his head in the softness of her stomach. He was attempting to breath through her body, taking in her fresh odour that was stirring his strength. Shortly thought, he held up his head and she started massaging his cheeks with loving hands. His face was smooth and she liked that. When her thumb reached his lops, he took it deep into his mouth and savored it with his tongue. She was getting used to this, for he seemed to relish all her fingers this way. He went on to take the rest of them, affectionately savouring each one in turn. Then his hands went to her waist and began the delicate act of removing her panties. Once at her feet, she stepped out of them. He held his head up and suddenly her breasts were hanging just above her face. His eyes hungrily sought hers. Jackie slumped to his knees, ,her breasts coming down in his face. He sucked at her nipple, one after the other and in no time she felt something coming alive inside her. It surprised her, the feeling grew and she felt them begin to hardened. He began pressing them with his mouth and face, kneading them in a wild passion. The flame grew and she lost control, issuing a little cry. She rolled from his knees on to the bed, but her body was a sweet magnet that kept him glued to her. As she laid back, he clung to her, his body stretching her out full length. Penman kissed her again, savouring her lips and ensuring her comfort. Then she felt the power of his loins working inside her, heating her up, driving the flames even higher. She melted and held him dearly. He expended himself quickly and his body became quiet. He breathed tiredly and undid himself from her.

Lying quietly, she could hear the sea making a great noise

under the hull. It had to be, since the ocean itself was too calm to be heard through the closed windows. She turned and looked at him, he was resting and breathing much better, more comfortable. His shoulders strong looking, his stomach slightly protruding, it's prominence disguised only because he was lying back. She was thinking that he was probably just over six-feet tall, and compared with herself at five-feet-seven, that their height were nicely matched. But ideally, he could do with losing more than a stone. He was about fourteen stones and would look much better at thirteen or less. That would mean losing some fat from his shoulders and arms, his stomach and thighs. As a yachtsman, he should really work on his body. But he seemed keener to work on hers. She smiled at her own thoughts. "Karl," she said. But her voice was just a wisper, and despite their closeness, it was inaudible. She repeated herself and found her voice. He murmured but made no movement.

She kissed him, then asked, "What shall we do?"

"Nothing," he murmured, And he meant it. For he was happy to remain there, lifeless, bathing in the knowledge that she was there for him, that her loveliness was all his. In a few moments his breathing got deeper, and she knew he had dropped off to sleep.

Jackie left the bed and drew up a plain sheet over him. She collected her garments and quietly slipped away to the shower. As she attended to herself, her thoughts pondered over her situation. She'd been on the yacht twenty days. It was the fourth time Penman had made love to her, and it was the first time he'd removed her under garment. Previously she'd prepared herself for him. And it had always been in the middle of the night. It was the first time they'd made love in the daylight hours. Perhaps he came to her when she wasn't expecting him. But he'd entered her quarters in daylight before. Only, this time he'd given her quite a surprise. It was the first time he'd taken command of her and she'd not had to coaxed him at any stage. She wondered if he had really overcome his shyness? Or was it that her own quiet temperaments had made things so wonderful for him?

She'd noticed that over the past few days, when they'd spend many hours together, though he had not tried to make love to her, he had been cautiously exploring her body more and more, caressing her almost everywhere, and getting great pleasure from his little acts. His lips had savoured every inch of her body from her navel upwards. She's becoming aware that he may well start at her feet and worked his way up with his lips, for only the day before, he had

150

played with her feet and had kissed all her toes. There were clear hints that his lips might soon work their way up. The great pleasure he derived from removing her panties now, made her realised that she must be on her guard. Only once had it happened to her and she must never again be overcome with such surprise.

It suddenly occurred to her also, that it was important to use little make-up as possible, or perhaps none at all. And certainly no body cream or lotion. Then she remembered that plain olive oil, or even coconut oil should be safe for him.

Dressing herself now, Jackie became aware that she'd put on some weight over the past two weeks. She was seeing it at her waist, and in her cheeks. Her preferred waist was twenty-six, with half an inch variation. She must take special care. Perhaps the few pounds she'd lost during the first few days had been restored, for she was eating two good meals a day. But she'd lost the taste for alcohol. She was probably back to her ideal nine stones; there was no scales to confirm it. But she was happy with her looks, and her body felt free and buoyant.

Chapter Seventeen

At eleven-fifteen the Grey Lady cautiously approached Calicos Island. Built by the islanders, the harbour would accommodate small vessels up to seven thousand tons. Two island tugs met the Grey Lady two miles offshore, guided her in, and had no difficulty pulling her to the quay. There were some problems, though: that of the small rowing boats which swarmed the harbour, each with one or two rowers, getting in the way and ignoring the importance of leaving a clear area for the incoming yacht.

The island was sun drenched, with a large mountain to the left of the harbour, some ten miles in the background. From the quay two men attached a large wire-braided hose to the yacht's water inlet, and for one hour three thousand gallons were pumped into the tank. Meanwhile, fresh supplies of fruits and then food products were taken aboard. There was a personal request from Miss Cary for a basket of flowers which she arranged into three vases, placing one in Jackie's quarters, one in hers, and one in the dining hall. As for Jackie, while there was no inclination to go ashore, with the aid of the binoculars she had spotted something which made an interesting souvenir. It was a red and white wooden carving of a mermaid which she was able to see on the stalls forty yards away. Karl had it brought aboard by the steward who was the only one to go ashore.

Two hours later they were heading south through the Windward Passage, steering between Cuba and Haiti, and making straight for Jamaica. The last two days were delightful. Jackie carried the binoculars continuously. Like a new hobby, she scanned the area ahead, then on both sides, picking out the small islands. Karl was always close at her side, explaining the sights. For comfort and freedom she wore only bikinis beneath her beach jacket that reached six inches above her knee.

Jackie at first made a deliberate effort to stay close to him, knowing quite well that he considered himself fortunate. But over the last few days they'd been spending much more time together, in fact she was spending half the days in his arms. And she was discovering that Penman had not lost much of his shyness. Whenever he wanted her, he would approach her with keen instincts, usually at three or four days intervals. For the days in between, she would stay close to him, but it would take one or two hours for him to get comfortable with her and then he would begin to enjoy her closeness. Whilst she would not intrude on his privacy by going to his quarters, she was happy for him to have the freedom of hers. In the late nights, after they'd enjoyed several hours of relaxing together, watching films, reading books and magazines about the islands, she would stay on his arm, and more often than not he would guide her to her quarters and then divert to his own. She was even beginning to relish the many nights by herself. For once in bed, she was falling to sleep very quickly. Jackie felt sure that the gentle rocking and rolling of the yacht was somehow therapeutic; she was sleeping soundly, for six or seven hours. Occasionally when she found herself awake, she would quickly drop off to sleep again.

Penman had no difficulty with her. Once together, it seemed she was a permanent joy. Jackie enjoyed his collection of films and his small library of books and magazines. Her true personality finding expression, she was very generous with her smiles, which sometimes breaks into quiet laughter; then her twinkling eyes, pretty teeth and perfectly curled lips, simply fascinated him. He discovered a way of telling her on many occasions that she was much like an expensive Christmas tree, that her proportions were very neat and curvaceous. He had even told her that her natural flair and style was doing something to him. But he wasn't brave enough to spell it out. She sensed what was happening in his heart and mind, and she simply told herself that it was up to him. But he went on to disclosed that he wished he had the talent of an artist, that he would love to be able to capture her on canvas, full size. Of course, he had never considered purchasing a movie camera, but it was a special item he was planning to collect once they were in Jamaica.

Jackie was entirely herself. But she was beginning to think that he seemed to be representing more than she'd thought possible. Of the affairs she'd indulged in before Pascoe, only one man had actually commanded a part of her. He was the doctor who had given her up with considerable reluctance. On quick reflection, she had been in her mid twenties, and he had been twice her age. Penman was much older than her, yes. But they seemed to have more in common. She was beginning to sense that he was very caring, doing everything to please her, and was always thinking about her likes and dislikes. Their emotions seemed to be slowly fusing together, perhaps because they were spending so much time together. Jackie was very impressed with the way he made money and still have all the time in the world for recreation. She was impressed with the way he spent it. She was able to recall the night at the charity ball, which had left her convinced of her ability to live up to certain ambitions. He had introduced her to some people whom she had thought she could like and respect, though they were much older than herself. Jackie was beginning to think now, that the cruise was destined to change her life, but she needed to contemplate how.

They were already off the Jamaican shores. There would be no need to shuttle back and fore in the speedboat. The authorities were favorable to yachts owned by reputable people, and checks were often made, since countless vessels were anchored off Port Royal, an area popular with divers, treasure-hunting being the sport of all seasons. The Grey Lady respectfully avoided them and made for a reserved pier two miles east of Port Royal. At five-thirty pm. the sun was a large amber balloon already half-sunken behind the Blue Mountain. By the time Penman had made the pier, six o'clock and gone. Darkness had fallen. Here, as soon as the sun was down, darkness followed, with scarcely a moment of dull skies.

A large sedan waited for Penman. It was a white Lincoln Continental, with a black convertible hood. The black chauffeur held a rear door open and Penman who steered Jackie in. An hour ago she was still in bikinis and beach jacket. But for the landing she wore a red cotton dress, low at the neck with a wrapped skirt. The temperature was warm, about ninety degrees, and would cool down a little as the night air took effect. But getting into the car, she felt a slight chill.

Penman in his sports shirt, also felt the chill and quickly told the chauffeur to switch off the air conditioner. The fellow apologized for his over-enthusiasm.

Leaving the small peninsular of Port Royal, they turned right and went into a series of hill climbs. Jackie paid little attention to the scenery. It was dark, and apart from the cluster of lights behind them, which was Kingston, there were only few houses on the mountain side. However, the few looked exclusive, large and particularly handsome, great mansion. Jackie glimpsed an out-door swimming pool, well lit, and two women in bathing costumes.

The Lincoln Continental turned slowly into a sheltered driveway. The area ahead was a beautiful recess on the mountains slope. The headlights traced the trimmed edges along the short drive, before coming to rest on a large terrace. The driver pulled up so that the rear door on Penman's side was directly in front of the large veranda entrance. Further back the chromium handles on the door reflected the light. The doors were all glass, several panes, and a yellow light shone within. The terrace too, was well lit.

Penman already had his door opened when the Chauffeur held it back fully. He was the fellow Penman had hired in the middle of his last stay on the island. He now smiled happily and watched Madam get out of the car.

The chauffeur was a black fellow of about thirty, who came from Spanish Town originally. Proud of himself, Penman had found him driving a bus to Palisades Airport, taking school children on excursions. Penman himself had been driving the Lincoln Continental and had picked up a puncture. The bus, empty, and heading back to Kingston, had pulled up. Then the driver approached the Lincoln cautiously, seeing the white man standing by with hands in his trouser pockets, and looking down at the flat tyre.

"Want to earn an extra pound?" Penman had asked.

"Sure."

And Penman had stepped back to let him get on with it. By the time the job was done Penman had already decided to hire him, having liked the way he had changed the wheel. His name was Lloyd, and his Jamaican colleagues called him Lloydie.

He closed the door after Jackie and, while Penman looked around the premises, having left it for so long, went ahead of Madam to the veranda where he opened the right half of the twin glass doors. Jackie walked into an enormous drawing room where the four intricate chandeliers formed a square. She stopped under them and turned slowly, fascinated. The housekeeper was also black. She was American and did not intend to go back, having got the job through answering an advertisement; her credentials impressive, she had been housekeeper and cook to a wealthy American who had run for Governor. After that the job was no longer attractive: too much had been demanded of her, and she was no longer getting much rest. In Jamaica her new boss was there only four or five months a year. Moreover, she had liked Mrs. Penman, a typical English woman who was entirely different form her previous American mistress.

Expecting Jackie now, she appeared through a door at the far end of the drawing room. "I must welcome you," she said, smiling by way of salutation. "Mr. Penman did tell you about me, I hope?"

"Good evening," said Jackie. "No, Karl hadn't mentioned you."

"Oh, Mr Penman must have forgot. It's been a long time. I'm Betsy, the housekeeper, I'm here to look after things for you."

She displayed a proud grin. And it didn't take her long to appreciate Jackie's disposition. It was quite plain that she had not handled a housekeeper before.

"Ah, you two have met, I see," said Penman, coming in at that precise moment.

Jackie looked at him.

"Well," he announced, "This is Betsy. She will be looking after you."

"Delighted to," said the woman, still displaying her proud smile.

She was aged about forty-five, and actually worked best with a mistress who took pride in her home and wasn't wasteful. She would expect her mistress too to command a sense of responsibility to her husband and family. But on the other hand, Betsy had never served a mistress who was not a real mistress, that is to say, an unmarried mistress. However seeing Jackie, she was suddenly respectful to the younger woman, perhaps because Jackie appeared warm and in no way frivolous. She excused herself and departed from them.

Penman went straight to a corner of the room where a wide recess gave access to the cocktail bar. It was openly displayed and a bottle of Demerara Rum caught his eye. Next to it was a bottle of Planter's Punch; he seemed to drink rum only when he's in Jamaica. It was not his favourite, but no bar was complete without rum. He found a bottle of Wray & Nephew coffee rum liquor, which he preferred after desert. Searching further among the shelves, he came up with some Blanquette de limos from which he filled two slender glasses and handed one to Jackie who had planted herself in a soft leather chair.

"This is an aperitif," he said. "It will open your appetite for a good meal."

"No, no. I couldn't eat anything now," she protested. "I must settle in first."

"That is just what I mean. Without this, you won't be settled in before tomorrow. But this will condition you for dinner in quick time."

Jackie took the glass but didn't intend to drink it down. She'd lost the taste for alcohol and didn't want to disappoint him. She waited till he had drank half the content of his own glass, then she put her's to her lips and her usual smile of contentment did not appear.

"You would really prefer fruit juice, I can tell," he observed.

She nodded with a slight grimace. "What will this blend with?"

He considered for a moment. "Grape juice, white," he suggested.

She nodded.

"I'm sure Betsy have all the juices here for us." And he left her side and disappeared towards the dining room. He returned quickly with a tall glass, half full with grape juice."

Jackie filled it with the contents from the other glass. After putting in some ice, she sipped it with more appreciation.

Penman was looking on. "Does this mean my favourite lady has lost the taste for expensive drinks?"

She nodded. "I'm afraid so." For a moment she was looking into his eyes, then to his stomach and back to his eyes.

"You have a message for me, my dear. Tell me, I want to hear."

"I've never asked you before, but for the past few days I've been thinking about your weight."

"Ah," said Penman, "You're thinking that I'm drinking too much? And eating the wrong food."

Jackie gave a nod.

Penman fell silent for a while. Then he said, "I can only take it as a compliment, my dear. To know you're concerned about my health. What do you think I should do, change my diet?"

"You could alter your diet a little, and enjoy more fruits."

Penman rolled things over in his mind, then said, "I like what you're saying, Jackie." He leaned towards her and kissed her forehead, then allowing his face and chin to linger in her hair. It seemed he was becoming addicted to the feel of her hair against his face. He also breathed deeply, taking in her perfume. "That's a great compliment, and you're a wonderful example for me."

"How much do you weigh?" asked Jackie.

"You know, I think I'm just over fourteen stones."

"You should be down to about twelve and a half stones."

"Okay. Let me think about it, I will certainly start on something."

Jackie went on sipping her cocktail, while Penman was beginning to wonder about what was going on in her head. It soon occurred to him that she might be experiencing something similar to what he was feeling, though on a much lesser scale, no doubt. He suddenly thought of something that would excite her and help to ensure her happiness.

"Come," he said, "You can have a quick run through the house, see some of what there is to see. Then you can use the phone to contact your favourite number at home."

Jackie suddenly lit up. She uttered an exciting cry and flew to his arms, kissing him gratefully. She began playing with his hair. "It is so thoughtful of you, Karl. You're fantastic." And she kissed him again.

"When you're ready to use the phone, remember, my dear, the time in the United Kingdom is five to six hours ahead of us. It's eight o'clock here now, so it's well past midnight over there."

A little while later she was sipping her drink when she notice a sparkle through the glass. It seemed to be reflecting a light from outside. Along the far side of the drawing room were three wide double doors, their bottom halves were polished wood while the top halves were panes of glass. She looked at Penman.

"What's on the other side of the doors?"

"A swimming pool, my dear. You do swim, I hope?"

"I can't wait," she said. "Do you know, I haven't gone into a swimming pool for some years. I did swim a little when I first started carrying Constance. That would be at least three years ago. Not since."

"You will have all the opportunity to practice."

"That's exactly what I shall be doing, only practicing. I'm not a strong swimmer. I can float very well, but I haven't developed any speed."

"You will have the days to practice. Come, you must see the house."

Jackie rose and straightened her dress. She took his outstretched hand. He directed her through a carpeted hallway which took them to the foot of a staircase. The stairs were made cozy by fresh flowers in vases and three or four local paintings on one side.

They soon entered into a large luxury room with two sets of windows on each side and a large bed at one end. The bed looked about eight feet wide, by eleven or twelve feet long. Penman chuckled as he showed her the bed.

"I'm sure you're wondering about the size. It is specially made by a local cabinet maker. It's made in three sections and bolted together. When I commissioned him, we sat down and designed the head and posters and the canopy to suit." He could see Jackie's amazement. The blue piled carpet was much enhanced by the shades of light blue throughout the room. Also bordering the canopy were rolls of light blue net materials. Penman made his way to the head of the bed. He pressed one of the four buttons in the head panel, and they watched as the rolls of netting unfolded slowly, all three sides simultaneously. The bed head reached up to the canopy and did not need netting at that end.

When all the netting unfolded to the floor, screening off the bed, Jackie asked, "Is it because it's such a big room why you screened the bed?"

Penman chuckled. "In a tropical country like this, you have one serious enemy, the mosquito. They're blood suckers. Humans are their favourite treats." He reached for Jackie's hand, the sleeveless dress allowing him to smooth the back of his hand up to her shoulder." These creatures love juicy people, and I don't want them touching you, my dear. If we don't take this kind of precaution when sleeping, they could easily destroy your beauty. I wouldn't want to see your skin breaking out in spots."

"I know of mosquito, but I didn't realised they could be such a menace."

"Don't worry about them. When awake you can keep them at bay. But once asleep, without netting like this, they could take over."

"Are there nettings in my room?"

Penman was caught by surprise. He fell silent for a moment.

Jackie was showing some innocence. "Oh, you haven't prepared any for me." Her arms were folded as she looked about the interior with admiring eyes.

Penman heard himself saying, "I decided this would be right for both of us, my dear."

"But your wife! Surely, this was set up for you both."

"Indeed, it was. But she's a million miles away. The situation is very different now."

Jackie was suddenly thinking fast. She hadn't planned to give up herself completely to him. "I really like the arrangement you have for me on board the yacht. It is very convenient for both of us."

Well, he considered, it should be easy to remedy the situation, not a problem at all. Then he remembered: "All the bedrooms are equipped with nets, my dear. Next door is much the same arrangement, somewhat smaller, that's all."

"Can I see it?"

"Sure, through there." He ushered her through an oval shaped opening at one corner, and they were into the boudoir.

This was quite grand, though much smaller in size. The decoration was light pink and off white. "Yes," she said with excitement. And she rushed to him and kissed his cheeks. The boudoir was equipped with everything she would need, it also had it's own adjoining shower room and all amenities.

So much for that! Jackie wasn't sure why she'd asked for a separate room. Perhaps it was because she'd adapted herself to the arrangement on board the yacht and liked it very much. When she had first stepped on board, she wasn't sure what to expect. Maybe she had expected a single cabin to start with, and then, once he had enticed her into his quarters and they'd made love, she would have been expected to stay there with him. But the separate quarters had been great, and she'd become used to it. The first time they made love, she had expected him to remain there in her bed, and that she would have waken up next to him in the morning. But he had gone, and she'd learnt to appreciate the convenience of waking up by herself. Now she did not want to feel that she was giving herself completely to him. And besides, over the past two or three weeks, her sixth sense had been telling her that for much of the time he preferred his own privacy.

After they'd gone through the top floor, they came back down the stairs together. The maid invited them to the dining table, but Jackie had no appetite for food. She simply wanted to carry on through the house. But she realised she could not leave Karl to eat alone. In any case, she found herself worrying about what he would be eating. Detaching herself from him, she quickly ran through the other rooms, just glancing in to see how they looked, what they were. There were two servant's quarters, a games room with a snooker table and some exercise equipment. There was the pantry, a store room, a large garages for two or three vehicles, and as she returned to the far end of the drawing room, there was his study, with radio equipments, a television and a collection of books, etc.

Deciding she needed soft shoes, Jackie dashed up the stairs and rummaged through her personal things. She found what she wanted and was quickly back in her soft felt slippers.

Between the kitchen and dining room, she soon discovered that there were quite a vaiety of vegetables on the island, that the gardener grew carrots, turnips, sweet pepper and other local things that were unknown to her. They looked good and she promised herself she'd be trying something new at every meal. Also, whatever vegetables they did not have they could easily buy. She was even keen to sample something new right away.

She made Karl settle for a light dinner of chicken cocktail and just two boiled potatoes, carrots and white beans. She herself was having a vegetable pie which the cook, Betsy, had made. Karl could also have one if he so desired. They both finished off with fruits and juices. No alcohol was taken.

Penman felt somewhat flattered. No one had previously showed any interest in his eating habits. He was considered unapproachable, too aloof. But secretly she was getting to him and he felt good about it. Afterwards, he went off to check how things were in his studies, if the short wave communication set could be made to work after his many months absence.

Jackie looked out at the pool and was very impressed. It was covered above, and partially shielded on the far side. Part of the balcony above formed a section of the roof, while the outer walls were built in sections with a series of round openings. The building blocks were also stylish with air vents. The outer wall went up about eight feet and sloped in to join the balcony floor. The whole area of the pool looked private, being adequately shielded from heavy rain and winds. Under the lights, and with the air outside quite warm, the water looked inviting. Despite being on her own, it was drawing her in.

She went off to her room to change into a set of bikinis. But it took her a while to get her hair all tucked into an extra large protective cap. The effort made Jackie realised that she really needed to have her hair shortened by at least two inches. A promise she'd made herself a week ago came to mind. She smiled to herself and decided she would see to it in the morning. For the time being, she collected a large towel and went back downstairs. She stopped by the kitchen where Betsy was still washing up, and told her she was sampling the pool. The older woman looked at her and couldn't help voicing her secret thoughts.

"Oh my, you look very glam', Miss Jackie."

"Thank you, " Betsy," she laughed, being her usual self.

"I t'ink we're gonna enjoy havin' yuh here, Miss Jackie."

Jackie smiled. "I'm going to enjoy being here, Betsy."

161

"Oh my; you must be careful now, Miss Jackie."

Jackie declared that she would. And she went off to the study where she found Penman. He was seated in a chair in front of the communication set. The BBC World Service station was broadcasting the news.

"I'm taking a dip," she said.

His features lit up as she presented herself in front of him.

"It is late, my dear."

"And it's hot, I want to cool down before bed time."

"D' you want me with you?"

"Not really. It looks nice and safe out there."

"Stick to the shallow end for tonight."

"I will," she said.

Penman watched her walked away, very pretty and pleasing. She remembered what he had said about the time back at home, that the difference was five to six hours. She worked out that if she were to spend an hour in the pool, she could use the phone at about midnight and probably get her parents up for six in the morning.

At the edge, she put her towel on a rail and climbed down the ladder, cautiously. Her bared feet tested the water, it was neither cold nor warm, perhaps the same temperature as her body. She went down three steps to her knees, her feet felt a little coolness; two more steps down and the water just touched her bikini, another step down and the water was warm at her navel, but cool at her feet. Another step down and it was level with her breast, and then she detected the difference. It was slightly warm at her breast and cool from the waist down. She smiled, knowing that she would have to play about in it before the real coolness would be felt. One more step down and she had reached the bottom, and the level was just above her breast.

She let go of the ladder and walked off. When she'd gone the full width, she turned and did a little jump, then launched out and started swimming. It was a long time since she had gone into a pool, it felt good and testing.

Jackie played about for a time, swimming tentatively across the width of the pool, at the shallow end. She occasionally stood up for a pause, the water up to her chest. It felt good, very cool and caressing. On two occasions she went under, diving for a few seconds at a time. The plastic hair-cap seemed to be holding, but she was not happy with it, tied beneath her chin, it kept her hair in too tight a bundle. She was checking it when she spotted Penman.

In truth, she was in the water for more than half an hour when he came out. Her features brightened as he walked towards the pool. In his white shirt, blue shorts and flip-flops, he stood at the edge and looked down at her. "How dose it feel?" he asked.

"Very nice." And she explained how it felt when she'd first got in, and how she'd paddled about to get it all cool and enjoyable.

"The sun blazing down all day had warmed it up. They filled it and got it ready for us yesterday. It's been empty for months, because you weren't here."

She laughed aloud. "Are you telling me off?"

"That's how it is when I'm not around." He turned an drew up a chair to the water's edge, then sat down.

"Are you going to stay and watch me?"

"I can't imagine anything better for entertainment."

Jackie explained she was only going across the width of the pool, because her swimming wasn't strong, that she'd be crossing four times. "Make sure you keep your eye on me," And she was off.

Penman watched her with proud eyes, her legs trailing elegantly together, her arms reaching out with each stroke, the fullness of her bikinis, her whole body kept his eyes sweetened and attentive. When she'd turned and was swimming back to him, he started counting the strokes to check how many it would take her to reach him. As she got closer and closer, Penman could see that her serious expression was not changing, and even as she approached him and turned, her face had not softened, for a while he was puzzled. Then he remembered that she was concentrating on her swimming, that staying afloat was serious enough. He went on counting until she was back, completing the return leg. The moment she reached out and held the rails, Jackie's face lit up to her usual self. Penman's secret fears were allayed. Then he told her:

"I've been counting the number of strokes you were making to complete each length, my dear."

She stood in front of him, "Am I doing well?"

"Very well, considering you haven't been in a pool for more than three years."

She was dripping, and she looked healthy and exciting. She was making sure her head cover was tight. "How many?"

"Nineteen and twenty to each length. You crossed four times, about eighty in total. Feeling tired?"

She shook her head and droplets of water reached him.

Penman's hand automatically went to his forehead and wiped

the spots. Jackie simply put her wet hands to his cheeks and, bending her knees, she planted a wet kiss on his mouth. "You're not to wipe it," she said, "I'm going to do another four lengths, and I must finish before it dries." She turned from him and, jumping back in the pool, started swimming again.

He counted her strokes through the first length, on the return length he was in two minds: Should he keep counting, or should he time her. It wouldn't mean much. He was also tempted to wipe his cheeks and mouth, but decided to leave well alone.

Jackie completed the four short lengths and decided to carry on for another length, to complete a hundred strokes. Then in the middle of the fifth length, she remembered that the final return would make it six lengths. By the time she returned to him, she was so tired, and had even forgotten that she'd left her water mark on his face.

"Were you counting?" she asked in her tired breath.

"Yes," he said with a smile. "You made well over one hundred strokes."

"How many?"

"One hundred and twenty-nine."

She was surprised. "Oh, was I much slower for six lengths?"

"Just a little. By the time you did the fourth, you were tired going into the fifth, and even more tired going for the final length."

Jackie's breathing almost returned to normal. "Shall I take off my cap?"

"Not yet, I want to get you dry first. Pass me the towel."

"Oh," she laughed, "I did promised to finish before your cheeks were dried." And she wet her hands with the beady droplets on her thighs and smeared his face again. "Don't touch it, let it dry on it's own." She passed the towel to him.

Drying her off, Penman was a happy volunteer. He hardly touched her face, leaving it to dry in the temperate night air. He rubbed the towel all over her body, down to her ankles. Then he told her it was time to get her feet into the slippers, it was twelve midnight, time to call it a day.

Back in her room, Jackie removed the bikinis and, still with her head-cap on, she went under the shower for a final rise. Then it was just a matter of tidying her hair and getting into her nightie, nothing else.

She sat on the bed, upright, with legs folded beneath her. As she picked up the telephone, she was well aware that Karl had gone to his room, probably just to change. He was aware of her plan to make the Trans-Atlantic call. He told her it was something she could do every night, as a special treat for her and her children. He expected her to be on the phone for about half an hour. As Jackie placed the call and gave the operator her parents number in Bedfordshire, she was expecting him to join her any moment. More so, since already four days had gone since he'd spent time in her room. It would be nice for him to be there, lying next to her while she's making the call.

Chapter Eighteen

It was midday when she took the opportunity to see some more of the surroundings. And discovering that, not only did she have the convenience of a swimming pool, but she also had a tennis court prepared on a well kept lawn. Penman had certainly provided a very adequate retreat. There were some two acres of land, and about half of it was the gardener's pride and joy. While the house, the pool and tennis court were on level ground, the fruit and vegetable garden which occupied about half the property, were on slopes. The gardener liked the situation, for there were two seasons of the year when heavy rainfalls were expected. Then the root of the plants would be nicely drained. It was for that reason he had dug three trenches down the slope, and a series of narrow ones across the beds to ensure good drainage. Furthermore, water would be diverted from the house to safe areas.

The fruit trees along the drive from the main road were laden with fruits, common oranges on one side, and on the other side, a variety that was bigger and sweeter, which the gardener called 'navel fruit', because it had something looking like a big navel at the bottom. And there were two grapefruit trees at the rear of the property. For the time being the fruits were a rich green colour, as they were out of season and wouldn't begin ripping for another five or six weeks. Along the drive, all the tree trunks were painted white up to three feet off the ground.

The gardener was always at work, trimming the foot paths, pruning the plants and flowers, even removing weeds which, after the rainy season, tended to spring up everywhere and could quickly over-run the place. There were also three or four sections of lawn which were kept low and trimmed.

The view form Jackie's bedroom was excellent. Unhindered, it extended to the horizon, across endless blue seas. But before the sea, and slightly to the right, was Kingston. With the aid of binoculars, she pressed herself to the window sill and scanned the area. Palisades Airport came into view. Jackie held her breath. It was something unexpected. With the naked eye, it was merely a cluster of tiny square specks, indistinct. Now she was able to pick out the larger buildings, and a stream of vehicles heading along the Palisades Road. There were some five aeroplanes looking like shrimps on the ocean bed. It was interesting. For over on the horizon was a small peak, a dark patch; it wasn't clear, it might even be clouds. But the door opened behind her and she didn't look around. She already knew who it was.

From behind, an arm circled her waist while another hand got inside her hair and guided it aside; she felt her neck being kissed. Then his voice broke the silence.

"Fascinating sight, isn't it?"

She lowered the binoculars and agreed. Penman was in white shirt and short khaki trousers.

"I have a fitness plan," he said. "I'll be back in a little while to explain it."

"Where are you going?"

"Just a few yards along the path, to the other end of the property. I want to speak to my gardener." And he slipped away easily.

She lifted the binoculars again and trained it a little to the left. She found the yachts. They came in clear and, from this angle, they seemed scattered. There was some activity on one deck; three figures in black, their wet suits reflecting the sun. Jackie shifted the binoculars round to the right and tilted them slightly. There was a glimpse of coastline, then the harbour, with cranes along the pier, and ships of various sizes, one already sailing out, trailing a long path of white foam.

Kingston was a cluster of buildings between which, scantly spaced, were high trees, intersections, roads, moving vehicles, buses with baggage on their roofs. There was even a moving figure on the top of a stationary bus, tossing down bags and boxes.

Tilting the binoculars even more, a factory of some sort came into view. It was close to them, almost at the foot of the mountain. A container moving on a kind of conveyer belt, while white smoke belched furiously from a giant chimney. She stayed there for a while, scanning the area, seeing what she could see.

He had only been gone about fifteen minutes when he came back.

"Where are we?" she asked. It was a spectacular view.

They were on the side of the Blue Mountain, he pointed out.

She had heard it mentioned vaguely. It was famous for the best coffee in the world. "How high is it?"

"Seven thousand feet, perhaps a bit more at the highest point."

Jackie re-employed the binoculars, this time looking down almost directly below them. Between trees she spotted large houses.

Their roofs, were interesting: They were painted red, green, blue, even the occasional yellow.

"This was a romantic spot," Karl went on. "Three hundred years ago, even at the turn of this century, there was a look–out point form just above us. The watchmen would scan the seas for approaching pirates. In the early days the buccaneers used to visit the area regularly, to convince themselves they were gallant sailors. From Port Royal the British sea-dogs would launch counter-attacks to drive away foreigners. Nothing could get near; Port Royal was the strong point."

She brought into her view the remains of the old port, taking in the moored yachts once more. "But how do they expect to find treasures out there? Were they not all sent to Britain?"

Karl laughed. A lot of battles were fought in the Caribbean, ships were sunk, some laden with silver and gold. Port Royal was a fort where they had stock-piled the treasure, but a large part of the port was sunk by earthquake, and a lot of treasures were still under the sea.

"Are they finding much?" asked Jackie, lowering the binoculars.

"Oh, one or two old ships have been located offshore; treasures have been recovered; A few Spanish ships were sunk further out."

She handed the binoculars to Karl. "Why Spanish ships?"

"Well, the island and a lot of others in the Caribbean were first discovered by Columbus, about the year fourteen ninety something."

She remembered vaguely, probably from history lessons, that Columbus sailed in Spanish ships, under the spanish flag. He discovered the islands and most of the America's. Then for a couple of centuries there had been battles between Britain, Spain, even France, for possession of these islands, or something like that.

After scanning the horizon for a while, Penman gave the binoculars back to her and pointed in the direction where she should look. She followed his instructions and soon located a spiky area well beneath the horizon which was supposed to be the island of Haiti. He explained that the coastal town was Les Cayes, but the higher grounds further back would be Mt. De la Hotte.

"How far away is Haiti?"

"Les Cayes would be less than a hundred and fifty miles."

Not very far, she agreed.

"The original name for that island when Columbus named it

was La Isla Espanola.   Over the years it got shortened to Hispaniola.. In swashbuckling years of the sea-dogs, the island was partitioned into two separate territories. Now they speak French in Haiti, and Spanish in Dominica."

"The result of all those years of fighting between foreign nations?"

"Yes," he said. "When battles are fought settlements have to be reached."

Jackie lowered the binoculars and thought for a moment. Then she turned and looked at him. Her feminine features, normally gentle and inviting, was distant, vague and contemplative. It was only the second time that Penman had seen her like this, as if troubled. Her eyes sought his.

"Karl," she said.

"Something's troubling you?"

"What happened to all the people who lived on these islands before the Europeans came?"

"Don't worry yourself," he said hastily. "There were very few inhabitants in those days."

"What do you think happened to them?"

"I suppose they couldn't cope with being made slaves. They probably died out."

"One way or another?"

"Yes, one way or another."

Jackie looked out to sea and he pondered over what could have made her asked such a question.

"Come," he said, "I have something to tell you. We must go to the drawing room."

They went to the drawing room. But with the three twin doors wide open, the space by the pool seemed more inviting. They went out to the easy chairs and sat on the patio. A lovely white pussy cat squatted by the chair as they sat down. Jackie was tempted to pick it up, but suddenly remembered that her beach jacket left most of her thighs exposed and it's paws might easily leave her with scratches.

"Right, here it is. I've decided to take up running…"

"No," she said, objectively.

"It will be good for me. It's a way to get some of this off." And he put both hands to his stomach and agitated the excess flesh. "It will be easy for me to get two or three pounds off here, and everywhere else."

"You're not going by yourself," she said with a worrying look.

"It will be good for me, you must agree. But I have a plan. In the mornings, starting tomorrow, about six o'clock while it's still cool, I will get the chauffeur to take me down to the yacht. Rayno will join me, we will go along the beach. I will run about two hundred yards, then rest for a few minutes, then another two or three hundred, and so on. In a couple of weeks I should be running two to three miles. Furthermore, by this time in the afternoon, or late evening under the flood lights, we could be playing tennis, or swimming. In seven weeks time when we're ready to sail, I should be a stone lighter, I'll be going back fitter and looking more upright."

Jackie's features softened with admiration. "Do you think you can do it?"

"It's much easier to do it here than if I was trying to do it back in England. The hot temperature here will bring me down to size much quicker."

"What am I going to do when you're gone in the morning?"

"I'll be gone for two hours at the most. You could stay in bed, or take to the pool."

"An idea is coming to mind," she said. "When the chauffeur takes you down to the pier, he could bring Deidre back. We get on well. We might even practice at the nets when you are out."

"A great idea," said Penman. "You could be fully occupied. And I won't have to worry about you getting bored. But remember, you may find it difficult to get up before seven o'clock. Every other night you'll be speaking to the children. It could be one o'clock before you get to sleep."

"We'll see," said Jackie, happily. "And there's something else that came to mind yesterday."

"I need to say something more before I forget yet again. Are you phoning your parents tonight?"

"Yes," she said.

"Keep a pen and paper by your bed. Ask for their bank account number, the sort code and the address of the bank. I want to transfer some money to them. I don't want them straining their resources to look after the children."

Jackie was pleasantly impressed. She would get her mother's account number.

"Now, what else did you have in mind?"

She held the hem of her beach jacket. "I only have three of these and it seem the only comfortable way to dress out here. I've decided that I need another four, one for every day of the week, preferably all in different colours. Is Deidre familiar with shopping in Kingston?"

"She should be. She and Rayno would have gone to the stores once or twice. You should really stick together, she's a trained nurse, you know."

"Yes I know."

"She can sleep here if you want her to. And she could get the chauffeur to drive you to the stores."

It was settled. They've devised a simple plan to occupy themselves for the few weeks on the island. Jackie agreed she would not go out anywhere by herself. She would call Deidre and ask her to come up to the house, every morning that is, if the nurse preferred to sleep on board the yacht.

The following day as planned, Penman went off early, apparently at five-thirty. He had spoken to Rayno the day before, and it was the steward who had advised him that the sooner the better, that it was broad daylight by five-thirty, and that the cool mornings were better for running.

As far as Penman could remember, it was more than twenty years since he had attempted to run any distance. But over the past few weeks, an important part of his life that had been so long neglected or ignored, had been joyfully revived. Now he was full of enthusiasm to get himself in trim.

They started off exactly as planned. And they had covered about one hundred yards when he had to stop. They walked another hundred yards and commenced jogging again. After covering about the same distance, he was again forced to stop. Then he sat down on the edge of the sand, his legs stretched out while his body and head laid back amongst the weeds. There they rested for about fifteen minutes, But once he'd recovered his breath, Penman started talking.

He discovered that Rayno liked his job very much. In his wildest dream, he had never imagined he would have found a job that was so cushy: Sailing the oceans, and so many days and weeks doing very little. Then Penman asked how he was getting on with Deidre? Penman sat up and found him grinning. He also reckoned his steward was blushing, but couldn't be sure, as his dark complexion failed to show the colour change. But he quickly agreed that Deidre was a very nice girl, they were getting on fine. They were a very good team on board the yacht.

They decided to push on once more and after another two spells of about a hundred yards, Penman felt his body aching all over: His stomach ached, his jaws ached, and worst of all were his knees and ankles, even his insteps. All because he had not attempted to run for such a long time, those muscles and joints had never been forced to carry his weight at any more than walking pace. Rayno assured him it would get better by the day, and that he should not attempt to run every morning. It should be every other day, so as to give his joints and ligaments time to heal. They ran on some more, but the next hundred yards were just as painful. Then, after trying to rest his joints, Penman felt himself aching so bad, he could scarcely walk. In the end he managed to hobble back to their starting point. So the first morning was severe torture, but was considered a worthy effort.

Rayno assured him that the ginseng tablets were very good for all-round fitness, and it would prove itself in a week. That it was his stomach and joints that were aching because he had not been flexing those muscles, that he really had the stamina to run three miles once his joints had got used to the strain.

Penman liked the steward's explanation, it made good sense. And he was looking forward to running three miles in a month or so. Sweat poured from his body and a lot of impurities were drained from him. The small sweat towel had been saturated and, luckily, Rayno had brought a spare towel for him. So much for the first morning.

It was about nine o'clock when Penman returned to the house.

He was comfortable with his aches and pains, he was able to move about without exhibiting any obvious discomfort. Of course, he made his way to the dining room before Jackie became aware of his arrival. But she had instructed the maid to let her know when he arrived, and that she would take charge of his breakfast. Jackie soon presented him with a small dish of grapefruit segments. He went on to enjoy the appetizing starter while she quickly prepared fresh scrambled eggs and toast for both of them. She removed her blue and white bib to reveal herself in a light blue sleeveless dress. They chatted while they ate and finally, while they enjoyed their glasses of ice cold orange juice, she told him that the children and all at home were fine. Her mother's bank details were on the desk in his study. Then she told him she and Deidre were heading off to Kingston, to the stores. They may be gone for about two hours.

It suited Penman well, he had things to do and would work

better without her there. For nearly two months he had neglected his work, finding it difficult to switch his mind from her. He was still reveling in the novelty of having her to himself, having taken her over completely. But she was clouding his mind. Every time she put on a different dress, he seemed to be looking at her anew, the picture she presented seemed so fresh and tantalizing. He needed the break while knowing she was safe.

He went to his study knowing he could work for a couple of hours without being distracted. He needed to contact his stockbroker to get some figures and to make one or two important decisions. But first things first, he arranged with his bank manager to transfer five thousand pounds into the lady's account with immediate effect, thus complying with the first part of some instructions Penman had left him the day before his departure from Sandgate. That done, he got on with his other business.

It was just after midday when Jackie returned. Out on the patio, next to the pool, she sat in front of him and, much like a pretty teenage daughter who was very close to her well loved father, she explained everything in a mixture of excitement and disappointment. Firstly, the only items of clothing she brought back for herself were two sets of bikinis, two scarves and two sets of slippers. The only beach jacket she found in the two top stores they'd visited were the same three that she'd bought in London. Nothing else. But the manageress in one store came up with a fantastic idea. Jackie was to choose the materials and the jackets would be made and ready in four days. The manageress had explained that she was in contact with a local dressmaker who would make the garments, providing even better quality than those from abroad. So there! She had chosen lovely materials, in four colours, to be mixed so that she would have a different colour for every day of the week.

Then she gave him a soft parcel. "Open it," she said, "it's for you."

He was curious. "What is it?"

"It's a surprise."

He followed her instructions and began to unwrap the soft paper parcel. Slowly he went on to reveal three sports shirts of light Caribbean colours which immediately excited his thinking.

"I didn't imagine you were shopping for me?"

"I couldn't resist them." She laughed. "I had to buy them for you." And she took them from him and put another parcel on his knees. "There's another one for you to open."

"Jackie, my dear, you've gone out of your way."

"Open it, please," she said with loving insistence.

Karl opened the second parcel and there were three pairs of shorts, different colours with discreet patterns. He could not disguised the fact that he liked them. The combinations of shirts and shorts would transform his outlook. "I've never bothered with golf, my dear, but you've suddenly made me recall that there are three or four good courses right here on the island. I might even get around to visiting one or two."

Penman attempted to put on one of the new shirts right there in front of her. But Jackie refused to let him. She pointed out that the garments smelt of textile, that she would have them rinsed right away.

Jackie and Deidre were soon changing into sports outfits, they went on to practice on the tennis court. Particularly for Deidre, it was good for her to play at something rather than to stay in one place in the hot sun. Her complexion was a delicate white and she was aware of it. The two were to spend many days together, swimming or playing. This was also good for Penman. For along with his new training programme, it allowed him time to get back into phase with some of his previous activities.

Two mornings later, at five-thirty, Penman was back on the beach with Rayno for his second outing. This time they jogged for more than two hundred yards before he needed to rest. And he was pleased with his progress. They rested for about fifteen minutes, chatting away and commenting on the yachts that were off shore. When they took off again, he jagged for about two hundred yards before agonizing with pain. They rested another fifteen minutes and went on jogging for another two spells before deciding to walk the return leg. He was contented with his progress, for this time walking back was not as distressing as before. Penman was happy with his breathing too, if only his joints and ligaments were strong enough, he could easily have gone on for three miles before running out of breath. He would keep on taking the ginseng tablets, but would ignore the egg flip drink for a while. He hadn't drank any for nearly a week. He laughed when disclosing this information to Rayno. He sweated as much on this run as he did before, and already his senses were telling him that his body was melting down.

Penman kept up with his running for the next three weeks. He played very little tennis, but he swam in the evenings and enjoyed the pool with Jackie. She had improved her strength and was swimming the length of the pool a dozen times in the evening, though at a leisurely pace. And this was how they spent their days in the warm Caribbean climate.

Jackie was enjoying her fresh look day by day, with her full set of beach jackets and bikinis. She took special care with her appearance. Using no make up at all, she resorted to just the two oils. The olive oil she would use one day, and the refined coconut oil the next. After her morning shower, she would apply the oil to the parts of her body that would be covered by the bikinis, she would put them on and then the jacket. At about midmorning, after their late breakfast, she would go off to the private balcony where Penman would join her. She would simply remove the jacket, apply a little oil to her face, and then lie flat on the extra wide sun bed. Penman would pull up a stool and got on with the exciting job of applying the oil to the rest of her body. He would start at her neck and worked around the bikinis, all the way down to her feet. Then she would turn over and simply close her eyes while he enjoyed the ritual.

She soon got used to looking forward to these late morning relaxation, knowing full well that on the private balcony, he was enjoying her as much as he wanted. And always, just before finishing off with the ritual, Penman would spend time savouring her toes in his mouth, one by one, before finally anointing them with the oil. On the mornings after his run, these sessions would also prove extremely relaxing for him.

One morning when he was back from his run, before having breakfast, the maid, Betsy, presented Penman with two letters. He opened them straight away, seeing that one was from the UK. But the second letter contained an invitation card from the Jamaican finance ministry. A dinner and dance function was being held at the New Kingston Hotel, to celebrate the continuing success of the Corporate Development Programme. The date of the celebration would be in two weeks time. The ministry was also apologizing for the late invitation, as they were not aware until recently, that the millionaire was on the island.

As Jackie was busy preparing breakfast, Penman chuckled at the thought. He placed the invitation card on her side of the table. The decision whether to go or not to go, would be hers. At length, when they were finishing off their breakfast, she looked at it and suddenly decided that they would go. She'd not been to a ballroom dance in more than three years. And she does have a dress that was suitable. She was also aware that he had brought at least one suit that would fit the occasion.

The invitation became the subject of discussion on the balcony, with mutual agreement that they would attend. She was indeed looking forward to it. They were both fit and she needed to stretch her legs.

Two weeks later, on a day when Penman was not running, he was in a particularly good mood. For he had ran four miles the day before, in two sessions of two miles. Such was his fitness, and he had lost a stone in weight over the many weeks of running. He had spent most of the day in his study while Jackie was reading through a book of romantic poetry she'd found in his small library.

It was the day of the dinner dance, to be held in the late evening. In the middle of the afternoon, Jackie put the book aside and threw herself in the pool for a few quick lengths. Then she came out and dried herself briefly before putting on a long blouse over her bikini and throwing the towel over her shoulder. As she paused on the patio, she carefully removed a rose from the vase by the door. Holding it to her nose, she inhaled deeply and admired the purple columbine before walking off. In the drawing room, she poured a long glass of grape juice over three cubes of ice and carried it with her. At the door to the study, she told Penman she was going to her room, that it was near the time when they should be getting ready.

Jackie was especially carefully with herself under the shower. Afterwards she applied a small amount of texture and combed her hair purposefully, finally using a ribbon over the top, so that it disappeared at the sides under heavy tresses. She applied just a little oil to her cheeks. More than half an hour was spent in front of the mirror. This profound care was unusual; it was done with enthusiasm. But she disagreed with her own look when finally she gazed at herself. It was the kind of image she would have frowned upon two or three years ago, for it actually expressed a little more then her real character. Not only was it pleasing and rich, it was dazzling, bewitching and sexy with a hint of aggression. In the white dressing gown she appeared quite sensual. Yet she smiled fondly. If Karl had never seen her like this, it would be interesting to note his reaction.

The small clock in one corner of the dressing table showed her it was near five pm. On the other side of the mirror, in a similar position, was a small barometer which hardly ever read anything but fair or dry. While the sun was low on the horizon, she was in no hurry to dress, knowing of course that it would take only a few minutes to slip into a silk dress.

According to the invitation card the dinner and dance was schedule for seven pm., an invitation from the Corporate Development Committee. The occasion would mark an important stage in the island's development programme; of which Penman was a significant investor. Five years ago when the island had launched itself on a giant civil engineering and development drive, some thirty million pound worth of shares were offered to the public. This sum was largely raised from overseas investors and Penman had been generous in throwing in a million pounds that had been lying idle in Britain at a time when the British economy had been depressed. I fact he had been speculating seriously on getting it across to Africa where prospects were good and the promise of a fat return was only threatened by unpredictable government policies. But British economic policy had made it impossible to transfer that kind of cash, and it was then that he had thrown the lot in the Jamaican Development Fund as a panic measure, since the island was in the Sterling Area, the investment was for ten years and was now in its first half term. Karl was therefore on the list of important guests and would receive a grand welcome. The journey to the New Kingston Hotel would take about fifteen minutes, twenty at the most.

This was their first engagement since arriving on the island two months ago, an important engagement to which Karl was looking forward. So was Jackie. It was a chance to see something of this sun-drenched island in all its beauty and splendour.

When the door opened and Karl walked in, already dressed, Jackie greeted him in a most unusual manner. She sprang from the dressing table where she had been merely passing the time, her white gown trailing on the carpet. Karl stood in his tracks by the side of the ottoman, to receive her.

"Well, I thought you'd never get here. You might have told me you were ready."

But he soon pointed out that there was ample time. "We don't leave for another half-hour."

"Oh good." She straightened his bow tie and kissed his cheeks.

He held firm. "You surprise me."

Jackie smiled a tempting smile. "You like it, don't you?"

Karl stood back a little and let his eyes fell to her lips. Her complexion was remarkably dazzling. The very cleft where the floods of her gown went low, jolted him. There was no sign of anything beneath the grown and her cool, golden flesh rose forcefully before disappearing under the white folds. When at last their eyes met, he found her rich and dreamy. Jackie went to him like a child, with her arms reaching inside his dinner jacket and circling behind his shoulders; meanwhile Karl had found her lips. It was more than three days since he had made love to her, the gap was immediately apparent. As his face fell to her hair, he inhaled the new fragrance and, quite intoxicated; he plunged himself quite suddenly to her neck and shoulders.

It was a remarkable episode, for he soon slumped to the ottoman where her very nearness was particularly effective. He worked himself through the folds of the gown to her flesh, and was buried there for a time. Jackie felt the sensation and held him fast. Then, without a word, he hastily removed his clothes, tearing away everything down to the boxer shorts where he found himself ready and impatient. They worked themselves onto the bed where they remained in a tremendous orgy. The feeling that had driven her from the pool was further inflamed by the grape and passion fruit mix. She might even have passed off the attack, but despite the cool shower, the heat of the day had made it so impossible. It had not been intentional, yet she had stepped form under it with the uncontrollable propulsion of a full blooded demand. It was no wonder that she had surpassed herself at the dressing table, and had thus emerged with a burning flesh that had even astonished and frightened her.

Up to now the two months on the hot island had been good to her. Along with her activities in the pool, on the tennis court and in the gardens, she had also passed a few evenings watching movies. Karl had even allowed her to add words to the few feet of film he had taken of her, and she had been going to bed tired and sleepy. But today an old feeling had got the better of her. Thus unable to decide what had sparked it off, Jackie was startled by the very thought of the chauffeur, even when he was nowhere in sight.

Embedded in her now, Karl was powerful and restless. She clutched him and frantically arched her body to him, took his heavy thrust, and relaxed with impatience. Yet driven by his own demand, he was hardly aware of her. For he pressed on without a pause, furiously, ungratefully, while her mind took on the full weight of his relentlessness before collapsing under exhaustion. Then, as he lay back, quite inactive, she turned and huddled her head to his chest, her breast softly compressing his stomach. After a time she glanced at his lifeless face, kissed him happily and resumed her moments of absolute peace.

Despite their plans, they had actually forgotten themselves, quite abandoned, sunk deep in the rich luxury of their own flesh. Karl had dozed off while she had quietly relapsed into unusual meditation. When at last he stirred and felt her softness against him, the room was dark, ghostly, and lit only by a grey light that came from the half moon that was already high in the sky. The temperature had taken a plunge and a chill wind blew though the open window. He reached a hand to the padded shelf and felt for the light switch. Unsuccessful, he reached himself up further, so that his head now rested on the pillow, then his hand went back to the shelf and found the switch.

It was the bedside lamp that came on, its cool orange shade flooding the room with a romantic hue. There were two of these lamps, one at each side of the bed. Jackie raised her head and covered herself with the dressing gown. Karl showed little awareness. He merely gazed at her, her face a delicious peach, soft and delicate. He extended a hand to pull her to him. But she protested.

"It's very late," she pointed out. And secretly reflecting that he must have slept for more than an hour while she had lain there in silent meditation.

"It can't be undone," he said, sounding regretful. But the remark conveyed none of his true feelings. He was proud of what had happened and his inner self was overjoyed. "It is late, I know. We've missed the engagement."

"There's still time. We could catch the last couple of hours."

Karl chuckled. He rose and found his clothes, but this was only in response to a greater instinct. "The worst thing a man can do under the circumstance, is to arrive an hour before the end of a banquet. It is absurd."

She was about to leave the bed, to get ready. But his last words struck her. "You mean we're not going at all?"

"Precisely."

She sat on the edge of the bed clutching her gown to her body, quite bewildered. It was already nine o'clock. Karl took off towards his bedroom. Suddenly Jackie dashed off to her bathroom where she spent five minutes. Then she was back and putting on her clothes, the very clothes she'd laid out for the evening. She wasn't sure why, but it seemed the right thing to do.

In a few minutes Karl had gone, he had simply put on some casuals and had done a quick dash to the drawing room cabinet where he drank two small glasses of his favourite primer. Back in his bed room, he poured a glass of port and was sipping it slowly when he returned to her room to find her at her dressing table.

"Oh, you've given up completely?" she observed.

He chuckled. "This is no time to be rushing off, my dear. We must forget it. I will make some excurse."

"What kind of excuse?"

"Anything to remedy my absence. I am a busy man, they all know that."

He was tempting her with a drink, but she shook her head, preferring only fruit juice.

"It will have to be a good excuse, you know. It was an important engagement."

"The Jamaican authorities won't be entirely disappointed. They know I am here simply because I love the island. If anything, only the High Commissioner might consider himself hard done."

"But what will you say?"

"I will you write a letter, tomorrow."

"No, Karl. That won't do. You're a very important guest. Surely they will be expecting you, even at the last moment."

He searched his mind. "Perhaps you're right. They'll be expecting to hear something tonight."

He put the glass aside and went up behind her. With just her hair left to be tidied up, she was already looking grand. He put a hand on her shoulder, then lowered his head and kissed her neck.

"Please go and do something now, Karl. Don't leave it any longer. Get Betsy to phone them, say you've taken ill." Jackie suddenly recouped. "Ah, perhaps it's best if I ring the hall and tell them you're ill. Yes, it should be myself, or Deidre. And it wouldn't be right to call her now."

"So, I'm to leave it up to you?"

"Yes," she consented. "It's best if I do it. We will go to the drawing room. I will do it from there."

Jackie managed to re-do her hair, back in the style it was before he'd got into it. She stood up from the dressing table and he was mesmerized. Penman stood back and allowed her walking space. The ivory silk dress, sleeveless with a modest neckline, was stunning. The skirt flowed easily, dropping just below the knees and fitted her freely.

"Come, come," he said proudly, "we must go to the drawing room." And he gave a bow and a flourish, allowing her to lead the way.

Jackie walked away, in her normal gait. And it was enough for him to scold himself for missing the ball. Even without a tiara, she would have stood out amongst the women, a perfect star. Her sheer beauty would have made him the leading man.

In the drawing room she was a picture of elegance. But she was more concern with repairing the damage he had done himself.

"Will you find the letter, please. It should have a telephone number on it."

He found the letter and brought it to her. Jackie seated herself at the telephone table and rang the hotel, asked to be put through to the grand ballroom where the function was taking place. She asked for a name and made a note of it. Then she passed on the information that Mr Karl Penman was taken ill four hours ago. It was not considered serious, as he was still expecting to meet his engagements. But a stomach bug was causing him great inconvenience. He sends his apologies to the High Commissioner, the Finance Minister, and the Development Committee."

During the phone call, Penman, in white trousers and sports shirt, leaned against the back of an easy chair and watched her with tremendous admiration. His heart was no longer in his body, he had removed it and placed it in her. As she completed the phone call, he made towards her, to take her in his arms.

But Jackie avoided him. "I want to go out."

"We can't go out, my dear. Not before tomorrow."

"Why not? I need fresh air."

"I'm down with a stomach bug. We might be seen."

She stared at him for a moment, then softened with a clever smile.

"I think some good music would help you get over it." And he went over to the stereo deck which was situated next to the drinks cabinet.

Penman quickly found one of his favourite music tapes, it was 'Manuel and the music of the mountains'. He inserted it in the cassette deck and switched it on. He turned the volume up in order to fill the room with romance. It had to be right for her. Then he poured a glass of fruit juice for her and put in some ice. For himself, he had iced Dubonnet. By the time the second piece of music came up, Jackie's eyes were gleaming, reflecting the light from the chandeliers. She took his glass from his hand and put it aside, then lead him to a section of the floor where they began dancing.

The next half hour she floated through Penman's arms like a cool breeze on a warm day. So light on her feet, her suppleness was all the more enhanced by the easy flow of the music. Then her twisting and turning, the occasional whirl, made him recalled that she had once danced for a living. As for him, had he not been working on his body, enough to have been able to keep pace with her. Not only was he lighter and fitter, his feet movements reflected it, and he was relishing every moment with her.

When at length she decided to have a break, he was glad. For he needed the break some four dances previously. But she had made him follow her movements. He didn't have to work hard, he didn't have to follow her every move, but he had to stay with her. Then he knew for certain that she would have been in her own element at the ball. He wouldn't have danced more than two consecutive pieces with her, for others would have taken her off his hands. She would have loved the big occasion, the grand presentation.

As they sat down, Penman knew she was only giving him a rest. She crossed her legs and the ivory shoes with their inch and a half heels, shimmered under the lights. He left his chair for a moment and turned the music down so that they could talk.

"I can see from this gorgeous dress, and shoes, you came prepared for the odd night out."

"When you said two to three months, the thought did cross my mind that we might go out on the odd occasion."

"It seemed I've kept you cooped up when you really wanted the odd night out. I will do something about it. Shall I."

"No," said Jackie.

Penman looked at her seriously. "You don't want me to do something about it?"

"Not because you feel obliged to."

He reflected suddenly. "Sorry, my dear. I was being silly."

Jackie sipped her drink. Penman emptied his glass and helped himself to a refill.

"How many of those have you had?" she asked.

He seemed puzzled. "Three or four, I'm not sure." He knew she'd been keeping an eye on the amount he'd been drinking ever since they came ashore. And he was rather flattered. In fact, because of her, he had reduced his intake by half. "This is my last for tonight," he decided. "If I need another, it will be your fruit juice."

The tune that came on was something she liked: 'I Talk To The Trees.' There were set movements lodged in her subconscious for this one. She rose to her feet and did an elegant turn.

"Can I, please Karl."

He straightened up and hastily went to the music deck, turned the tape back a little, then increased the volume and came back to her.

"Your wish is my command." And he followed her to the dance space.

She floated into him, they clasped their hands in each others, and she went off on a waltz. Penman simply followed her movements, holding her, supporting her, positioning his hands and feet for the graceful twists and turns of her body. He became engrossed in her movements, his mind and body lost to her. His features took on her smiles as he lost himself in the magic of her suppleness. They did the waltz and a slow waltz, the cha-cha, wherever the music took them. Then he was totally lost in the rumba, for it brought her body into him, their pulses phased and his senses heightened. But Jackie was very much in control, and shielding him so that when the music ended, she lead him to the lounge chair.

Jackie removed her shoes and remained in stocking feet. They quenched their thirsts with the Dubonnet and fruit juice.

Penman gazed at her seriously. "I think it would be a good idea for me to take you to a couple of places tomorrow."

"Why tomorrow?" she asked with a smile.

"You're very much in the mood to go out and the morning is not far away."

"Karl, you have me to yourself. You can take me wherever you want, whenever you choose."

Her statement was suddenly the sweetest music Penman had ever heard in his adult life. He took it to heart." You do me a great honour, my dear. You've made it very clear. I don't have to guess and run the risk of getting it wrong. Now I want to say something that I haven't mentioned before."

Jackie's face changed slightly, but her eyes still twinkled.

She thought of putting her feet up and resting her head in his lap, but she was in her best dress and wouldn't feel right.

Instead, she sat at the other end of the lounge chair and,

leaning back against the padded arm, she raised her feet to his lap. She'd developed a great skill of knowing how best to please him.

"You're going to tell me something important about yourself, so I need to make myself comfortable.

Penman smoothed his hands along her legs, one after the other, down to her feet where the silk stockings protected her toes.

"I haven't told you before that I am separated from my wife. Now you're hearing it for the first time."

"Separated," she echoed, quite astonished. "How long?"

"Three years."

Leaning back, Jackie folded her arms. She was having to digest the statement. "Am I hearing you correctly, Karl? You're separated from your wife?"

"That's correct. We're separated."

"Has it been made public?"

"Discreetly."

There was silence. Karl was confident and demanding no sympathy. He had stumbled onto something very precious. Now he must rid himself of everything in order to grasp it with both hands. Toying with her legs, he studied her closely.

"Does it mean anything to you?" he asked, breaking the silence.

She was thinking seriously. But the news wasn't affecting her. She had never met the woman. Mrs Penman was an unknown person. He had said very little about her. Only that she was sometimes in Australia, and was pursuing a project of her own making.

"Three years is a long time," she said. "Are you planning a reconciliation?" Her question was automatic, it didn't reflect her feelings, merely protecting them.

"I am planning a divorce, as soon as possible."

She was shocked into silence. She didn't expect such a forthright reply. But he was studying her and noticed that her smile was still there, the twinkle had gone from her eyes.

He went on to say, "I've found a very important pearl and I want to keep it. Something very precious. Believe me, I don't want to lose it."

"You found a pearl, without diving?" She heard her voice asking.

"Sometimes the tide does bring ashore something precious."

"But the coastline is endless, Karl."

"Fate, my dear, brought me to it."

"Where is it?"

"The pearl is right here, in my arms." Lowering his head and bringing her legs up from his lap, he kissed them both.

"Karl, are you being serious? I hope you're thinking properly."

"I want you to be my wife, Jackie. I don't want to lose you at all. If you think back to our first meeting, and look closely at the developing stages, I am sure you will find my proposal justified. It certainly wouldn't seem strange."

She reflected quickly. It was true. Her first opinion had been right. He was a man of considerable strength and self-importance. He had been alone for a long time and naturally she had failed to understand why he had taken to her with such profound interest. She was utterly confused, and hadn't really considered whether she would want to surrender her whole self to him, forever. But what else could she do with her life? Only the night before when speaking to her mother, she'd learnt that he had transferred another five thousand pounds to her account. He was more than capable of providing for her and the children. And besides, she had not imagined herself spending another day with Pascoe.

"I don't like the sound of the word 'divorce.' It sound quite horrid, like complete rejection of another person. It's distasteful."

"It is really not as bad as it sounds, my dear. It simply means giving ourselves the opportunity to marry each other."

He could have put it differently, but he was really making a persuasive effort to condition her into digesting his plans. She occupied his mind so much that, when he was not with her, Jackie's image, her loveliness, seemed to travel with him. Her calm and gentle nature had become the essence of his existence.

Penman knew that in a few weeks he would have to return her to Ashford, and the longer it takes her to agree, the longer he may have to stay on the island, just to have her to himself.

He suddenly remembered that they had not eaten for six hours or more. He did not want to break the spell they were in. Discussing their future together was exciting. She hadn't yet agreed, but he was concerned for her well being.

"It's time I got you something to eat, my dear."

"No," she said. And she hastily swung her legs from his lap and stood up. "You're making me feel ashamed, Karl. It is I who should find you something to eat. I need to change, can I leave you for a minute?"

"Of course." He conceded.

"And you mustn't go to the kitchen, not till I'm back."

"I shall obey your every word, my dear."

She took her shoes to hand and fled to her room.

He did not have to wait long. In less than five minutes she was back, wearing a plain long blouse. They spent an hour in the kitchen where Betsy had left them a light meal, eventually retiring to their separate rooms, very tired.

The outdoor life was disturbed only momentarily. It rained on few occasions for which the flowers were thankful. It also cleansed the atmosphere of dust and burnt air. The garden bloomed with freshness even before the spring, gracing the front of the great house with splendid verities. Acting on instructions form Jackie, the gardener had planted a huge bed of African marigolds which came out in yellow and orange. Along with these were two beds of hydrangeas, and in each, the blue and shocking pink bloomed over broad green leaves. Some were even white. And along the front patio loomed purple salvias and scarlet geraniums. Then, lining the path and steps, in narrow beds, the gladioli grew straight with absolute freedom.

All this provided rich background to the movie film. Karl employed himself impetuously, sprinting and dodging behind trees, catching her candidly in spectacular moods. She often emerged from the pool in blue or red bikini under a glossy beach jacket, and at times even in white swimsuit and cap. But whatever the attire, the shapely contours of her majestic profile delighted him most.

Even the gardener regarded the season as his most successful ever, for he had often found himself working next to her; when she would stand close to him while trimming the dead leaves. At such times he would keep his head low for fear of catching her eye, which would only cause him some embarrassment. Yet seized by her nearness, his face often took on a staunch ecstasy.

Only on the tennis court did Jackie show any restriction, for although she admired the game, she was actually out of touch. Now she refused to take long strides and was certainly not prepared to toss herself about. Not that the demand of the game was too much; she was merely playing reserve while exhibiting a childlike naivety which Karl regarded as one of her best aspects. Nevertheless, she played well, with increasing fluency which he accepted as the product of his gentle tuition. After an hour of this they would make for the pool. They often relaxed on the patio, or in the huge drawing room, the balcony outside their window being reserved for cool evenings, or early mornings when the full blast of the sun was not too severe.

In fact, the balcony was ideal when they were up early to catch the golden rays, for it was high and undisturbed; and caught the sun first thing, while the shaded areas remained cool and at nine o'clock were still wet with dew. But with the purple curtains drawn over the white nets, the nights travelled on: and only when they were thrown back, sometimes not before eleven, was the daylight effectively convincing.

Weeks and months rushed by unnoticed. Not once had they visited Kingston. Though less that fifteen minutes in the big Lincoln, the chauffeur actually ran errands, fetching all the time, even making decisions on behalf of the millionaire.

The house was an excellent hide-out: snug and well placed, its romantic surroundings spoiled them. And with the aid of the binoculars they viewed the great harbor.

Chapter Nineteen

Towards the end of April the vacation took the final turn. Jackie boarded the yacht with uncertainty. She tried to enjoy the final weeks, the glorious days of homeward sailing, and for the few nights Penman had stayed away from her bed, she had actually slept peacefully.

He was now anxious to get back to England. He had neglected his affairs, having left instructions that he should not be disturbed. But after six months he was suddenly restless with the lack of news. Yet having accepted Jackie as the woman in his life, he was pleased with himself. She was close to him, their understanding firm. But one other matter would affect their illicit love!

Nursing the dream of a new yacht, he would seek news from the Italian makers as soon as possible. He was sick of the Grey Lady with only two luxury cabins and limited facilities. His extravagance had rocketed and a thousand things must be rearranged to satisfy his new longing. They landed on the south coast in the last week of May and Penman moored the Grey Lady as though it had made its last voyage. True enough, the enthusiasm to sail her again had weakened. She was regarded as not good enough to accommodate his mistress, and he left the crew on board without instructions.

It rained miserably and they came off the sand with two crew members bearing a large plastic sheet over their heads. The drive to the house at Sandgate was short, only a mile or so. Karl could scarcely withhold his enthusiasm. He looked at Jackie with apparent fondness. "You might not take another trip in the Grey Lady, my dear. Perhaps you'd like to see the end of her!"

She returned his friendly smile, but did not share his opinion. She could not imagine why he should have thought that. But he soon explained that it was small, hardly enough to keep her occupied, and she must have been bored. While in fact this was not true, and she endeavoured to make it clear. She had enjoyed every minute of it. He must have noticed that she was impressed. Yes, he said, but only at the start. Coming back, she did not seem entirely herself.

So he had noticed. "Yes, you're right. But the yacht had nothing to do with it."

"No? You didn't think it was too small? You didn't think your quarters lacked anything? And the lounge. It was ridiculous. The projector was always in the way. Even the deck was narrow. And the stairs!"

But he was forgetting one thing: that it was her first experience on a private yacht. In fact it was grand. She had hardly noticed the small inadequacies.

He suddenly reflected. "True, I suppose it would have been very interesting. After all, I was taken in when I took it over myself."

They'd reached the house. Karl escorted her to a small drawing room that was carefully decorated. Then he showed her into a large bedroom at the top of two flights of carpeted stairs. It was the master bedroom, with two principal beds and a table between. He studied her reaction.

"If you want the whole thing rearranged, it will be done at once."

In order to please her, he had forgotten himself.

"But why? This is quite satisfactory. I love it."

Still he was curious. He wanted to know what was wrong. "You haven't been yourself in the past few days. You're obviously not happy. Why?"

Jackie fled to his arms. It had not occurred to her that she'd been so obvious. But after a moment's embrace, she drew away and observed the interior with a little smile. "This room is spacious and well prepared. Why, it even smells new." She looked at the carpet and wondered if it wasn't really new. The wall was an immaculate cream, the ceiling freshly painted; the whole interior had a distinct newness. Why was everything freshly prepared for her?

"Well," she continued, "perhaps I ought to tell you that you're not to blame. The truth is, it grieved me when I thought I might have to go back to the bungalow. I was actually forced to consider my situation seriously."

"That was unnecessary. You knew you were coming here before we left the island."

"Yes, but I still have to visit the bungalow. And the reality of it bothers me now that we're back. I could not take my mind completely away form it."

"Then you'd prefer to have stayed in Jamaica?"

"It is more than that; it's a feeling that is unavoidable. No matter where I was, it would have been no different. If I had left the bungalow for good, I would have experienced this feeling at the beginning. It isn't something that can be driven away before it is apparent. But I'm already getting over it."

Karl smiled happily. The picture he was looking at gave him new energy. He was madly infatuated. The white and grey floral dress caught his eye. He was aware of his great fortune. It was a brilliant idea; she would be his entirely.

The next day he restricted her movements. He persuaded Jackie to remain in the house, to make herself familiar with it. There was no need to rush back to the bungalow, they would visit it at the weekend. Then they would call on Mary. But she reminded him that Mary would be in Spain. It was that time of the year. He accepted with a smile, and in a kind flourish persuaded her to take over the house and dismiss the idea of ever returning to the bungalow.

From her new bedroom window she watched the purple Rolls Royce out of sight, and then threw herself full length across the bed. The ecstatic life would prevail. She had every intention of making sure it did. The matter of the bungalow was taken up by Karl. He gave instruction to this lawyer to settle the overdue rent with the estate agents; then a man was sent along to drive Jackie's car down to Sandgate.

A fortnight later, when she had ventured to leave the bedroom, Karl drove Jackie up to the bungalow for a final look. Her memory of the place, though vivid, seemed long in the past. She felt even a little embarrassed at its smallness, its shallow atmosphere and bourgeois furniture. Her position with Karl seemed so well established that the past must be forgotten at all cost, since it triggered unpleasant memories, unhealthy events which she was eager to forget. She walked about the bungalow with folded arms, sealed lips, a superior air, only putting out a hand now and again to open a door, or remove a picture.

The sight of two tins of fruit in the larder unbalanced her; they represented much indignity. To think that she had once called this home and the scant little kitchen had been the heart of her life! Afraid to open the refrigerator, she quickly ran her mind back to the day she had left, wondering whether she had emptied it before switching off the electricity. The details were hard to trace and nothing was clear. Then, undecidedly, she pulled back the door, it was empty. Mary had seen to it for her. Now she closed it with a sigh of relief.

Karl was somewhere in the living room. Heaven knows what be must think of her! Suddenly she wanted to get away from the bungalow. To be haunted by such memories was unnecessary.

He was standing next to the cabinet which was in fact the drinks shelf. He had found a bottle of Martel and had used his handkerchief as a duster. It still had its original seal.

She looked at him. "Shall we go?"

Karl held up the bottle. "Perhaps we should have a final drink, don't you think?"

But she shrugged and gave no inclination that she wanted to get involved with anything at the bungalow. How strange it all seemed, now that she'd escaped from this place which had tormented her so much.

But he had no such thought in mind. Naturally he wanted a glass, but had simply swung open the cabinet door, took out two glasses, inspected them carefully and decided that they were clouded by a film of dust. He glanced at her enquiringly and went through to the kitchen, hardly knowing where it was, but intent on finding it.

Suddenly Jackie realized her indiscretion: had she chosen correctly she would have kept him away from the kitchen. Now the thought of him washing his own glass in front of her actually appalled her.

He was back with the two glasses, spotless, in one hand, his handkerchief in the other. She regretted the simple misunderstanding but watched as he uncapped the bottle of Martel and filled the two glasses. He handed one to her. Jackie looked apprehensively at the bottle.

"You know very well I don't care for that," she said.

"It is harmless, my dear. Besides, it's the last one you will have here."

She took the drink and stared at the room with a critical eye. Karl pretended not to notice

Putting the glass to her lips, she suddenly stopped short. The smell of he rich liquid stung her.

"Well, perhaps there's something more to your taste." And he began another search in the cabinet.

From the bottom shelf he came up with a new bottle and dusted it off. "Champagne?" but the bottle was less than half-full. He removed the cork and put the bottle to his nose for approval. "Perfect," he said, and looked at her for consent.

Her lips were sealed.

Using the empty glass to sample the champagne, he nodded a further approval and filled it for her. Then, as she brought it to her lips, he said sportingly:

"We'll drink to the dust of this graceful bungalow," and he treated himself to the glass of Martel that she had previously refused.

"Graceful!" she echoed at length.

"Naturally. It seemed an ideal seclusion."

"Convenience is a better description."

Karl recapped the two bottles and returned them to the cabinet.

"There's no need to leave them there," she reminded him.

"Oh, the removal chaps will consider themselves fortunate, I'm sure."

The removal chaps indeed, for with her approval, he had arranged for the furniture to be auctioned off. It would be collected shortly. A week later the estate agents would reclaim the property.

They were late getting back to Sandgate. Once back in the spacious drawing room, her gaiety returned.

Karl occupied himself with interesting plans. Having taken action before they'd left Jamaica, the final documents of his divorce were now in his hand. He prided himself on his new freedom. He would marry Jackie at all cost. His infatuation with her was on the increase, for he rushed back from London daily.

Jackie had not been unyielding towards her own proceedings. The lawyer Karl had recommended was skilful and, according to him, the matter was a simple one. Pascoe was in jail. That alone was a crime against her own integrity.

She drove the Fiat on one or two occasions when Karl was out, but her taste had actually outgrown the little car. Being noisy and very light, there were little room inside for real comfort, and the suspension seemed to fall into every little hole in the road. She was dissatisfied with the cheap upholstery, and besides, in such good weather, a convertible was preferable.

Returning from Folkstone one evening with all the widows down, there was still an apparent lack of cool air. The result was that she perspired greatly from the heat and felt terribly uneasy. Then, arriving at the house, she left the car in front of the garage, slamming the door in disgust. An hour later when Karl arrived he was forced to park the Rolls behind it.

He mentioned the situation to her at the dinner table, and pointed out that there was ample room in the garage for both cars. But she simply made it clear that she had to get out quickly, that she had been roasting with the heat. When he eventually caught on, he readily agreed that a convertible would be more appropriate. She was in no hurry to disclose her real desire, however, but he, nevertheless, maintained that it ought to be, adding that she could have had the hood down and another thing, that it would suit her well. He actually scolded himself for not having thought of it before.

Jackie said nothing. But as he pressed her further, she did make a gesture of reservation, saying, "Oh, I doubt if the weather will hold. It is so unpredictable."

But it was settled. She would drive up to London and make the choice.

There were other ideas, too. With great enthusiasm, he went on to list other things he thought she ought to have. And shortly after the new Mercedes 28OSL was delivered, he came in one evening with special champagne for her birthday. Later, he presented her with a diamond necklace, with stones of pale blue. They were rare diamonds, selected for their superb colours. It looked particularly grand against her cool complexion.

Jackie accepted it with a little sigh, as though it was long overdue. It was striking when worn with a low-necked dress. She needed it. Then, before she had got over the excitement, he presented her with a matching ring, slipping it onto her finger himself. She agreed with the utmost sincerity that it was more than a replacement for those she had conveniently removed before the voyage; it also removed any doubt of his intention. Almost at once he pressed the point amiably and suggested that they be married at the first opportunity, pointing out that the solicitor was an efficient chap with a knack for unwrapping those things. It would be an easy matter for him.

Then, with only a dim light in the room, Karl climbed into her bed. The occasion had made it inevitable for them to share the restricted comfort of only one bed, so that he half lay on her, his head supported by an arm while she, resting comfortably, was more concerned with the new diamonds. Now and then she put a finger to his cheek, twisting herself so that the stones would catch the light.

"Are you planning a big wedding?" she asked. It was the first time she had spoken seriously of it.

Karl smiled cordially. "Perhaps I should let you decide."

"Well, we could do it secretly if you wish."

It was a good move. Anything would satisfy him. But to conceal the real bond between them was an even greater satisfaction. It would be good to have his friends guessing. Her indifference to them would please him, and it would tickle them to have others guessing at the real truth.

"Yes. A quiet wedding would be ideal."

"With just three or four witnesses."

They made love well into the night and slept late. It was Jackie who was awake first. The dim light in which they had passed the night was a grayish mist in the room. With faint traces of daylight, the atmosphere was ugly, loathsome.

She untangled herself from the sheets, leaving him undisturbed. Then, over the small nightdress she quickly drew on a dressing gown and fled to the dressing room. In front of the large mirror, her first reaction was to spread her fingers and review the ring. Quite enchanting. With the new air filling her lungs and the natural light from the window, she smiled perfectly. She retrieved the necklace form the bedroom and, baring her neck and shoulders, even to the top of her bosom, she fastened it so that the cluster of diamonds fell neatly to rest above her breast. Yes, it suited her.

Chapter Twenty

Two weeks later Jackie was heading up the A20, sitting back comfortably in the soft leather of the Mercedes 28OSL, with the hood down. She was heading towards London and, having cleared Ashford, the area become nostalgically familiar. At the old turning which led to the abandoned bungalow, she could do nothing to avoid taking note of the little road, but suddenly, with increased speed, she hustled along towards the city.

Crossing the river at Vauxhall Bridge, she was soon in Grovernor Place and going onto Park Llane. At the very top she crossed to Oxford Street and into Baker Street, making her way to Wigmore Street. But she finally found a parking space at the bottom of Harley Street where, releasing the scarf from her hair, she collected her purse and inserted a coin in the parking meter before walking off.

Several blocks down she turned into a small gate and up four steps, then gently turned the handle of a large white door and entered the house. There was a small passage with a recess from which a flight of stairs descended. Down in the passage now, she knocked gently at the door of the reception room. Then, having been invited in, she opened the door and walked through. The waiting room was empty. Quite unusual.

The receptionist, a tall dark-haired girl in a trouser suit, was cordial. 'I take it there hasn't been an appointment?" she asked, courteously. It was merely a formality, since in her appointment book the hour was unlisted.

Jackie admitted there was none. She had chosen a good hour, nevertheless, for the doctor was alone. She would see if he would accommodate her. What name should she say?

"Jacqueline Stewart."

"Mrs?" asked the receptionist in an obvious voice.

Oh! Why must people ask? And before Jackie was able to reply, the girl went off curtly.

Quite alone now, Jackie looked over the room. She was in excellent mood and wouldn't have minded having to wait, especially since she had not bothered to make an appointment. Presently, however, the girl was back, saying that the doctor would see her. Jackie was led down two flight of steps to the basement floor where she was shown into the second room on the right. It could not be mistaken for anything but a surgery. The usual smell was most familiar.

An ancient looking fellow, bearded and scholarly, came forward.

"Good afternoon, Madam."

Jackie accepted a chair.

"What can I do for you? Problems, troubles, they're all under the same heading." Then he added: "I don't usually receive patients without appointments, you know, but you've chosen the right moment; my pleasure."

She returned a thoughtful gaze. "I don't want an examination, just to leave a sample. I could ring for the result, if I may."

'I see. I thought there was nothing wrong. The complexion is quite brilliant; too healthy to have internal suffering." And he considered for a moment. "You're hoping for a confirmation?"

"It would be nice."

The doctor smiled sympathetically.

When she had left the surgery she sat in the car for a time. There was another matter she had in mind.

She drove carefully through the traffic. Fifteen minutes later she was at Trafalgar Square where she parked in a central reservation on Northumberland Road. Towards the square she considered the first jeweler on the left, and entered the store. But the jeweler was attending to a customer. Removing one of her gloves, she looked around the store. Then, after a while the jeweler turned to her:

"Yes Madam, can I help?"

She searched inside her handbag and came up with a small jewellery box, opened it carefully and handed him a gold ring. It was a wedding ring, brilliant, with tiny patterns.

The jewelers eyed it with interest, lowered it to the counter, inspecting it. She presented him with another. This was even more interesting. From a shelf behind him he came up with a small flat box, opened it out on the counter and, with a pair of tweezers, lifted both rings, one after the other and laid them in the felt-lined box. He then held a magnifying glass over them.

"Well, the gold is worth its value, and more. It is very good craftsmanship. The design is recent."

"Can you make an offer?"

He reviewed them thoughtfully. "Thirty-five pounds."

"And the diamond?"

"Yes, the diamond. Will you give me a moment?"

"Certainly."

He lifted the box containing the rings and disappeared to a private room, to inspect the stone under the jeweler's lamp. It was a large stone, mounted with supporting ones at each side. He was soon back. Yes, but it would need careful   cleaning, and the value would be considerably less than its new price.

"The design is modern," Jackie pointed out.

"That is true."

"Well?"

"Four hundred in cash for the two."

That would be fine, she said, without hesitation.

But his lips trembled. "You accept, Madam?"

"Yes, I will take four hundred."

Well then, he would make out a cheque.

"Just a moment," she said, stopping him on the move. "Make it payable to the Orphans' Institute."

The jeweler was confused, curious. He made out the cheque all the same, in accordance with her instructions.

"You're from the Orphans' Institute, Madam?"

"No. It is a donation."

It had been her intention to give the proceeds to some charity, but had never decided which. She had given him the first name that came to mind. Then, leaving the jeweler's, she called at a store for writing paper and envelope. In the car she scribbled a short introductory note, called at the post office for the address of the nearest Orphans' Institute, and mailed the letter containing the cheque.

The heat was scorching. She got back to the car and opened the quarter-light to direct a stream of cool air to her face. Caught in the thick traffic, it took more than two hours to get back to Sandgate.

The visit to the doctor was only a formality. The symptoms were already clear. When she rang a week later it was confirmed. She was pregnant.

The precise day of conception was easily traced. It had actually happened three days before they had left the island, when they'd stayed in bed all morning. Her last menstruation had been a week earlier and she had neglected all precautions. It was no accident, neither was it planned; she had merely left herself open while vaguely anticipating the possibility, knowing that Penman would be complacent, quite jolly. Now she was waiting for the correct

197

moment to break the news. It came at the weekend when he talked about plans for the new yacht. Inspired, she portrayed a certain warmth, and, with perfect calm, she broke the news, saying she had called to see a physician last week.

"A physician?"

"Naturally?"

"But why? And why wait till now to tell me?"

"It was not necessary, then."

"But I should know these things. Anyway, what is the matter? You've never looked anything but healthy."

"There's nothing the matter, Karl, only a development." And she gave him time while keeping her smile.

"Are we expecting a child?"

"Would it please you?"

He was impatient.

Later he rebuked her for not letting him know earlier. He was entitled to know, even if it had been mere suspicion. Why had she kept the information until now?

"There was no certainty until today."

"I have a personal doctor, an old chap; excellent. I could have had him down here. What sort of retarded doctor did you see? Three months! The symptoms should have been obvious."

"There was no examination. I merely left a sample and told him I would ring for the result."

He got out a bottle of champagne and they celebrated.

His plan was to sail for the Mediterranean in a few weeks. Not that he had to, for it was easier to have the ship builders send an agent to negotiate the design of the new yacht. But no: he favoured the opportunity. He would visit the shipyard and see the famous establishment for himself. It would increase his knowledge of the builders. And why not? He was giving them a six hundred thousand pound contract to build a new yacht. He would see the lay-out of the establishment, understand the origin of the craft and appreciate the care and enthusiasm that had made the reputation of the firm.

On a brilliant afternoon Jackie drove back from the little village of Hockliffe. She had visited the two girls. Arriving back to Sandgate, she parked the Mercedes carefully, so that the Rolls Royce would have adequate space. Then, walking to the front door, she saw a white car in the middle of the terrace, almost blocking the entrance. Having to go round it to get to the door, she was far from pleased. The car was low-slung, with a long bonnet and fat tyres.

The wheels had spokes of stainless steel. It was a genuine two seater, expensively designed and looking more like a racing car.

Who could have taken a liberty to park it there? Why hadn't the butler told him to move it?

She went straight to the drawing room.

He was seated in a sofa, half-reclining, with feet up, his face hidden behind the magazine he was reading. His expensive brown suit caught her eye, but he showed no sign of awareness.

She cleared her throat.

Still no reaction.

Then she went up to him. "Well!"

The magazine was lowered slowly and his eyes raised. He sprung to his feet.

"Hello."

"You must have heard me come in?" said Jackie.

"Yes. I was absorbed in an article." And he raised the magazine convincingly.

His identity was obvious. He was Karl's elder son. His photograph portrayed him well. He held out a hand.

Jackie did not return the courtesy. "You must be James," she said with certainty.

"Yes. And you're Jacqueline. My father mentioned you." He was suddenly making amends for the initial reluctance.

But Jackie would not be bought off easily. She was about to mention the car on the front terrace when she had second thoughts. Instead, she turned and went out of the room.

He had got there an hour before her, arriving from the continent. As it was, he had never met Jackie and had justifiably assumed that she was probably glamorous and floating from one man to another. He was hard hit by his father's action; his mother's detachment was a disappointment to him. He had swallowed the news of the divorce with reservation. Then, on the way from Dover, having planned to appear indifferent, even disagreeable if necessary, he had parked the car on the front terrace and had gone round the house with hands in his pockets.

When he had entered the house the butler greeted him, and after a little chat they soon got to the point.

"Your father is in London," the butler had assured him. "He's up there most of the time."

But James was actually looking for signs of the new mistress, and he made no secret of his expectation.

"Where is she?" he had whispered confidentially.

But the butler spoke up with a smile. "She's out, sir. Can't say exactly where, but she left early; much earlier than usual.

"Oh! What is she like? I mean, would you say she's worthy of your service?"

"She's rather splendid, sir."

"You mean you've accepted her right away?"

"Well, she is, in your father's word, exquisite."

"I see."

It was the first time the butler had used the word, and it fitted the occasion well.

Then he had gone from to room, looking in without touching a thing. Jackie's room expressed a great deal. He felt more and more indignant, thinking all the time how remarkably easy it was for a woman to move into rich circles. This one obviously had her head screwed on; straight off the street and she was suddenly mistress of the house, occupying the best quarters. He'd be damned if he was going to be nice to her! He made himself a drink and carried the glass to the drawing room.

When Jackie arrived he had paid no attention. Let her introduce herself, he decided. But when he had lowered the magazine and his eye had caught hers, he was immediately taken aback. Then he had hesitated while the accumulated indignation escaped from his mind. He had hardly known what to say. Should he apologise for the unreasonable presumption? She was undoubtedly refined, undeniably graceful, with inexplicable simplicity. And he found himself speculating on her age.

When Karl arrived home, he met James in the same drawing room.

"What is the occasion this time?" he asked proudly.

"Practise, tomorrow."

"Brands Hatch?"

"Yes, A big event the day after."

They had not seen one another for a year. James was spending most of his time on the Continent.

"Well, any recent luck?"

The racing driver smiled regrettably. "I don't understand it, but I think a long spell of bad luck is coming to an end. I had a second last week."

"A second? Was that important?"

"Well, it was my first finish in six events."

"I see. You still have time to throw it in if you feel like it. Come to the dining room: dinner is served."

On the way Karl said softly: "You've met Jacqueline, I hope?"

"Yes. We met earlier."

"And?"

"Well, she's extremely good taste…"

"Good. She's the only choice I could have made, remember that."

Jackie was already seated, waiting for them. After the first course, Karl eyed them speculatively.

"What did you two talk about, anything in particular?"

Jackie glanced at James. A moment's indifference gave way to thoughtful acceptance. "Apart from a magazine, we didn't get round to anything else."

James looked at her warmly.

"There was hardly time to pay her compliments," he said happily. "She was rather busy."

Jackie shunned his daring eye. The butler was serving the main course and she quickly assisted, serving James first.

Later, when she and James were alone, her holiday in Jamaica was the main theme. She freely discussed the island with him, for he had spent a couple of terms out there some years ago. But that was before the big house on the Blue Mountain. He hadn't visited the island since. Seven years in motor racing, including two years go-carting at North Luffenham, had kept him busy. Furthermore, he had no plans to go out there at present.

She handed him some pictures of the house, the pool, the garden, the surroundings, and the great view from the mountainside. The following day he invited her to Brands Hatch where he was doing practise runs.

"Are you suggesting I go round the circuit?"

"Of course. I'm sure you will enjoy it."

"But a racing car will only accommodate one passenger. He would take her round a couple of times after the qualifying laps, in an adapted car. She would find it exhilarating, quite fantastic on the first experience. There was nothing like it to stimulate excitement. On the other hand, he could take her round in his road car. Of course, it was not exactly race-bred, but the luxury would suit her.

But Jackie had to refuse. Her present mood rejected anything that was so out of this word! And with the winter creeping on she was preparing to leave the country.

When she was given the small scrap of paper which said briefly that the marriage to Pascoe was annulled, that the divorce was absolute, a cold tremor went through her breast. The seven long years seemed so uneventful; they were dull, actually marking a long cessation in her life. Glancing back through the long depression now, she was suddenly convinced that she had actually died and been transported to hell when she had gone to the little village. She would have rotted there had Karl not found her. Resenting the place more than ever now, and vowing never to set foot back there, she expressed her feelings in a letter to Mary who would understand perfectly, since she herself had played a part in her reincarnation.

The marriage to Karl was indeed secret, with only James, her parents, Mary and the butler witnessing. Then the next day, when the crew members aboard the yacht were told to celebrate, they sailed for the Mediterranean.

Chapter Twenty One

The contract for the new yacht was settled. Karl dismissed Jackie's chaperon while he himself escorted her to the dinner given by the Italian boat-builders to celebrate the big contract.

After another two days in the ancient capital, they sailed west out of the Mediterranean. The new craft would be ready in less than a year, and already Karl had decided that this voyage would be the last in the Grey Lady. The new yacht would be named Lady Jacqueline, with an impressive head carving of the raven-haired beauty to point ahead majestically.

When they had cleared the Mediterranean Karl ordered a course south west to the tropics. Already it was cold, a clear sign of a bad winter closing in. The area was occasionally misty, especially in the early mornings, with the ocean showing signs of turbulence.

In Italy Jackie had indulged in the country's fashion by collecting three maternity dresses. She was hardly impressed, but they were needed and buying them in Italy meant taking something of the visit with her. Apart from special exercises, she relaxed for most of the journey. The trip was enjoyable, however and Deidre Carey had naturally set herself up as her personal nurse.

Jackie looked forward to the birth of the child, estimating that the confinement would be early January, and would give her approximately six weeks on the island.

In Kingston, however, Karl made arrangement for her to receive a doctor, hardly regretting the unavailability of his own physician, To Jackie's relief, the doctor turned out to be a Jamaican woman. She immediately proved interesting, for she knew England well, and besides, she herself had had confinements on the island and knew what to expect from the climate. She examined Jackie and assured her there should be no complication.

But what was unforeseen was the fact that the doctor was to be called urgently on Christmas Eve. When the chauffeur collected her and rushed her to the house, she was actually anticipating an accident to the millionaire's wife. Unable to visualize any complication, she rushed to the room rather worriedly. Then, assessing Jackie's situation, it become clear that the child was due at any moment.

Karl was happy with the news; he had certain ideas on premature births. The very next day, amidst the Christmas decorations, the baby was delivered at 3:30 pm. It was interesting, since less than twenty-four hours ago Jackie had been active, hardly anticipating the event so soon. The child was born two weeks prematurely.

A few days later Karl explained that the child was destined to be brilliant. "Yes, when it's a premature birth they usually are. This boy should develop fast. By the time he's four, the signs should be clear. The fact that he's two weeks."

Jackie shook her head. "Seventeen days, precisely."

"Ah, that's even better. And a good eight and a half pounds at birth. We must watch him closely."

"You mean I'll be very proud of him?"

"Undoubtedly, my dear."

Jackie was delighted with her first boy. There was even a moment when she felt particularly blessed. Three weeks later, when she had completely recovered from the confinement, she was already her usual self. The swimming pool and tennis court were again absorbing her. Then she seemed to have acquired new energy, for when Karl was tired or disinterested, the chauffeur provided some challenge. He was active and robust, and sported a certain flamboyance. Jackie resented this at first, but gradually found it less interesting, especially when he showed little aptitude for tennis, though he liked the game. She put this down to his lack of early opportunity. After all she could easily remember when, he was totally unfamiliar with the game. However, he was learning fast, though his shots were confined to two types and his serving tediously inappropriate. But within two weeks he was making challenging returns, and soon become impressively skilful. Even Karl sometimes called on him for assistance in his early morning work-out.

In the convenience of the mansion, Jackie was actually taking everything for granted. The local scenes were absorbing her. In time she even visited some historical places. A trip to Spanish Town, the original capital, was interesting. When not absorbed with the picturesque mountainside, she floated to other parts, among the wild flowers that were always so abundant. Even the banana trees produced giant white flowers before separating into small ones at the tip of young fruits. The doctor bird was a fascinating creature. With its long, slender tail and almost equally long beak, it moved from flower to flower, a daily visitor to each bud and, without ever landing on any, simply employed its wings at fantastic speed to maintain a steady poise over each bud as it suckle the sweet nectar. Jackie had taken several pictures of this display, to make huge photographs for the drawing room. A year out here had thrown her past into oblivion.

A letter form the Italian boat-builders said the new vessel was awaiting delivery after a two-month delay. This gave Karl immediate reason to head north. He would sail in a month. First to take delivery of the yacht, then to negotiate the sale of the Grey Lady.

How long would all this take? Asked Jackie, who was in no hurry to leave Jamaica, for the novelty of the new yacht had lost its significance as far as she was concerned. But in truth, however, there was no desire to have Karl go off without her.

"Three or four months, maybe. It doesn't matter," he decided.

It was the end of February and well over a year since she had settled on the island. Now they would leave only for a few months. She would keep him at his word, disregarding the fact that he was considering himself a free traveller, refusing to be bogged down, and was giving little importance to time.

The child was a year old, walking strongly and already showing little traits of Karl himself. Karl was spending long hours with his son, speaking softly to him, watching him laugh, even teaching him the significant movements of the lips. Undoubtedly, indeed, the child was learning fast, for already he was laughing out loud, with a happy twist in his tone.

Sailing south of Haiti, Karl steered into the Mona Passage, the first time he had taken the route. He was handling the yacht for the last time and taking the longer course would extend his knowledge of the sea. He made for Tenerife and steered a straight course to reduce fatigue in the control room.

The new yacht would eliminate the constant need for attention. A sort of automatic pilot would be installed by a firm in England, an electro-mechanical box would engage the compass and speed indicator with a direct bearing, and would employ a miniature radar device to sense objects up to three miles ahead. It would mean that the control room could be deserted without fear of losing course, and would trigger off an early alarm if there were the possibility of a collision.

Before leaving Sandgate Jackie had transferred five thousand pounds to her mother's account. Karl had also made two transfers of five thousand each time. Eighteen months had elapsed, but there was no reason to suppose that the account would have gone down. From the Mediterranean she telephoned her parents in Bedfordshire. Her father answered and she spoke to him at length. Then he explained that her mother had gone to collect the children from school.

"Are you cabling from Jamaica?"

"No. we're in the Mediterranean, just off Capri. Did you get the cable yesterday?"

"Yes. It surprised us a little."

And she briefly explained her position: Karl was taking over a new yacht; they would be in England in about a month."

The two girls were very well, always jolly. They were looking forward to playing with their baby brother. When she had thanked him for the news, she rang off.

Anchored off Capri, the new yacht was an eye-opener in the blazing sun. There was no scarcity of yachts in this area: but Lady Jacqueline was new. With three decks to the usual two, and more in line with the small ocean-going liners, its high hull and sleek water-line gave it an attractive magnificence. Painted white, with a red water-line, it floated high in the shallow waters. The funnel was brilliant red, while the mast-head sported the British and Jamaican flags.

New supplies were taken on, as well as three stewards and two cooks. Karl made it known that he was giving a party on board. As well as two officials from the boat-builders, there would be a couple of tycoons and their associates, and James was expected to come down from Turin.

Jackie was enthusiastic. "Why, is he here in Italy, or have you invited him specially?"

"He's here. He's driving for Maserati."

Instead of finding a new dress for the occasion, Jackie delayed her choice until the final moment. The fact that expensive women would be around interested her a great deal, but not in the usual way. She had no intention of particularly impressing her guests. She was unknown to them and would show herself in something ordinary. That way they would see that she needed little help from the cosmetic and fashion stores. She finally chose a fine summer garment, with a low back and a large bow. It had a wrapped skirt, while the front was quite plain and flowed smoothly to the waist. It was a shocking red without trimmings. She also ignored her jewellery.

She greeted her guests with natural warmth; then the wife of a tycoon, in a heavily sequined dress suggested secretly that she felt over dressed. Jackie liked her all the same, perhaps because her flowing black hair was styled the same as hers.

Dancing commenced with the first cocktail and Jackie was left out until a prominent Italian collected her. Later Karl guided the same fellow to a corner of the lounge where they chatted for the remainder of the evening. Then at two o'clock in the morning, with the light, dimmed, Karl congratulated his wife.

She had done nothing more that was expected of her, she protested.

"You did much more than that," he insisted haughtily. "You flattered him; you were courteous, and what's more, you kept him close for more than half the night, at least until I relieved you of him. It turned out that he had had the most expensive night of his life."

"In what way," Jackie asked, rather concerned.

"He's agreed to pay me in sterling, two hundred and forty thousand pounds for the Grey Lady, three hundred and sixty million lire."

"He's buying it outright?"

"Naturally. It won't break him; he's a wealthy fellow, owning a chain of stores and supermarkets. He makes that in a week."

"Well, was the Grey Lady worth that much?"

"Every Lire."

Jackie raised her eyebrows. Was the deal closed?

"Not yet. But it's certain. I'm to visit the yacht with him in the morning. He will look it over and decide whether to pay two hundred and ten thousand, or go up another thirty thousand. I want you there."

"He's agreed to a figure without having seen the yacht?"

Karl shook his head. "He knows it. And besides, he also knows something about the builders, and is impressed by that particular craft. It is undoubtedly the fastest of its size, with unrivalled capability. He won't be disappointed."

They were expecting James, she pointed out, and he had not even arrived late.

"There was a telephone call he was unable to make it. Some trouble with the car. He had to spend the night working on it."

Was it feasible? She enquired suspiciously.

"Well, if he's racing he has to see that his car's in order. No doubt he was doing practise runs yesterday. It sounds feasible, all right."

Jackie had seen James only once. Though they had chatted well, there were doubts as to whether he accepted her fully.

She was tired and slept well. Rising late, the Mediterranean sun was high. The white sky showed the horizon closing down on some folded mountains. Below the window were small sailing boats. Already it was May, and she suspected that Karl would spend the season anchored there, between the exotic island and the mainland.

At eleven o'clock she decided to take a bath. Then she had a light meal with fruit juice and an apple. The next hour was spent with the child.

By one o'clock she was dressed in a printed cotton suit, the colour brilliant and flowery, and with her hair tucked up under a blue and white straw hat.

Karl directed her to the small craft on the boat deck before getting in himself. A member of the crew, piloting the small craft, gave the signal to lower them. Less than a minute later they were heading towards the Grey Lady, anchored two miles along the coast.

The Italian was already on board. He had made a point of getting there early, before the agreed time. The guard had admitted him. When Karl and Jackie arrived, he had already seen half the vessel.

"Welcome," he said broadly showing the gold tip of a front tooth. When they were in the dining hall, "We go to the deck above, eh, now that you and the lady are here. I look below. I come early, you know. It is important business. You don't mind, I am sure."

Then he showed Jackie the stairs. She went first and while they inspected the place, she continued ahead, into the lounge. She was surprised not to find his wife there with him, but suddenly remembered that the Italians were customarily detached from their wives when doing business or negotiating important matters. On the other hand, Jackie felt a special importance at being the only woman on board. She asked for a drink when the men entered.

The barman held a tray to each in turn.

The men graduated to the control room for a while. Returning after a few minutes, Karl made for the bar to ascertain that everything was in order. His guest remained with Jackie.

"You enjoy sailing?" he asked, charmingly.

"Very much. It is different from anything ashore."

"Yes, quite different. What is the most time you spent at sea?"

"Five weeks."

He smiled, impressed. "Ah, that is a long time for a lady. The English are good sailors; you know, they disappear to the ends of the earth, never to return for one year, sometimes two." He laughed. "Italians are not made that way. You see, the English sailor takes a lady on board, the Italian leaves the lady at home. Because of that, he can only sail to the mouth of the Mediterranean. Then he is too far from home, so he turns back."

Jackie was amused. She admired the casual way in which he injected flavour into his words. Will you travel further than the Mediterranean?"

"Oh, naturally. In this yacht, if I go at full speed, I will be out of the Mediterranean before I can stop, so I will just keep going."

Karl joined them and ordered another drink. The deal was soon settled. Two hundred and twenty thousand pounds would be paid into Penman's account.

Half an hour later a party of two woman, ceremonially dressed, a young boy of fifteen and a young girl joined them on board. The Italian introduced them as his wife and family, along with his sister-in-law. They would celebrate. They spent the afternoon and evening on board, watching films and taking cocktails between conversations. The men discussed a hunting trip to West Africa.

Jackie was apprehensive. She was counting on being back in England as soon as possible. In fact, the telephone call to her parents a month ago had committed her. Yet she was having to accept that she would be away for at least another month.

Karl was non-committal. The weather was good, the company excellent. He was particularly pleased with the new yacht. He was also discovering new people. The ancient   region had a kind of fascination. He even talked about visiting Greece, then south to Egypt, and down the Nile. All this meant they would probably not arrive back in England for another year.

The new yacht, Lady Jacqueline, was a floating chateau, styled in a Chinese fashion. The pilot's house was high above, out of the way. The third deck had a master lounge, with a projector room directly behind, and a luxurious bar. The second deck incorporated a spacious dining hall, kitchen, crews lounge, and other facilities four spacious living quarters were on the main deck, with crew quarters below. The powerful lightweight engine was also tucked away down below. For very slow cruising, at twelve knots, maintenance could be minimized. With the automatic pilot and radar to be installed, the vessel would require no manning for twenty-four hours, and then only observation checks would be necessary. Each warning circuit would trigger an alarm.

Significantly, however, there was a reason to sail up to England very soon. Penman considered having the electronic equipment fitted at the earliest, with immediate emphasis on the ship-to-shore radio. This he regarded as vital for world-wide communication. He said nothing more of the West African hunting trip, since the Italian was busily adapting himself to the Grey Lady, and had not followed up his suggestion.

Karl attached himself to the control room and hugged the wheel with pride. A couple of long voyages should free the engine and machinery and thus make for a good response. Her twelve knots cruising speed would then be effortless. He steered watchfully up the Dover Straits, drifted calmly past hythe and anchored the yacht within half a mile of Sandgate. Then in the speedboat lowered from the deck of the yacht, a party of four went ashore. After dispatching Jackie, the child and nanny, the craft sped back to collect Karl.

Less than ten minutes later he joined them in the Rolls Royce. They were soon home, to be greeted by the butler who had prepared the place well. After two years of absence it was necessary. Dust and corrosion would have set in, the beds needed shaking up, wardrobes needed cleaning out and windows and doors had been opened occasionally to prevent seizure.

Now they were only in England for a short spell, a month at the most, the yacht would be available to the electronic people for the new fittings.

Already Karl was busy. After two years there were situations to clarify, trade records to catch up on, reports to be read. Though changes to the money market must be studied, opportunities missed were few, but he must know about them all the same.

Jackie was delighted to be back. She would use up the few weeks as much as possible. Alone in bed, she was deep in thought and, getting up, she threw back the curtains. The late March weather was mild.

Without caring for breakfast, she backed the Mercedes out of the garage where it had been looked after by the butler for almost two years, and she headed north along the familiar London road. More than an hour later, instead of turning off the motorway at

Dunstable, she continued to the next exit and took the country lane to Hockliffe. This route avoided the tedious drive through Dunstable.

Hockliffe was a quite village, looking almost deserted. Her parents' home was a large farmhouse, built some years before her time, and quite respectable, with comfortable accommodation. Off the main road at one end of the village she turned the Mercedes into the long driveway. The house ahead looked quiet and nostalgic, and the Humber Hawk owned by her father was parked at the front. She pulled up behind it, gazed ahead for a moment, and then got out of the car.

A large Alsatian racing towards her stopped abruptly, wagged its tail happily, and followed her to the door. Then her mother, still strong and healthy, greeted her and showed her into the living room. It had been such a long time.

"I thought you'd forgotten us altogether."

Jackie smiled, reminiscing. She had expected Karl to sail much earlier, once the yacht was proved, but she was wrong. They had spent months off Capri.

She fell into her mother's arms. They embraced. Then she stood back and looked at her.

Her mother understood. She, too, was wearing the new fashion: a dark, full-length dress that looked warm, with high collar, and buttoned from the waist up.

"What would you like to drink? Coffee, tea, a glass of wine?"

"No wine. I had no breakfast. I haven't eaten yet."

"Then you must have tea, and dinner afterwards."

And over cups of tea the mother looked at her daughter proudly. She was particularly receptive and suddenly went into a flurry of compliments, singing high praises for her only offspring. Jackie, on her part, certainly wished that her mother would spare the details. Her knowledge of the world had broadened her mind, and such emotions seemed unnecessary. She had stripped off her gloves, not wanting to appear out of place.

How are the children?" she asked when the emotions had subsided.

Oh, they were little darlings; quite the dream of the house, and so well loved. Of course they would not be home till four. There were evenings when she had gone to fetch them, but today they would arrive home on the school bus,

Jackie was longing to see them, to know how they were getting on, especially Diane, who been so gay when they were down in Kent. She remembered how the child had been concerned and helpful in her bad days.

"Have they grown much?" she asked, panting for news.

"Oh yes; Diane's a good three inches taller. And Connie, she's grown a lot faster."

"They haven't forgotten me, I hope."

"No, no chance of that, my dear. They have two photographs of you in their room. They'll be delighted to see you."

Jackie reflected on the very day she had dumped the children there. Connie, three at the time, had been scarcely aware of the situation. But Diane, who was seven, and intelligent, had been fully aware of the desertion. The child had cried, rather bravely. Now, unable to switch her mind from the very day, she remembered the events that followed: how she had driven back to the bungalow, gone out with Karl, and then found herself alone in the middle of the night. The escapade of that very night suddenly turned her stomach; it took her mother's voice to switch off the unnecessary remorse.

Diane rushed to Jackie on sight, with a trickle of tears after a moment's hesitation. Connie was initially less enthusiastic; she contemplated her mother and studied her disposition, then, when her sister had received Jackie's warmth and maternal love, the younger child dashed forward with a great laugh.

At ten o'clock, an hour after their grandfather had arrived, Jackie left the house, he had insisted on keeping the children, unless her new husband demanded them.

On the way back she turned it over in her mind. Karl had known the two girls. He also knew where she had left them. But apart from his generous gift and cheerful words, he had never spoken seriously of them; neither had she attempted to discuss their further with him. Now she wondered if it would not be wise to send them off to boarding school as soon as they were ready. Diane would be ready in two years; Connie would follow later. It made sense under the circumstances. She and Karl would make the necessary arrangements. The children could then come to her at holiday times.

Although she was late getting back to Sandgate, Karl was still out. She waited up and passed the time arranging her things properly. Then she was aware of the light on the window. She rushed to the drawing room in her pink gown and scarf, and poured herself a drink. Then, as Karl came in, rubbing his cold hands, she went to him.

"Anything unexpected?" she asked when they were seated.

He swallowed a sip of brandy, looking eager and decisive. He smiled.

"No, nothing at all. Interesting, though, how things went up and down in the last two years. You know, I think it was far better that I was not here. The great speculation that the Germans were to devalue the Mark turned out worthless after all. I might have lost a great deal.

"Why, has anyone lost heavily?"

"You remember David Cimla? We met him at the party in Earls Court."

Jackie nodded.

"He went down heavily, with only a slight recoup. Mind you, from the record, the position looked good at the time."

Jackie refilled his glass and told him about the children.

"Damn selfish of me," he admitted. "I'd forgotten about them. You must get them down here whenever you can. We've only got a month here. You must see as much of them as possible.

"They're at school. We can only have them at weekends."

"That's understandable."

What would he say to the idea of a boarding school for Diane in two years time?

Karl supported the idea; it was wise under the circumstances. The small cost was not important. The first two years could be covered in advance, then for subsequent years the fee could be drawn from a trust fund. It was good traditional thinking.

For the weekend Jackie collected them, drove them down to London and fitted them out with new clothes, then took them back to Hockliffe in order to keep a tight schedule.

Karl had an engagement, a party, the kind she had gone to once before; this time in a Holland Park hotel. They were still there at two o'clock the next morning. Then, travelling back to Sandgate in the early hours, a car appeared in the driving mirror of the Rolls Royce and kept close.

Annoyed at this, Karl dropped his speed to a constant fifty, and to irritate him further, the car behind did likewise, only it kept further back. In Ashford, where the road was well lit by overhead lights, he was able to make out that the car was a Jaguar saloon. It kept behind them all the way to Sandgate, and continued on when they'd left the main road. Not knowing what to think, Karl decided that the whole thing was suspicious. He stopped the Rolls Royce in the driveway and stared after the Jaguar.

"Is something the matter?" Jackie asked.

But he simply shrugged. "Can't think who the devil that was!"

But Jackie was unaware. Why should he want to know who it was? she said, for despite the late hour, one could still expect a few cars on the road.

Karl agreed, for there was no need to tell her the car had been following them from London.

Would he have a night-cap?

It was a good idea. They would enjoy a glass of Tia Maria. It brought back pleasant memories. She found a new bottle and filled two glasses, then pulled a low table in front of the curved leather chair and sat close. It was after 3 a.m.

"Where are we going next?" she asked.

"We could sail straight to the Caribbean, on the other hand we might go to Capri, pick up the Italian and sail for West Africa. We could follow up the hunting trip."

"But you made no decision."

"It is still in the balance. I had to get the yacht completed before a long voyage. It's important for business as well as pleasure." He looked at her with a familiar smile.

Jackie knew the precise look, she had learned to recognize it. It meant satisfaction, a kind of exultation. A feeling he invariably showed when close to her. It often carried them off to bed.

He said at last: "Well, we've been married more than two years. I should have taken the initiative on our last anniversary, but we were busy, it seems like the ideal opportunity has only just presented itself. I want you to look back over the last two years and pick out the moments of dissatisfaction…"

"Karl, you're not serious?"

"Yes, you must tell me what you find unbearable. We should be able to compromise on one or two points."

Did he seriously think there were one or two aspects that needed altering?

Oh, there ought to be. He was deeply in love. And he was not entirely convinced that she was satisfied with every thing so far. Neither was it strange that he should be expressing his feeling.

Jackie laughed. She would give it a serious answer. And the truth was that she had been too busy in her new surroundings to notice anything unimportant. Conditioning herself to him and having his child had kept her elated. But really, it was only two years and she hadn't noticed the small flaws.

"So, you have no complaints, no regrets?"

"None."

He took her hand. "We ought to be in bed, you know. It is almost four o'clock."

She agreed and at once drew up the tail of her dress. Suddenly she was in his arms, cradled. And he climbed the stairs quite easily with her.

In the middle of the week Jackie was heading north, through London. She must be with the children as much as possible. She would visit them every day for the next three weeks. She was particularly fond of Diane. At nine she was pretty, with clear hereditary traits. The child was a lovely replica of Jackie herself.

The two girls had played with their baby brother. So deeply were they taken up with him that Jackie was having problems whenever it was time to return them to Hockliffe. Diane was continually lifting up the baby, cradling him, which seem dangerous at times. Furthermore, Karl was having second thoughts about boarding school, saying that they should all grow up together. Jackie was excited, they would explore the idea.

Now, as she drove through the busy streets, she was suddenly alerted by the last minute stopping of a Jaguar car behind her. It had obviously been travelling dangerously close. Now, only two inches from the Mercedes' rear bumper, she found herself staring into her driving mirror with uneasiness. What was further disturbing was that the blue car continued to follow her, dangerously close, onto Park Lane, and actually turned into Edgar Road behind her. With the hood of her car up, the rear window was restricted. A clear view of the occupant in the Jaguar was impossible. Furthermore, the car had a tinted windscreen so that only the heavy beard of the driver was apparent.

The Jaguar followed her for another mile or so and gradually faded into the distance. She calmed herself. It was not entirely unusual for one car to travel behind another through dense traffic and finally take the same outlet. Now that it was out of her mirror, she would think no more of it. She turned onto the motorway and headed north.

At nine o'clock when the children were put to bed, she left for Sandgate. Then, driving down the dark motorway, she was horrified by a new thought. Earlier the younger child had reminded her of

Pascoe. And there were actual moments when some old traits of her father were evident. Alarmed at the clear sign, her mind had flashed back to Pascoe. And throughout the evening the child's laughter, with contracted eyes and wide nostrils, had dug up disagreeable reminiscence of the dark years.

More than five years had slipped by since Pascoe was jailed. If there were a remission of twelve months, he would have been freed some eighteen moths ago. She was not aware of a definite remission. At the time of the sentence the judge had pledged that Pascoe should serve the full five years. But whatever the term, Pascoe was certainly a free man at this moment. He might even have started up a business under a different name. On the other hand, he had made it clear that he had money, and would hardly be desperate.

Driving through Charing, she noted that a car was gaining on her. The vehicle was some way off, and the lights somewhat dim, but it was clearly gaining ground. Then, on the other side of Ashford, the car caught up and she made allowance for it to overtake her, but it calmly settled in behind the Mercedes. This made her uneasy, especially since there had been two occasions when it ought to have gone past. In the well lit area of Hythe she was able to make out that it was a Jaguar. Her heart missed a beat, for it was the familiar blue, with the tinted screen. It was impossible to see beyond that, but with her earlier memories, there was nothing but fear. She considered stopping to let the car by, but instead, she drove on quickly. It was not a coincidence she would only be making things easier for the Jaguar.

She covered the three miles to Sandgate in very quick time. Accelerating hard convinced her that she was not mistaken, for the Jaguar was never more than twenty yards behind, its bright light flooding the interior of her car.

Then, slowing rapidly to get into her driveway, she anticipated a crisis, that the car might run into her. She was wrong. The Jaguar had read her intention and had braked at the same instant. She drove carefully up the driveway, stopped in front of the garage and peered back through the darkness. The Jaguar edged forward, reversed into the driveway and sped off back towards Hythe. She shuddered. It was barely eleven and Karl was still out.

Jackie left the car and instructed the butler to put it in the garage. In her room she threw off her gloves and shoes, removed the jacket of her two-piece dress and released her hair so that it fell to her shoulders. Then, finding her slippers, she went back to the drawing room.

The butler had carried out her instruction and was passing though the big room.

"George."

He turned to her.

"Do we know anyone who drives a blue Jaguar, a late model? it followed me to the driveway and quickly turned back."

George hesitated. No, no-one he knew drove a blue Jaguar.

"Do we know anyone at all who driver a Jaguar?"

"Only young Howard, but he's in Australia. He had the sports car. You're referring to the saloon, I take it?"

"Yes. Think about it. If you come up with anything, let me know."

"Certainly, Madam."

Jackie poured herself a dry Martini and drank it quickly. The taste was acrid. She rebuked herself and filled a glass with pineapple juice. Whoever it was knew exactly where she was turning off. She remembered the night Karl had stopped in the driveway and looked curiously at the car that had gone past. He had said something about a car following them and she had dismissed it outright.

Chapter Twenty Two

For more than two weeks there was no sign of the Jaguar. Perhaps she was silly to imagine that a stranger was obsessed with her movements. She made the same journey daily, arriving back at the same hour. Well, it had to be something that happened once in every woman's life. In three days they would sail for the exotic regions, away from this horror which frightened her so much. But she was scarcely able to forget her driving mirror.

Then it suddenly came to mind: Phillip Russell owned a Jaguar, the very model. How had it escaped her? He was the scientist she'd known briefly before Karl. Could there be a connection? Phillip Russell had admired her. But what did it mean? She was confronted with the thought. Phillip Russell was an amiable man, hardly the type to frighten her in this way. But was it not true that a man could go out of his mind with obsession, any man? Perhaps the years had made him thoughtless. Yes, it was not impossible that he might even have grown a heavy beard.

Karl was out. He had gone to the yacht, to test the new installations. She got out of bed and ran the bath, then came back to the dressing table. A quick look at herself made her wonder if Phillip Russell could ready have gone out of his mind for her. She smiled strangely and went back to the bath.

First she washed her hair, and then buried herself in the thick foam of the bath. It reminded her of the Blue Mountain, how she had missed the open-air pool, the picturesque surroundings, even the tennis to keep her trim and active. Once at sea she would insist on going straight there. She treated herself to the full essence of the bath salts, its rich and extravagant foam. Under the shower she took special care with her breasts; they were still firm. Her body was firm too, even after the last birth. She credited this to the constant outdoor activities on the Blue Mountain. Swimming had widened her shoulders a little and seemed to have rounded her breasts. Suddenly, under the raining warm water, she was aware of an old feeling. Her breasts grew and filled out before her. But she struggled with the heightened feelings and eventually went to bed. She slept well, undisturbed.

The next morning she prepared herself calmly and thoughtfully. Using the mirror she brushed the heavy black tresses into a respectable flow. Then dressed carefully to finish in a green

218

three-piece, with stylish jacket and elastic waist.

At about twelve, he had a light meal, with fruits, and suddenly decided that she was not ready to go out. She spent two hours with the child, coaxing him to formulate difficult words, expressing her maternal instinct with great affection.

Then, on her instructions, the butler got out the car and ran the heater. He was an enthusiastic servant, proud, and full of admiration for her. He wished she would spend more time at the house instead of rushing off abroad.

Finally she drove out at four o'clock, the waves of early thoughts creeping on. The idea that her follower was the amiable Phillip Russell had brought the events back to mind, setting her eyes alert in the driving mirror. How easy it would be to go past his gate, had she known his address. Only three days more, however, and she would sail. If only she could speak to him, for there was no doubt of it, it would be three days of hell! Oh, she was nervous.

Yet the Jaguar failed to appear. It took two hours of tedious driving to get to the centre of London. By then it was dark and cold with a slight wind. She drove carefully, picking her way towards the motorway. Normally she would have collected the children before midday, but she'd been shaken with fear and only found the enthusiasm during the two hours with the baby.

Appearing in her mirror was a brilliant yellow sports car. For a moment she had forgotten the mirror in her contemplation of the traffic, and hadn't seen it come up behind. But it caught her eye when jets of water squirted onto the screen and the wipers were suddenly switched on. And behind it all was the only occupant, bearded, there was a sudden shiver as her temperature fell. Was she being followed? Could it be Phillip Russell? If only the car would go past and remove her fear!

Along the carriageway she took the slow lane and dropped her speed to a crawl, attempting to induce impatience in the yellow car. But it did nothing of the sort. Instead, it reduced speed even more and settled further back in her mirror.

Moments later it was up behind her. A flash of head-lamps and it was already alongside, cutting sharply across her bonnet, red lights flashing. When she had halted to avoid a crash, her assailant reversed quickly back, to the right of her, and pulled up.

But he was in no hurry to get out. Then the door slammed and he stood up. Suddenly, under the street lamp, her mind jolted with vague recognition.

Pascoe came forward, his hands in leather gloves, his face disguised under the beard; his body reduced to slimness, in a respectable dark suit. The eyes were strange; they were hard and cold.

Jackie was frozen. She made no movement. She had never been afraid of Pascoe. She had resented him, yes, but had hardly been afraid.

"Well?" he said, lowering his head, "Aren't you going to say a word or two?" His voice was high and directed through the closed window.

She fumbled for the switch and lowered the glass. Had he gone crazy? Was he out of his mind?

But he smiled coldly, taking a hand out of the gloves, and saying it was no coincidence that she was still in one piece. She knew him better than that.

What was it he wanted?

Only to talk to her.

It was out of the question.

"Look," he said, waving a hand to the car that was blocking the lane, "do you want to cause a disturbance?"

And he got the door open and hustled her to his car, wrenched the door open and forced her in. Then he paused abruptly as a passing car swerved to avoid him. But he was quickly in the car, behind the wheel. Meanwhile, she was struggling to get her door open, resenting the way he was driving off with her.

"What are you doing? My car is unlocked."

He said nothing. Pascoe was busy manoeuvering the car, turning round, and in a moment they were rushing back to the city.

"Where are you taking me?"

But he took no notice. He drove on, harder than ever. Without glancing at her, he said harshly, "I must talk to you. It is important."

They had halted at a red light, and again she fought with the door.

"Forget it," he growled, "the door's jammed. Solid."

What did he mean, picking her up like this? Oh, he wanted to discuss certain matters with her. And she was thrown back in her seat. Now she was horrified. She had nothing to discuss, nothing to say. But he drove fiercely all the same, cutting in and out of the traffic, braking hard, swerving madly. His intention firm.

Jackie was indeed forsaken, quite helpless; yet it was best to remain calm. Before long they were turning into a road she knew well, the very road she had travelled less than an hour ago, the A20. He was heading south, hurriedly. Where was he taking her? It couldn't be Sandgate. Did he intend to confront Karl? Pascoe had never been entirely stupid.

The lights penetrated the darkness, picking out the road, lighting up the bends. Jackie stared ahead with horror. She sensed Pascoe's hand reaching for the gear lever, then the high pitched roar of the engine and the rapid deceleration. At the old familiar junction he swung right. It was Lenham, the very place she hated. More that two years ago she had given up the bungalow. Was he trespassing? There was a dim light in the living room. He pulled up on the terrace in front of the garage. Suddenly they were in darkness. He got out of the car and held his door open.

"You'll have to come this way."

Jackie showed no interest.

"Come on. That door's jammed, damn it!"

Oh, but he had opened it to get her in.

"I tell you, it's jammed. It was fixed for the occasion."

Reluctantly she worked her way across the cramped interior, not without difficulty. Then, leaving her seat, he grabbed her by the arm, yanked her out and slammed the door quickly.

Pascoe rushed her to the front door, wrenched it open and thrust her into the living room, locking it behind them and putting the key in his pocket.

All the curtains were closed. He simply flicked the switch and a brilliant light flooded the room. Then he looked at her coldly.

"Well, as you can see, it is just as you left it. It is nice to have you back."

"Why have you brought me here?"

"It's your home. You chose it, remember?"

Jackie was confused, quite astonished. But he quickly excused himself, saying he would make a telephone call. Her eyes followed him. As well as his dark suit, his black shoes were new, his beard unhealthy looking, strange, it frightened her. His hair was freshly groomed, his hands looked clean now that he had thrown off the gloves. He was using the telephone.

Jackie removed her gloves; it would be foolish to remain indignant forever.

He put the phone down and came back to her. "Your car will be collected by one of my friends. There'll be no damage, I assure you." He smiled cynically and looked her up and down.

"You know, my dear, it is difficult not to adore you. You're as beautiful as ever." And he showed her the armchair. "Please."

After a time, Jackie took the few steps to the armchair, reluctantly. Everything was exactly as she remembered it. The two armchairs facing, and two sofas completed the arrangement. The table was in the middle. There was a smaller table at the side, in front of a third sofa.

"Make yourself at home," he emphasised.

But her lips were sealed.

"Let me see," he wondered aloud, "five, five and half years. It's a long time; almost a generation! But you haven't changed, no, not much. I must congratulate you. You know, Jackie, you remind me of the early days… interesting." He was silent for a time, studying her. "I've lost weight, you will noticed. I had to get new clothes when they let me out of that damn place."

"How long have you been following me?"

Pascoe flashed her an appraising glance; a tense silence persisted.

"I ought to entertain you," he said at last. "Let me see," he made towards the cabinet, "you only like soft drinks. Dubonnet, Martini, champagne? Ah, that would be more suitable. Yes, the occasion call for it." And he opened the cabinet. It was well stocked. He brought over two glasses and a full bottle.

"You will have a drink, won't you?"

"I'd rather you get on with what you have to say."

"Pity, I was hoping you'd make yourself at home."

He placed the two glasses on the table, opened the bottle carefully, and filled one. He emptied it in one gulp. "Hmm, not exactly my taste, as well you know." And he brought out a half-bottle of brandy, replenished his glass and sat down in the armchair, opposite her.

"You know," he continued, "I went to a lot of trouble to keep track of you. I had you followed since you arrived from Capri."

"You did most of the following yourself," she said harshly.

Pascoe stared at her. "Yes, I was behind you most of the time."

"In a blue Jaguar!"

His eyes widened. "In a blue Jaguar, yes."

"And the bungalow?"

This annoyed him even more. "The bungalow!" he shouted. "This is something I must hold against you. It will take time to forgive you for this."

"What do you mean?"

"You send a man to jail, and then dispensed with his home. That was a thoughtless act. It is impossible to forgive you for that. You put me in a position from which I had no chance of recovering; giving up this house, so that I had no home to come back to."

"I had nothing to do with your sentence!"

Pascoe's eyes were ablaze. "For whatever reason I went to jail, you were the cause. I was striving to support you, your damn high standards." He smiled ruefully, thoughtfully. "You know, I've always taken a dim view of men who get themselves ruined by women. It happened to the most successful men. A woman's looks sometimes create strange burdens. My burden was not exactly strange, but I suffered where it hurt most. Not satisfied with giving yourself to another man, you dispended with my home, rejected it, rejected me. Five years in jail is not easy for a man of my temperament.

"Do you know, since I came out I've had to avoid all the places I used to go. It is not easy. I had to find new friends. There was no one I could trust.

"How long do you intend to keep me here?" she cried.

Pascoe simply emptied his glass, refilled it, and sat back in the armchair.

"Five years is a long time to harbor hatred for a man. You have no sympathy for me, I can see that. What I am saying means nothing to you; I'm having no effect at all. But really, I want to hear what you did while I was away."

"Must you persist in this ridiculous manner?"

He repeated himself; he was interested. He had always been preoccupied with her.

Jackie was pale. She wished there was some way to get out of the house, to avoid the repugnance.

"Come, come," he said, "I want an account of your movements, how you lived. I am entitled to that."

"I am not your wife!"

"No? But you were. And in my view you're still my wife. You married me for better or worse, till death. It was a solemn oath we took. You promised to obey and I damn well expect you to obey."

"That was legally terminated," she spat furiously.

"Terminated?" he cried. "Think again, Mrs. Pascoe."

But she flew from the armchair and made for the door. Pascoe leapt to his feet, caught her at the door and hurried her back to the armchair. Overwhelmed by his great strength, she slumped back into the chair under the force of his arm.

He leaned against the table, two feet from her, breathing heavily.

"What do you intend?" she fumed.

But he regained his composure quite easily and soon recovered himself. "I think you should have a drink. It will calm you down. Maybe you will change your mind."

He got back to his chair, swallowed half a glass of brandy and settled back. The table was low, the same height as the chair; and she was in full view, her knees to one side of the cushion, her skirt drawn up. Jackie was perplexed, her eyes challenging. The jacket had given way at the waist. It was wide open, clearly revealing the thin blouse, her breasts heaving furiously. The sight disturbed him.

"Now then," he stammered, "Do you remember how many visits you paid me in that confounded place?"

God! He had expected her to count them. Her lips locked in anger. But his eyes were fastened on her.

"You don't want to remember, but I can remind you. You visited me once a month for three months, you missed the fourth and obliged only once after that. You were very thoughtful. I was seriously wondering what had happened to you, particularly the children."

Jackie stirred. This was flash point.

"Yes, the children," he reiterated, this time with great emphasis. "I was concerned about them too, after that fourth visit; you missed the following two months. No, correction: you were absent for three months. When you did arrive, I reminded you for the second time that you were to let me know when your account was low. I offered you support. But the next news I had was a confrontation with a solicitor acting for you. My wife was divorcing me. I had never heard such a joke." Pascoe smiled ironically, quite sadly. "My wife would never consider such a thing, I insisted; it was impractical. Then the next visitor was the estate agent. The situation was urgent. My furniture was going up for auction; they were taking over the bungalow. Well, I had to agree that they were to be regarded as security against outstanding rent till I was out. Then, if I were unable to pay within a month of getting out, they would be sold." His eyes pierced hers.

The short silence was agonizing. For the first time since his great strength had planted her in the chair, Jackie twisted herself.

How long would he keep her there? What was behind it all? The children were expecting her. She pulled her jacket to and vainly attempted to straighten her skirt, to cover herself.

Pascoe emptied his glass. "Fifteen months I've waited for you, reliving the good days all over again. Yes, it happens even to the strongest men. The bungalow is exactly as you left it. Would you care to look it over?" Pause. "Come now, I'm not holding too much against you. I am willing to forgive a great deal. Of course there are certain things I could never forgive. But I am ready to overlook the small points. I am not such a brute after all."

Pascoe left his chair and came round the table, closer to her. But her superior air belittled him. Her stern obstinacy disturbed him.

He said coaxingly: "I wish you'd take a drink, it would ease the situation, it would make things easier. Come," he begged, "you've always liked champagne."

And he moved the extra glass to the edge of the table and poured the drink into it. Jackie sat with an arm along the side of the armchair, the other in her lap. Hardly abandoned, she was thinking hard. But his nearness, this bearded face frightened her. His madness shocked her.

Seated on the edge of the table now, he learned forward and held the glass to her lips. "You must have a drink with me. It is the one honour you can do me now. It will at least convince me that there was a time when I meant something to you, the times when I was proud of you. Believe me, I loved you beyond words. I could be easy on you. I might even drive you back to London. You could go on from there."

"You could be easy on me," she echoed. "what d'you mean?

Pascoe's voice was suddenly calm, full of confidence. "I have a plan for you."

Jackie considered him ironic. She sat uneasily in the chair. "The least I can do is listen."

"Good," he said easily. "You're beginning to sound like the woman I once married." He looked at her seriously, "I am hungry. How about fixing me something to eat?"

"You're out of your mind."

"Go and look in the kitchen, it won't take you long to rustle up a steak, or fry some eggs, anything." He gestured to the drinks cabinet behind him. "There's plenty of good wine in there."

Jackie suddenly smiled. The whole thing was ridiculous. Pascoe hadn't change much, despite the years. She took the glass of champagne from his hand.

Sensing that she might throw it at him, he held her hand gently, their eyes met one another. In that instant he got her up from the chair and slowly led her to the kitchen door. Suddenly she stood firm.

Jackie expected to find the kitchen exactly as she'd left it. But no; it was neatly fitted, all in white and cream. A striking yet impressive contrast. Everything was automatic. Ideas flashed through her mind. Surely, he must have done this himself. His remarks stopped her thinking.

"You don't have to tell me you like it. I can see it." She did not look at him; she pretended not to hear him.

He slapped her cheekily on her bottom. "Hurry now," he said, confidently. "I must use the telephone. I will only be two minutes"

But as he made to move, his face caught the full splash of the champagne.

Quickly, her hand was in his pocket. She tore the key from him and made towards the door.

It took Pascoe only a moment to recover some sight. He caught up with her by the front door. Suddenly she was thrown back, almost losing her balance. The key slipped from her hand as she saved herself from falling. He was quickly onto her, his face wet, his eyes half-blinded. Fleeing with one arm out of her jacket, she heard the sudden rip and the garment was left in his hand, torn from her, leaving just her flimsy blouse, so inadequate.

For a moment they gazed at each other in shock. Then he mopped his face with his handkerchief. He went shakily to the table and emptied the bottle into the glass. He sipped and let the brandy run through him. Then he removed his own jacket and unleashed his tie before abandoning himself in the armchair, calm but alert.

Meanwhile, huddled in one corner, Jackie peered at him with terror. Her mind had suddenly collapsed, and only when he was motionless in the armchair did she come to herself.

She moved forward with uncertainty and parked herself at the table, opposite him, beside the vacant chair. For a moment she stared at the half bottle of champagne. The glass she had held briefly was on the carpet. She retrieved it. Then, ignoring him, she filled it from the bottle. Her flowing black hair had been ravished. She employed both hands to smooth it back before sipping the drink. This was her charitable act, to show that he had not been entirely forgotten; that despite the past, there were indeed blissful moments. Wasn't this what he had pleaded for?

Pascoe remained silently watchful, his eyes fixed to her breast, prominent now against the thin blouse. He had hardly noticed the little act of honour. Soon she was unable to withstand the silence.

"What is it you want from me?" she pleaded without looking at him.

Pascoe sighed wearily. He stretched forward to the brandy. When he had swallowed another heavy gulp, he rose and, avoiding her, walked briskly towards the door. He collected the key and reclaimed his chair.

"So, you're living well? I won't hold that against you. I could not expect you to confine yourself totally for five years. But tell me, why won't he marry you?"

Jackie was stung by this. In the chair she had crossed her legs. But Pascoe's eyes penetrated the flimsy white blouse, especially where her breasts rose momentarily with her heavy breathing. Her face, taut and restless, refused to look at him, yet she could not shut her ears. The question uprooted her emotion: so he was ignorant, no one had told him they were married.

"It is hard to see why a man should not want to marry you," he went on earnestly. "Are you refusing him? Oh, you're capable of that, you know. You can be very strange at times. Maybe he's afraid of you. Yes, that would be the case. His sort is usually clogged up with pride. Dignity they call it. They use their heads. They think up all the pitfalls. If there's a disadvantage that might deprive them of their dignity and jolt their pride, they're immediately afraid. That's why he's not marrying you. Damn him! Maybe he's afraid you'll reject him. Yes, that's more devastating for a man of his sort: to be turned down by the woman he loves, it would unbalance him for life, ruin his manhood."

Jackie's mouth shot open. The vulgarity outraged her; it made her head spin, tugged at her very nerve. God! How could she avoid his filthy tongue?

"But there might be another angle," he went on; "he knows you've been married before. He knows how easy it   was to get hold of you. If he was to marry you and after a year or two you were to wind up in another man's bed, he's the kind of man to put a gun to his head." He peered at her and saw the horror. "And that would suit you. You'd be entitled to his money…."

Jackie fidgeted in her seat, her nerves vibrating. She collapsed in the armchair, abandoned; the same armchair that had cradled her so many times in the bad old days, the days when she'd often drank herself to sleep. Now, choked by her own words, she could find no voice. She clasped her hands and uttered a cry. But that was all. Seized by a sudden bout of strength, she made for the bottle and tossed it at him.

Pascoe was quick, he leapt to his feet, escaping the impact. For a terrifying moment their eyes held each other, and then his heavy hands seized her shoulders and slowly forced her to her knees.

"Pascoe you're hurting me."

He suddenly came to his senses and eased his hands, almost letting go of her. But he stood over her, menacingly.

"You've been hurting me for five years. For all that time I wanted you.". I don't want to hurt you. I never want to hurt you, Jackie, always remember that."

She was still on her knees, one or two droplets of tears beaded down her cheeks. Her blouse torn away at the front, exposing her bosom.

Pascoe dropped to his knees in front of her.

"Don't touch me, Pascoe. You've gone mad!"

"I'm sorry, Jackie. If I've hurt you, it's because you made me do it. You've forced me into doing something I never thought I could ever do. "He took the handkerchief from his pocket and offered it to her.

She flicked it away. "I want nothing from you."

But he retrieved it from the new carpet on the floor, and decided to dry her eyes for her. "If you won't dry your eyes , I will do it for you." And he made a neat little pad and began gently to mop her eyes and down her cheeks. "I've thought about you for five long years, Jackie. And then I couldn't find you. "There, your loveliness is restored. And I promise I won't ever hurt you again."

"What do you want from me?"

"I want you back, Jackie."

"Impossible," she snapped. And her eyes were ablaze with horror.

"You're my life, Jackie. There's no way I can live without you."

The statement hit her hard, and she considered him mad. But she fell silent.

Pascoe rose to his feet, taking her hands with him." Come, come and sit down. Let's reason things out."

With encouragement, Jackie rose from her knees and allowed

herself to look at him. But Pascoe was filled with desire. So close to her, and with so much of her loveliness on display, the anger was draining from him. Desire filling his mind, taking over his whole body.

"You have to let me go, Pascoe. The children are waiting for me."

"Yes," he said, "I was forgetting my two beautiful girls. They're waiting for their mother." He was suddenly thinking hard. Letting her go was not his plan.

They fell silent for a while. He was trying to think, But her sumptuous body, so close to him, devoured his mind. Then he said coldly:

"I was planning to keep you here, till you come to your senses and realise we belong together."

Her hard eyes blazed at him. "You're really deranged if you can think that."

"My plan was to keep you here for as long as it takes: A week, two weeks, whatever. But you must go to the children. My children need their mother." He found a clear patch in his mind. "I'll tell you what should happen now."

Her eyes reached him again, horrified. "What are you planning to do?"

"I want to make love to you, then you can go."

Jackie didn't know whether to laugh or cry. She turned away from him and had to stifle a impulse to scream, knowing it wouldn't do any good. "The years you've been locked up has driven you mad."

"Yes, mad with desire for you. Surely, you can understand that?"

She turned to him suddenly. "Pascoe, the children need me. You must let me go."

"As soon as I love you, then you can go. That's what I want now, or you will stay here for a week or two."

Jackie was unable to think. How could he keep her there for a week, her whole life would end. She thought of the children, and her parents; Karl and everybody at home. Horrifying ideas flashed through her mind. "I don't believe anything you say. You're not the man I once knew."

She felt her hair being touched and stroked and she was afraid to face him.

"Your hair have always been lovely. And this earring is so

pretty, it suits you." He was caressing her earlobe and admiring the matching earring. He ran the back of his hand down her neck, and then he sensed she was trembling. He hoped it wasn't fear. "I will show you that I will keep my word. Watch me."

Pascoe left her side and went to the door, retrieving something from his pocket. "See what I'm doing? I am putting the key in the door." Then he parted the curtain at the window and peered out. "Ah, my friend brought your car back, the keys are in it, ready for you. And he's gone. It's just the two of us here." And he put out the ceiling lights, leaving only the dim bulbs around the walls. He made his way back to her, taking off his shirt and kicking off his shoes.

Pascoe stood in front of her, nothing on his feet, his chest bare. "Come, let's go to your room."

"No, never."

"The bedroom's been made up the same as when you left it. But if you won't go there, what then."

Jackie was frozen. She couldn't think what to do.

Pascoe slipped to the back of the wide sofa and slid the bolts. He eased the back down gently, turning the whole thing into a large double bed. Then he was sitting beside her, manipulating her, and she could not move. Confused, Jackie was numbed She allowed herself to be laid out, offering no objection. He removed her shoes and eased her legs up from the carpet. Then folding her skirt up to her waist, he set about removing her under garments. She did nothing to assist, but with the more than adequate lighting, he spotted the knots at her hips and simply pulled then loose. Suddenly she was there for him, and quickly he removed his trousers. As he lay next to her, he tried a gentle kiss. But Jackie caught the brandy on his breath and turned her head away.

Pascoe was offended. But he didn't let it bother him. The sweetness of her flesh drove him on. He found her warm and lush, and he went on to enjoy what he'd longed for. He'd been faithful to her in all the years they were married. And since his freedom from prison, he'd waited for this moment, never wanting to approach another woman. Suddenly now, he was in a frenzy as he got into her. In this wild mood, he was insulting her.

Eyes shut to the terror that began to rage inside her, she was being ravaged by a wild beast that had escaped! But she could barely shut her mind from the old Pascoe who had once given her little thrills. Now he was just an uproar in her flesh, an incessant force. Pascoe's thick beard was pressed up against her cheeks, threatening her severely. Such repugnance and no end to the agony inside, driving to the very depth of her flesh. For a moment she remembered that she had given in and thought, how foolish. What was she thinking of? Then her children came to mind. Her arms fell back in an effort to relive the pain. But the thundering he was creating inside her seemed to awaken something, an old feeling she thought had died. The feeling grew, creating a sensation. And without knowing it, her arms came up and was reaching behind his shoulders. Her legs rose from the soft cushion and curled around the muscles of his thighs. She was losing herself and hating it. For it was no longer abhorrent. Deep in her past, perhaps when they were first married, he did provide her with some thrills, if only short lived. But the feeling had caught her now, and it was carrying her away. She was hating herself. Suddenly she was screaming for him to stop. She twisted his ears and ripped at his beard in a frantic effort to stop him.

He did stop. For in a fit of passion he had summoned his last powerful urge. And that was what had frightened her. With a mighty strength of fright, she forced him away and drew herself up avoiding the worst.

Pascoe was laying there on his side, his back to her. He was blighted, quite a wreck, his mind watery, diffident, as though half the blood had seeped from his veins.

The moment she'd sat up, Jackie became fully aware and was disgusted with herself. Her clothes in disarray, she noticed her undergarment at one end of the sofa. She retrieved it hastily and set about putting herself together. There was a thought of going to the bathroom since it was familiar, but she decided there was no need, since she had avoided him. With his back to her, she found a little privacy. But her blouse was torn badly, and her jacket. She suddenly wondered:

"Did you buy me any clothes?"

Her voice was a compliment to Pascoe. He'd been thinking that she hated him so much, she would never ask him a question like that.

"Yes," he answered, "in your wardrobe."

She knew her shoes were on the other side of the sofa but, still only in his briefs, she decided it wasn't safe to go that side. Instead, she made off to the bedroom.

It was exactly as he'd said, everything was there. All new. But in the style that she'd left behind. The duvet, the same colour pillows, same carpet, same wardrobes, same dressing table, same draperies, everything. He remembered it well. His side of the wardrobe was stacked with clothes, and the doors were wide open. Her side contained a dozen or more items of clothing, all bought for her. She counted them and uttered a strange little laugh. His love for her was beyond!

There were five dresses, three skirts and blouses, and two sets of two-piece dress. She also noticed two coats and two dressing gowns. She selected a white embroidered blouse and a light blue jacket from one of the sets. Turning to leave the room, she looked at the dressing table drawers and wondered, just for a moment, if he had dared to buy underwear. She plucked up the courage and pulled open the drawer. Seriously, how could he! One side of the drawer was stacked with bras, while the other side, panties. So this is how he'd planned to keep her there forever. Men! She pushed the drawer shut and walked out.

Back in the living room, Pascoe had pulled on his trousers. He had fixed the sofa and was sitting on its arm, sipping a drink.

Jackie dropped the new garments on the chair opposite and first worked her feet into her shoes. "I am glad you've come to your senses, Pascoe.

"I thought I remembered your size, but I wasn't sure if you'd put on weight."

"I did, but I took to exercise and worked it off." She tried the blouse and, with the two buttons at the back opened, it went over her head very nicely. There was no need to do up the buttons, she was in a hurry and the jacket would cover it. Then she tried the jacket and that fitted too.

Pascoe gazed at her with proud eyes. "You're almost back to normal, Jackie, as lovely as ever." He was looking at the woman who still occupied his mind. Memories of their early days rushed to his mind. But she was ready to go. "It's going to be very late when you collect the children."

"You must blame yourself."

"You could call them from here, tell them you're late."

"No, it will only delay me. But listen, Pascoe, whatever you do, you mustn't follow me again." Her voice was cold and tempered.

"No need to, now. It's settled. But I have to see the children. You can understand that, I'm sure."

"No, Pascoe. You're not to creep up to the village and watch them."

"They're my children, Jackie. If I can't see my wife, at least I must see my children."

"No, you're not to go near them. When they're the right age, they will come and see you."

"Those girls are so beautiful, they remind me of you. That's all."

"I am telling you, Pascoe, you must get me out of your mind. Seek a new life for yourself. It's very easy, just put your mind to it."

"I made a pledge to love you until death. D'you remember any of that?"

"No. I remember nothing."

The children are all I've had out of you. You've never loved me. You would never have married me if I hadn't planned it well. Getting you pregnant was the only way."

"Don't congratulate yourself," she declared. "I was already expecting Diane when you first talked of marriage."

"Naturally, the result of my plan."

"I was three weeks pregnant when you invited me to Brighton."

Pascoe turned sharply, his face contorted. He had always prided himself on how well his plan had worked, when he'd managed to get her on their first weekend together at the seaside resort. She had been avoiding him for months and he had to find a clever way to have his first night with her. This kind of news was a horrible blow. She'd driven a steak through his heart and his pride was draining away. He swallowed the brandy and poured another glass. He reflected for a moment. At the time of the marriage he had considered her an honest woman, innocent, respectable, so beautiful, his pride and joy. He drank half the contents of the glass and went across the room to collect his jacket.

Her eyes following him, frightened for revealing it so badly. He was reaching for something in his jacket and she felt herself trembling. The thought that he might be carrying a gun suddenly crossed her mind. She rebuked herself for telling him the truth, and was beginning to think her extravagant life was suddenly a filthy crime. Three children, each with the blood of different men. What sort of woman was she? She glimpsed the gun in Pascoe's hand as he drew it out of the jacket. Images of her children flashed through her mind.

Pascoe was obligingly quick. Throwing down his jacket, he

was suddenly walking away from her. She could clearly see the gun in his hand. And there was no time to utter a final plea. No sooner had he disappeared into the kitchen, the sharp bark of the gun pierced her ears. Frightened, she cluched her breast. The second shot made her cry out. She rushed to the kitchen door. There seemed no pain, only the cold shiver of a bitter end. A moment's thought flashed to the two girls, even the baby boy. Then, held ridged and screaming, she watched in horror as the last convulsions signaled the end of Pascoe. His body twisted and contorted before straightening out on the floor.

Out of her mind, Jackie screamed and staggered to the sofa.

She doubled up, feet tucked beneath her, arms wrapped tight around her knees, she cried and cried.

Pascoe's horrible death was a shattering blow. How stupid! How could he! Why hadn't he killed her first? He could only have been thinking of the children!